Praise for *Para**íso***

"*Paraíso* has a story so compelling, so sinuou—, —ld and passing strange, you feel like you can't take your eyes off the road for a second. Wonder and dread pull you forward. You need to see what's around the next curve."

—William Finnegan, Pulitzer Prize–winning author of
Barbarian Days: A Surfing Life

"Gordon Chaplin is a brave explorer of the human heart. With his wickedly observant new novel, he leads us from East Coast to West and then south to Baja, where this strange and mysterious tale pulses with life. *Paraíso* probes the heart of what it is to be a sibling, what it is to know regret, how to take risks and how to forgive."

—Joanna Hershon, author of *The Outside of August*
and *A Dual Inheritance*

"Some will say of *Paraíso*, 'I couldn't put it down.' But Gordon Chaplin's novel is so good I had to put it down repeatedly—to think, to savor. It's an intricate story, rich in surprises, with passages that are too well written to read just once. Entangling and then disentangling intrigues past and present, it accelerates to a dramatic conclusion on a misty mountainside, closing with scenes that—I promise you—no other writer has ever imagined."

—Jonathan Penner, author of the story collections
Private Parties and *This Is My Voice*

"A misunderstanding between brother and sister evolves through twenty years of separate adventures, from the fall of the Twin Towers to murderous surfing off the coast of Baja California, from a past of American secrets to a present of Mexican tumult and resolution in the heights—delivering you to its hard won Paradise. This is a ride you won't want to miss."

—Bruce Berger, author of Almost an Island

"This novel may be the ultimate exercise in slacker picaresque, wandering from Maine to Mexico, chronicling middle-aging rich kids for whom responsibility and consequences are side issues. Against sweet backdrops of scenery and surfing appear murder, suicide, child abuse, drugs, squalor, and sex. Readers who enjoyed being unsettled by the ending of Chaplin's first novel, *Joyride*, will find even more to enjoy in the conclusion of *Paraíso*."

—Henry Allen, winner of the Pulitzer Prize for Criticism

PARAÍSO

ALSO BY GORDON CHAPLIN

Full Fathom Five: Ocean Warming and a Father's Legacy
Dark Wind: A Survivor's Tale of Love and Loss
Fever Coast Log: At Sea in Central America
Joyride

PARAÍSO

A NOVEL

GORDON CHAPLIN

Arcade Publishing • New York

First Edition

This is a work of fiction. Names, places, characters, and incidents are either the products of the author's imagination or are used fictitiously.

Arcade Publishing books may be purchased in bulk at special discounts for sales promotion, corporate gifts, fund-raising, or educational purposes. Special editions can also be created to specifications. For details, contact the Special Sales Department, Arcade Publishing, 307 West 36th Street, 11th Floor, New York, NY 10018 or arcade@skyhorsepublishing.com.

Arcade Publishing® is a registered trademark of Skyhorse Publishing, Inc.,® a Delaware corporation.

Visit our website at www.arcadepub.com.

10 9 8 7 6 5 4 3 2 1

Library of Congress Cataloging-in-Publication Data

Names: Chaplin, Gordon, author.
Title: Paraíso: a novel / Gordon Chaplin.
Description: First edition. | New York: Arcade Publishing, [2016]
Identifiers: LCCN 2015050649| ISBN 978-1-62872-598-8 (paperback : alk. paper) | ISBN 978-1-62872-612-1 (ebook)
Subjects: LCSH: Brothers and sisters—Fiction. | BISAC: FICTION / Literary.
Classification: LCC PS3553.H2797 P37 2016 | DDC 813/.54—dc23 LC record available at http://lccn.loc.gov/2015050649

Cover design by Laura Klynstra
Cover photo: Shutterstock

Printed in the United States of America

If my sister hadn't died in an auto wreck
And had been taken by the injuns
I would have had something to do:
Go into the mountains and get her back.

—Jim Harrison

PARAÍSO

On the Way

For an hour or forever the car has been rocketing along in the tunnel made by its own headlights in the desert night. The thorny scrub beside the road is as undifferentiated as a wall. The road is flat, straight, and empty.

The lady is alone in the backseat with a lot of baggage. Two boys from San Diego are in the front seat.

They pass a road sign for a place called El Zorro y la Peña. The boy in the passenger seat takes a road map from the glove compartment and turns on the overhead light. "It's the only sign we've seen for hours, and it's not on here. It gives me the creeps. Where are we, anyway?"

"In the middle of nowhere," the driver says in an Orson Welles voice.

"I mean, if we broke down out here, for Christ's sake."

"They'd find our bleached bones in a year or so," the driver says. "And they'd laugh and say 'Three less gringos.'"

"We're not going to break down," the lady says. "I know this car. The older it gets, the better it runs." She puts out a hand and massages the base of the driver's neck.

"They don't make them like this anymore," the driver says, grinning and hunching his shoulders.

The boy in the passenger seat just shakes his head. The car is a 1956 Mercedes Benz 220S convertible, dark green with cracked beige leather seats, peeling walnut trim, and rusty landau irons.

They rocket along in silence for a while. Suddenly, there is a man standing beside the road waving to them. They are past him before they can see him clearly. Looking back through the rear window, all they can see is darkness.

"Holy shit," the driver says. "Trying to get himself killed."

"Maybe he's trying to warn us about something up ahead," the lady says. "A herd of wild ass stampeding across the road. We're in a strange land here, don't you think? Anything could happen."

"Not that strange," the driver says. "Just a bunch of cactuses."

"Cacti," the lady says. "They're *very* strange. Haven't you seen them moving around?"

The boy in the passenger seat rolls his eyes. "He wanted a ride. That's how they do it here. They don't just stick out their thumb. They wave you down, like they have a *right* to a ride."

"Well, maybe they do here," the lady says.

"Maybe the guy's a *bandido*," the driver says. "He's probably got a gang waiting in the brush."

"That doesn't happen here," the boy in the passenger seat says. "In Sinaloa that happens. The dope country. This is more like the frontier."

"I think we should go back and pick him up," the lady says. "He'll know where we are, at least. Plus I need to practice my Spanish."

"No room," the driver says.

"There's room. I'll just push this stuff over."

"Going to be pretty close company back there," the boy in the passenger seat says.

"All the better."

The boy in the passenger seat laughs and shakes his head again.

"I think we'd be asking for it if we picked him up," the driver says.

"Well," the lady says, "Suppose it was you, walking out there?"

"We'd stop," says the boy in the passenger seat.

They drive on until the lady leans forward and whispers in the driver's ear. He rubs it slowly. "Well, it's your car. What's the Spanish word for 'sister'?"

"*Hermana.* Why?"

"We'll tell him you're our sister, okay?"

The lady doesn't say anything.

"Is that okay with you?" the driver asks.

"I've already got one brother," the lady says. "I don't even want to *pretend* to have any more. Besides, I'm too old to be your sister . . . he'd never believe it."

"Sure he would," the driver says gallantly.

The car swings onto the steep shoulder with a crackle of beer cans. For a second the lights shine on the large dark form of a cow or bull, through an arc of cactus and then up into the star-filled sky. Then they are headed back along the road.

They drive for what seems a long way without seeing the man. And turn back again.

Within a few seconds he is there, waving at them. They stop and back up. In the backup lights they can see him standing calmly, a lean thirtyish man in jeans, boots, a checked long-sleeved Western shirt, and a stiff straw cowboy hat. The boy on the passenger side gets out to let him in without saying a word.

"*Muchas gracias.*" He smells of brilliantine, horsehair, and cigarette smoke. The lady smells of Chanel, as far as she can tell. She always travels with a bottle of it to use when she can't bathe. She smiles and shrugs. "*De nada.*"

The boy in the passenger seat turns and points at the lady. "*Hermana. Comprendo?*"

"*Claro,*" the man says politely.

"So will you ask him where the hell we are?"

Her Spanish is rusty but serviceable. The boy's face hangs impatiently over the seat back, his eyes shifting back and forth with the words. "He says we're coming up on a place called Tres Vírgenes. Three Virgins. Check it on the map."

The boy peers at the map and finally shakes his head. "Not on here either. Where's he going?"

3

She asks again. "Piedra Negra, he says."

"Shit. I don't see it, for Christ's sake. What kind of map is this?"

"Well, *he* knows where it is," the lady says. "And when we get there, we'll know where it is too."

The boy flips off the overhead light. Potholes begin to rock the car like a boat at sea, and then the road surface changes to gravel. The sound of the gravel under the wheels roars in the cab. The Mexican produces a pint bottle of tequila, which slowly makes the rounds. In the backseat, the smell of brilliantine is feeling itself around the edges of the smell of Chanel. Every once in a while a pothole will press the lady and the Mexican together and then hurl them apart. His body feels lean, hard, and warm.

She made the bad mistake of going to bed with one of the boys, the driver, she remembers, because of the nice hollow at the base of his throat. She picked them up in a restaurant in San Quintin after their own car died, hoping they'd help with expenses (and noting the throat), but so far they had only helped with the driving. They were the cheapest Californians she had ever met.

Anyway, they were both good drivers. And the lady has always hated to drive at night. Though she enjoys being driven.

She told them she'd come to Baja for the ruins.

"But there aren't any ruins in Baja," the boy in the passenger seat said. "There was never any civilization here at all."

"Well," the lady said after a while. "I guess I was misinformed."

This exchange set the tone for the past twenty-four hours.

"What does Pancho do for work, anyway?" the driver asks.

The lady laughs at the answer.

"What's so funny?"

"He said he works with his hands."

The lady watches the pinholed sky. The tequila bottle makes another round.

One of the Mexican's hands, the one nearest the lady, rests calmly on his thigh and looks like a carved, polished piece of dark wood.

The next time the tequila bottle comes around she lets her own hand come in contact with it. The fact that it is warm, dry, and human makes the bottom fall out of her stomach.

"Oh," she says.

"Oh, what?" the driver says.

The lady doesn't answer.

"Shall we throw him out yet?" asks the boy in the passenger seat.

"It's all right," the lady says. "Everything's fine."

"We just want to protect your honor," says the boy in the passenger seat. "That's supposed to be important here, isn't it?"

"I appreciate your concern," the lady says. "I do." She feels her leg bump gently against the Mexican's, bump again, then finally come to rest against it like a plane landing on a runway.

The Mexican moves his leg away.

The tequila makes a few more rounds. "Ask Pancho if he knows any songs," the driver says. "We might as well get our money's worth."

It's a ranchero number. He's good, a strong tenor who knows all the outrageous harmonics and flourishes of the form. They're getting a little shitfaced, including the lady. The tequila is creeping up on them from behind. They all join in whenever they can.

As he sings, the Mexican's breath smells of tequila and cigarettes. His teeth look very white and clean. The hand that had been resting on his left thigh rises in the air with the high notes and lowers and spreads with the low ones.

When the song ends, everyone laughing and whooping and congratulating themselves on the last long agonizing fall of notes hanging in the air, the hand ends up on back on his thigh.

"That was a great song," the driver says. "What the hell is *leña de pirule*?"

"Let me ask him," the lady said, and did.

The Mexican answers with an edge in his voice. "It means pepper tree logs," she tells the boys. "Pepper tree firewood. It's about a woman."

"*Leña de pirule*," said the boy in the passenger seat in a thoughtful voice. The Mexican adds something more.

"What?" the driver says.

"Pepper tree wood is very smoky." She feels the blood in her face and is grateful for the darkness. "It makes people cry when it burns. It's lousy firewood."

Nobody says anything for a little while. The boy in the passenger seat finally repeats the phrase. The Mexican clears his throat and looks at his knees.

"He really does think you're my brothers," the lady says. "Amazingly enough."

"Good," the driver says.

"So, now I want you to tell him the truth."

The boy in the passenger seat starts to laugh. "Why don't you tell him yourself? You know the language."

"Okay, then I want you out of my car. He can drive."

"*Jesus!*" the boy in the passenger seat says in mock horror. "You'd make us get out *here*?"

"Just tell him the truth," the lady says. "The truth will set you free."

"The hell with it," the driver says. "It doesn't make any difference to me."

"How about a deal," the boy in the passenger seat says. "We tell him we're not your brothers, you keep us abreast of everything that goes on back there. Kind of a play by play."

"All right," the lady says.

During the next series of potholes, as if by accident, the Mexican's hand comes to rest on the seatback behind her. She can sense it as if it belongs to her. She lets a pothole jostle her inside shoulder against the Mexican's chest and the hand drops gently onto the other shoulder. She can feel each finger through her wool jersey. Her own hands are clasped together between her thighs.

"What's happening back there," says the boy in the passenger seat without turning around.

"Nobody back here said a word."

"Oh, come on now . . ."

"All right. He just put his arm around me."

"Aha," says the boy in the passenger seat. "And what's his hand doing?"

"Nothing. Just lying there."

Silence. In a few minutes he asks again. "What's his hand doing now?"

The lady doesn't say anything.

"God damn it," the driver says.

"It's . . . lightly caressing my left shoulder."

The driver hits the wheel with his hand. Then he slams on the brakes and stops the car. "That's it. Tell Pancho the ride's over."

The lady can feel the Mexican's hand freeze. In front of her, the heads of the two boys are also motionless. The headlight-lit road continued straight on.

"Now it's just lying there," she hears herself saying, "but I can feel each fingernail."

The driver rips his door open and gets out. He goes around to the passenger side and motions to his friend, who gets out too. He tilts the seat back and leans in. "*Vámonos*, Pancho."

"Come on, don't be silly," the lady says. "His name's Rogelio."

"I don't care what his name is," the driver yells. "Tell him to get the fuck out, or I'll drag him out."

"*Calmantes montes*," the Mexican says. "*Pájaros cantantos y alicantes pintos.*"

The lady covers her mouth to stop a laugh, but it bursts out through her fingers. At the sound, the driver pulls his head out of the car and straightens up outside. "You're going to laugh when he insults me?"

"He didn't insult you. Here's a literal translation: 'Take it easy, baby. Singing birds and spotted snakes.'"

The driver silently walks away from the car. She can hear the boy from the passenger seat: "I don't believe this." When she pushes her own seat back up and squeezes out, the shadows of the two boys are huge and indistinct under the stars.

Her laugh is absorbed by the space around them. "Shall we start all over again?"

"Gary?" says the boy who'd been in the passenger seat. "We just can't—"

"It's either Pancho or me, Scott," Gary says. "That's how it is."

"Gary. Do you know where we *are*? This isn't the place for this."

"Go on with them if you want to, Scott. Sooner or later somebody'll come by. I'll catch up with you in Cabo."

"*Jesus.*" The lady can see Scott's head bow and swing. "I . . . just . . . do . . . not . . . *believe* this. Will you tell *Rogelio* to get out now?"

"She's not going to, Scott," Gary says. "She wants him. And she's already *had* us."

Scott's face hangs palely in the air above his dark clothes. "*That's* the truth." She can hear him panting, a hot, dry rasp." Okay, let her go. It's her funeral."

A match flares inside the car, illuminating the Mexican's dark face from the bottom up. The lady takes a deep breath. The car idles quietly. In back of the engine noise is black emptiness, punctuated by the brilliant stars. The temperature outside the car seems subzero, the temperature of outer space.

PART ONE

Engine Trouble

Perfect silence when she turned off the engine. Afternoon heat lay on the desert with a crushing weight, squeezing pale blue, yellow, and crimson blooms from some of the cactus and scrub. The straight empty highway bisected the horizon ahead and behind.

The old car's temperature gauge was in the red for the third time since yesterday. So the leak in the radiator was getting worse, though she could never see any water dripping or puddling. Should have had it fixed in Loreto, but she figured she could make it to Cabo on two gallon jugs of water even in a hundred and ten degrees.

Sharp brown mountains rose in the haze to the southeast, and the air was absolutely still. She poured the first gallon of water into the radiator and started on the second before it topped out. She'd misjudged the leak badly, but the next town should be reachable. She could get enough water there to make it to Cabo, but where the hell was all the water *going*? Maybe evaporating into the air. The only comparable heat she'd experienced was eight years ago in the lava fields on the Big Island of Hawaii during the hundred-mile cycling section of the Ironman (she'd been shooting it for *Outside*).

On her map, the next town was called Paraíso. From the high desert the highway sloped slowly down to its bright green oasis, cupped by hard brown hills and fronted by the misty blue Pacific. The place seemed eerily familiar, but then she had that feeling a lot.

Was this the place she and her brother Peter had been aiming for when they ran away from home together more than twenty years ago? Well, she'd finally made it. It would be nice to tell him, but they weren't talking anymore.

Why had she chosen to come now, after all this time? Things finally had lined up nicely. Her big photo book had just come out, but she didn't want to be around for it. Much better to be unreachable, south of the border. Her friend Dave (whom she'd made famous with a shot of his agonizing fall in the Ironman) had offered her a week of free room and board at the luxurious Twin Dolphins in Cabo, care of Adidas. She could feel the old Mercedes champing at the bit, ready to take up the challenge of a thousand-mile drive through the desert.

How many times had she been on the verge of making this trip? It was unfinished business, but something had always come up and she'd backed off with a kind of relief. Now she was as ready as she'd ever be. Now or never.

Dave was just a friend; she'd made it clear they'd require separate rooms, and Adidas had agreed. It was all really an excuse to make the drive at last. She'd been going through men like a bowling ball for what seemed to be her whole life. They just scattered and fell down, although Latin men—Mexican men in particular—were more of a challenge. They had an interesting edge, and she'd heard of some *gringas* who had never come back.

As the car descended, the temperature eased. Large cultivated fields appeared on the left and on the right storage sheds and produce trucks with a rising sun logo and the words *Del Sol*. Twin lines of eucalyptus began to shade the highway as it ran along the side of the palmy valley. A vacant inspection station, a sign reading PARAÍSO 2500 HAB., a speed bump, and finally a paved town street fronted by old brick buildings with a row of young Indian laurels in a center strip. Now the temperature was actually comfortable, the lowest since she'd doubled inland from the Pacific in Guerrero Negro five hundred miles north, but the siesta had started and the street was deserted. The Mercedes was the only moving car.

The strangely familiar scenery unrolled: the cinderblock Bancomer on the right, the Casa de Cultura in an old brick school building on the left, an open-air taco stand, a pink plastered *mueblería*. The rest of the main street, featuring an old hotel, a church with a plaza in front of it, more shops, a restaurant, and a small hospital, spread out in front of her as she topped a little rise. As if she'd driven through here in another life.

When she saw her first human being, she had an extra-intense déjà vu. He was a strange, postcard Mexican, very tall and thin in loose white *campesino* clothing out of a Diego Rivera mural from the thirties and a straw cowboy hat. He was standing in the deep shade of a big Indian laurel near the church behind a red wooden pushcart laden with bottles and hung with silver bells.

Her déjà vus were stronger than other people's, this she knew, not that they were unpleasant—they added an interesting fourth dimension to things—but where did they come from? When did they start? *How* did they start? Had she really lived other lives? The first one she could remember was at thirteen, in a drugstore, picking out her first box of Tampax from a shelf of others. Her hand reaching toward the blue box with its white lettering. Click. The fact that she'd seen the exact same image before was comforting.

She stopped the Mercedes, got out, and walked to the cart, feeling a little travelworn in jeans, faded red tee shirt, old leather sandals. Rusty Spanish from college and various Latin American photo shoots, rusty voice, as if she hadn't used it for years. "*Buenas días . . .* I mean, *tardes.*" For some reason she was blushing.

The Mexican's thin face was half hidden in the shadow of his hat. "*Buenas tardes, señorita.*" Voice rusty as hers felt, like a boxer's who had taken too many hits to the throat.

Yes, there was a mechanic, half a block left at the end of the main street.

A good mechanic?

The man cleared his throat and shrugged. *"Más o menos."*

More or less. She paused, for some reason wanting to prolong the moment. And what was he selling in those bottles?

Why, honey, *señorita.* He pointed over her shoulder at the serrated mountain range rising behind the town and fading into shades of lavender to the southeast. Honey from the mountains where the special herbs grow. He uncorked a bottle and handed it to her with the saddest smile she'd ever seen.

The deal was already done. She sniffed the sharp bouquet, and his smile confirmed it. She'd take two bottles; how could she not?

Their hands touched in the exchange with a spark she already knew was coming, and the script called for her to smile and thank him. Then she was back in the musty smell of old leather that was the interior of the Mercedes. In the rearview mirror she could see him standing hat in hand, smile bared to the full sun, watching her drive away.

Peter Fails Once

The first time my sister and I tried to make it to Mexico was in our family station wagon, of all things, heading for the border two thousand miles away. I was on the lam for having burned down the chapel at my boarding school.

Here's the truth: I'd *planned* to burn it down, but at 2:00 a.m. in front of the altar I'd had a crisis of confidence, stashed my fuel oil–soaked towel in a crawl space next to the sacristy, and split anyway. . . . It was only a few days before the Christmas holidays. Imagine my surprise when, upon arriving at the train station in my hometown five stops out on the Main Line, I learned from the *Philadelphia Inquirer* that the chapel actually *had* burned down. Jesus! If I'd stashed the towel outside in the bushes instead of in the crawl space, the hoary old building probably still would be standing. I was guilty through thoughtlessness rather than direct action: story of my life.

I hadn't exactly been a pillar of the school community; I had no alibi. My absence from the dorm would have been duly noted, and I assumed the alarm would have been sounded. There were two things I could do: go home and beg my parents for understanding and help, or take off on my own out of reach of the law.

The first was literally unimaginable—the dialogue and images just weren't there when I tried to summon them up. What would my parents' faces look like? What room of the house would we be in? What would I say to them and how would they answer? Blank.

Impossible. The second option seemed to be all I had. I'd started down that road by leaving school in the first place, hadn't I? But still, I couldn't make up my mind.

I'd turned sixteen that September but my voice hadn't changed. I looked and sounded like a girl, something my classmates and at least one closet pedophiliac of a housemaster never let me forget.

On the eve of my arson-by-proxy, this master had come across me alone in the shower room just before dinner, turning pink under a stream of delicious hot water. "Hurry up, you're going to be late," he trumpeted as I twisted a towel around my waist. I could hear his heavy feet behind me as I hightailed it down the corridor to my room, leaving wet footprints on the brown linoleum. I tried to close my door but one of his big wingtips was already inside. All I could do was turn my back on him as I took off the towel and began to put on my clothes, and it seemed I could feel his hot breath on my shoulder blades as he stood there panting a few feet away. Waiting for his touch, it came to me that I had to make a move.

My sister Wendy would be fourteen the next April, but instead of getting soft and curvy like her classmates she just seemed to be getting taller and more wiry. She too came in for her share of ribbing, but let's face it: a boyish girl gets off easier than a girlish boy.

I hadn't planned to take her with me, assuming I actually went anywhere at all, but she was my closest friend and confidante and I couldn't leave without saying good-bye. We wrote each other every week when I was in boarding school, so she knew how much I hated it. (I was too embarrassed to tell her my classmates had taken to calling me "Peedie Pan.") She responded with tales of our mother's latest atrocities, although compared to my problems they seemed pretty trivial.

I walked from the train station to her school, about a mile, hid in the trees near the playground, and waited till school let out. It was a cold, bright, gusty afternoon but the scrubby pines broke the wind and I found a spot of sun, so it wasn't too bad. I'd been up all night, sitting in trains or waiting for them in stations, and my mind felt incredibly focused from fatigue and adrenalin. But it wasn't focused on anything specific, the way a car's high beams will shine on fog.

My sister was in the first group of girls out the door, the only one without a windbreaker or a jacket—just the black Brooks Brothers Shetland sweater with small, dark red, discreetly embroidered initials front and center I'd given her for her thirteenth birthday, over the school uniform of white blouse, blue and green Forbes tartan skirt, and green knee socks.

I threw a pebble across the asphalt to get her attention and all five of the girls turned to look as I stepped out from behind the pine tree. Then my sister had left them and was running toward me with her loose, springy, floating, track-star strides. When we collided she was almost as tall as I was (she'd grown two inches since the summer), but her light brown hair still smelled of soap like it always had.

"Omigod, what are you *doing* here. I thought your school didn't get out till Friday."

"Well, there was a fire. So there."

She leaned back and stared into my face, and I could see a pimple or two on her forehead and around the corners of her mouth. "A *fire?*"

"Yeah. They let us out early. It was even in the paper here. Didn't you see?"

"The paper here?" A little smile starting. "Your school's in New Hampshire."

I was grinning a little myself. She might look different, but she hadn't really changed. "Maybe they put it in because a lot of kids from here go there. I don't know. I don't write the paper."

"Was it a dorm or something? Was anybody hurt?"

I shook my head. "It was the chapel. Burned to the ground."

Silence. Then she snorted, we were both giggling, and finally howling with laughter. *The chapel. Burned to the ground.* It was something about the way I'd said the words that set her off, not what actually happened—the way she said things could have the same effect on me.

"They didn't really let us out early, though," I said after we calmed down. "I just kind of left."

"You just kind of *left*? Why?"

I shrugged.

"You left *after* the fire?"

"No, before. The same night. It was just—"

"Oh God, you're going to get blamed for it, aren't you?" Her blue eyes had the same lidded, squarish look as mine, but they were more direct. "You've got to go somewhere. If you don't take me, I'll never forgive you." Of course she never asked me if I'd actually done it. She knew I wasn't the type to burn down chapels. In fact, one of the masters had called me *bland*. After he said it, I'd just sat there dumbly. The answer came to me years later: how would *you* like being the last kid in the class to grow up?

It was as if my sister had been waiting for this moment for years, she put the plan together so fast. She'd always had a thing for our father's dark green 1956 Mercedes convertible—sitting in it for hours reading one of her horse books, windows rolled up around the car's musty smell of old leather, sonorous Blaupunkt radio tuned to forbidden rock stations—and she insisted on hijacking it for our getaway. Finally, I talked her out of it: the fancy old car was so conspicuous we'd be pulled over before we went fifty miles. On the other hand, the family station wagon, a little English Hillman Husky, had been registered in my name as a birthday present, and I'd passed my driving test in it. It was clunky and inconspicuous and we could repaint it somehow. We'd stick to back roads and avoid big cities, driving mostly at night. And we'd figure out some cool disguises. Our parents probably wouldn't call in the police for a day or two, hoping we'd turn up and aiming to avoid scandal.

As to where we were going, we both agreed it had to be Mexico. A border had to be crossed, a real border, and Canada just seemed like an extension of the United States. Our parents had taken us skiing there the last two Christmas vacations, whereas Mexico they would never have been caught dead in. Mexico was a *desert*. Nothing there that would remotely interest our mother, just an infinitude of dry, dusty, wide-open space. No fences, not many people, a straight black road across the plains and the red mountains in the distance.

Neverland.

We snuck the Husky out of the garage at 2 a.m. and drove all night through a light snowfall, listening to country music on WWVA and watching the big white flakes come at us out of a single point way ahead. By daybreak we were in Ohio farm country across the Alleghenies and found an abandoned barn where we could drive the little car inside and fall asleep in our seats.

My sister was the first to go under, and I remember looking at the pimples on her face as she lay close beside me and wondering not for the first time what other changes were going on in her body. If there were any, and I prayed to God there weren't, I'd be totally left out and left behind. Peedie Pan, the boy who never grew up, alone in Neverland, while Wendy flies back to the Darlings' house, gets married, and has children of her own.

But in spite of my prayers I knew there were changes. Thinking about them kept my mind in a churn, and what with the strangeness of everything else I hardly slept at all, although the down sleeping bags she'd smuggled out of the house (along with $150 from our mother's purse, two bags of clothes, and one box of canned delicacies from the pantry) were cozy as could be.

I must have finally dozed off, though, because when I opened my eyes my sister was standing with her back to me in a shaft of cold gray light from a high window, nude except for a pair of white cotton Carter's underpants similar to those our mother oddly used to buy for me (saving her the "endless walk" to the boys department).

Racehorse legs flaring into narrow hips, a long straight back widening to square shoulders brushed by butternut hair. I could see no changes. Her body looked the same as it had always looked, only more so. It looked exactly like mine—I'd been a track star too until my classmates started developing men's muscles and I couldn't compete.

The temperature in the barn couldn't have been much over forty, so she didn't stand there long, only a few seconds in fact. From the open bag at her feet she whipped out a red Duofold long-john set she must have gotten for skiing, pulled the bottom on, and shrugged into the top.

Over the Duofold top went an old plaid shirt I recognized as mine. Over the bottom a pair of button-fly Levis. Even though her back was still to me, I could tell she was fumbling with the buttons as if for the first time. White wool Wigwam athletic socks and Topsiders on her feet. Mine too?

Then she turned and came back to the car. I pretended I was just waking up. She was looking at herself in a side-view mirror and holding a pair of scissors.

"Good. You're awake. I was afraid I was going to mess it up if I did it myself."

"Did what yourself? Are those my clothes?"

"Cut my hair." She grinned. "For my *disguise*, moron. Yeah, they're your clothes, do you mind?"

I grinned back and shook my head. The idea made a lot of sense. She handed me the scissors, and with a weird rush of gratification I tried to cut it as much like mine as possible. Her hair was thick and curly like mine and our father's, so it took a while.

"Guess what? I've decided not to be a girl," she said, while I was sawing away. "I refuse to be one ever again."

I had to laugh, she sounded so sure of herself. Like the English king who ordered the ocean to stop rising. But I liked the idea a lot . . . staying children together forever, or at least just a little while longer.

"I don't want to be like our mother," she said. "I'd rather die than be like her."

I knew they fought all the time, of course, but still I was floored by the implacable anger in her voice. "Why? She's not so bad. She's just . . ."

My sister suddenly pulled away and turned to face me. Her eyes were narrowed and her teeth were bared—she looked exactly like our mother in the middle of a tantrum. She was hissing in our mother's way. "Don't you *ever* sssssssay that to me. You don't know her. You don't know *anything*. So jusssst shut up about it."

Wow. Okay. This was new, all right, and I couldn't even begin to process it. A protective shutter eased down in my mind, I cut my eyes sideways, then looked at my hands and to my relief saw I was still holding the scissors. "Let me finish cutting your hair," I said after a moment or two, trying to keep my voice steady. "It looks pretty good, if I do say so."

She took a deep breath and looked at herself in the side-view mirror. "Not bad. Take a little more off the sides and the back." I started snipping, and she went on. "So . . . what are you going to do about yourself?"

I knew there was a major problem, of course. I didn't look old enough to drive. The week I turned sixteen, got my driver's license, and was soloing, I was pulled over in the Hillman Husky by a smirking cop. He was so sure the license was fake he took me down to the Bryn Mawr police station, and my father had to show up personally to vouch for me. Maybe it was paranoia, but I felt that I, not the cop, was being blamed for the whole imbroglio, and he actually had the gall to pat my head on the way out.

But other than embarking on an intensive course of hormone shots recommended by at least one doctor but nixed by my father, who'd been a very late bloomer himself and was always in favor of "letting nature take its course," I couldn't see what to do.

My sister had the answer, and I have to admit it was brilliant even though she had to bluff me into it by threatening suicide if we were caught. In the late afternoon we drove into the nearest large town, stopped at a Sears Roebuck, and had me fitted out with a dress, a dark blue long-sleeved wool number loose fitting enough to disguise how flat my chest was, and a Bonnie and Clyde black beret to cover my short hair. We told the saleslady I went to an all-boys school and was playing a girl's part in a Shakespeare comedy.

In the changing room mirror I could see how right she'd been: as a boy I'd looked wimpy and immature; as a girl I looked like a French gamine in a Godard art flick, a ballsy eighteen at the very least. My bare legs and neck looked tough and strong, and my face under the beret looked slightly dangerous. I grinned at my reflection and raised a fist: *quelle garce!* I wanted to buy a pair of hood boots to complete the look, but my sister nixed it. Heavy black shoes with medium high heels to make me taller were all she'd allow.

Next stop: the hardware department, where we bought five spray cans of heavy-duty silver car paint along with plenty of masking tape, the plan being to two-tone the sky-blue Husky on the roof and sides ASAP. Mexico, we were on our way.

We never made it. Our little escapade ended just outside a place called Cairo, Illinois, where the Ohio River meets the Mississippi, ironically enough the same place Huck Finn and Jim the runaway slave aimed to escape to, and missed in the fog.

It was foggy, too, when we arrived before dawn and hunkered down for the day in a grove of willows on the riverbank south of town. There were fields of harvested corn behind us, but we couldn't tell how far they went or what was on the other side. Somewhere pretty close, a flock of geese honked and gabbled like a crowd of people at a party. Fog hung and curled on the surface of the water and wrapped cozily around the car.

My new Sears Roebuck dress, even though fairly thick wool, was drafty and cool compared to what my sister was bundled up in, so I was inside my down bag pretty fast. I could see her silhouette moving as she arranged herself, saw it freeze, heard a little cry.

"What?"

"Oh God, *no*."

I turned on the overhead light. "What is it? What's wrong?"

She held up a finger wet with blood.

"Jesus. Holy shit. Did you cut yourself? What on? Show me."

Just at that moment, there was a fusillade of gunfire from the field behind us. The gabbling and honking of the geese changed to frantic calls of alarm, and the air filled with the sound of beating wings. Thousands of invisible birds siffled close above us on their way out over the water. All up and down the bank from us, more gunfire, more panicked geese, one flock after the next. We could hear men's voices shouting and see muffled lights in the fog. I snapped off the overhead light.

My sister and I lay in each other's arms and waited. "Good," she said. "I hope we die."

"What?"

"Anyway, we're together."

After a while the noises died down. "What are you talking about?" I said. "They must be hunters. The geese. They're not after us. Now will you please show me the cut?"

"I can't."

"What do you mean, you can't. You might need stitches."

She didn't say anything. Her short hair tickled my nose, and I smoothed it away.

"It's going to be okay," I said.

"No it's not."

"Sure it is. We can drive into town if we have to. There's gotta be a doctor."

She suddenly sat up, and in the gray dawn light I could see she was crying. "Goddamn it," I said.

"Oh, you stupid ape. You don't understand. You don't understand anything."

I started to get very angry. "So tell me. Just tell me. Then maybe I can stop being an *ape*."

"Okay." She screwed a fist into an eye. "It's my period. I've got my period, okay?"

I sat up myself. The word was nonsense. No one home. "You're kidding, aren't you?"

She didn't say anything.

"How could you have your period? Impossible. It's impossible, isn't it?"

It wasn't her first. The month before, she'd woken up between bloody sheets and, terrified, had gone to our mother's bedroom door. I wasn't surprised it had been locked—she always did lock her bedroom door at night; I'd tried to open it once myself—but my sister had called and knocked, finally pounded and yelled. At last she'd heard our mother's cold voice on the other side: "Go away. My door and my heart are closed to you."

Miss B found her asleep in front of the door and very gently confirmed everything my sister had heard at school about girls and periods but had chosen not to believe. "You mustn't blame your mother for the way she acted," Miss B said. "Some women get a little . . . well, their feelings might get a little out of control at her age, you know." Smiling and raising her eyebrows: "She's very likely envious. You're a woman now yourself." She said my sister would be menstruating every month from now on for the next forty years or so except for pregnancies and nursing; my sister chose not to believe that either.

We sat in the car, frozen. Every once in a while there was more honking, more shots. "'My door and my heart are closed to you,'" I repeated finally. "Jesus. She really said that? Did you just have a really bad fight or something?"

My sister took a ragged breath but didn't answer.

"She couldn't have said it." Our mother's face appeared in front of me so solidly I could have reached out and touched it. "It doesn't sound like her at all. She's just not like that."

As soon as the words were out, I wanted to snatch them out of the air, snatch them back, make them disappear. Even if they were true. Because they were true. Okay, I was an ape. Even an ape could see that those words were going to change things between my sister and me for good.

I never found out what my sister was going to say to those words. Suddenly there was a shotgun blast, nearer than any of the others, followed by the thud of something heavy hitting the ground right next to the car. We looked out to see the body of an enormous Canada goose on the grassy bank twenty feet away. In no time at all, a big man in camouflage appeared out of the mist, took the goose by the neck, and turned to look at us. He was holding a shotgun in his other hand.

"Wall now," he said in a kindly way, walking toward the little Husky with its amateurish paint job. "So what have we here?"

I knew it was all over, and at that point my strongest feeling was relief. I didn't look at my sister's face as I admitted everything to the goose hunter, but I could feel her presence burning beside me as someone whom I frighteningly didn't seem to know anymore.

The names our mother had given us showed pretty clearly what was going on in her mind at the time we were born, or at least the name she gave my sister did. I was Peter. Peter by itself had no real significance, just one of our father's two middle names. It was when my sister came along and she named her Wendy that her state of mind became clear. Peter and Wendy, in Neverland, on the Isle of Lost Children. Oddly enough, I always loved the idea.

Second star to the right, and straight on till morning. A very romantic dream, no? My sister began to not live up to it when she was only a few weeks old, kicking, screaming, refusing to nurse. "I'm at my wit's end," I overheard our mother saying to a friend. "You know I'm afraid I really don't like her very much."

Whereas true to form, I was the opposite. I was only two at the time, but I half-remember lounging on the sitting room couch with my pregnant mother, running a toy truck down the hill of her belly, being unexpectedly offered a breast, latching onto it joyfully, and associating this piercing bliss with the imminent arrival of my sister. Maybe it never happened. The fact was, though, I loved to nurse. Not many kids grow up knowing this; probably all the better for them.

My mother and I both loved artichokes, persimmons, shad roe, Silver Queen corn on the cob, Maine lobsters, and blueberries. We loved the dawn. . . . I'd see her on early spring mornings walking around the place, but we'd rarely talk. We loved long perspectives: long dim hallways in hotels, long piers, long straight tree-lined roads, skyscrapers, bridges, plowed fields, flat country. Sometimes she took me on long, aimless drives or walks. We'd follow a road or trail, but it wasn't the place they led to that really interested us.

Glorious was one of her favorite words. So was *loathe* . . . I think she liked *loathe* better because of the way it rolled off her tongue, not so much because of what it meant, but I could be wrong. Anyway, she used it a lot with my sister.

They hated each other for reasons I'm only just beginning to understand, but I've always known one crucial thing: I needed my sister's hatred of our mother really to feel my own love. Two sides of the same coin.

The Kindness of Strangers

She had to ask a few more times before she found the garage. It wasn't right on the street but down a sandy track in a kind of nook, hidden by palms and scrub and shaded by a huge, gnarled mimosa-like tree. There were the usual car skeletons and body parts strewn around, a little cinderblock house, and a cluttered workbench underneath a palm-frond *palapa*. The man at the workbench was working on an extracted carburetor and didn't look up as the Mercedes drove in. She couldn't help feeling slighted.

When she walked under the *palapa* with an irritable "*Buenas tardes*," he just increased the pressure on the screwdriver.

She put a sentence together in her head, then spoke it. "*Creo que hay un hoyo en mi radiator.*"

The screwdriver snapped free. He swore and looked up. His skin and hair were dark, but his eyes were light greenish yellow.

When he still didn't speak, she constructed another pair of sentences: "*Necesito que llegar a Cabo está tarde. Puede usted ayudarme?*"

His eyes moved to the car. "That's a fifty-six, right? First year they made it." In perfect California English.

"Wow. Ahmm . . . right . . ."

Tapping the screwdriver on his palm while he took a closer look. "You must have a good mechanic up there in gringolandia."

"I do. But I think all I have now is a leak in the radiator."

He knelt down and looked under the car. "Don't see any water."

"I know. I was wondering about that."

"When did you first notice the leak?" Looking up at her.

"Yesterday."

"How many times have you filled the radiator since then?"

"Maybe three."

He uncoiled to his feet. "Open her up."

Checking the dipstick, he whistled a boyish fall of notes. "Look here," he said, holding it out to her. The substance at the end was a light *café au lait* instead of dark oil. He rubbed it between finger and thumb. "You got water in the crankcase. Feel."

The substance was slightly sticky. He offered her a rag to wipe it off, and she felt he might pat her gently on the back as if she'd just learned she had cancer.

"Jesus. How did it get in there?"

"Probably a rust pinhole from the water pump." He pointed to the side of the engine. "See, the pump is integrated to the block. Bad design."

Bad design. She swallowed and handed back the rag. "So that's where all the water went. Into the engine."

He nodded slowly.

"I guess that's not good news, is it?"

"Nope."

"What does it mean, exactly?"

"You'd have to take the engine down and see." Flicking his hair back with a little head toss. "Probably new bearings at least. Maybe a new crankshaft"

"Oh my God." She thought for a minute. "Can I get to Cabo like this?"

"If you want to really wreck it. Better let me do the work."

Turning, she laid her hand gently on her car. Take the engine down. Put in a new crankshaft. A huge job, even for the Del Mar mechanic. Yet she knew nothing about this guy, not even his name. Where did he get his green eyes, anyway?

28

"Well." She gave him her brightest smile. "I've always depended on the kindness of strangers. Give me a night to think about it?"

The mechanic gave her directions to a bed-and-breakfast back across the valley in the old part of town, merrily run by a fortyish gringa named Judy and her two teenaged daughters. Wendy had left her bag in the Mercedes and hadn't wanted to deal with the mechanic again until she made up her mind, so after a hot walk Judy's younger daughter lent her a clean blouse and toiletries. Their three Mexican boyfriends squeezed limes for margaritas and mashed avocados for guacamole, and one of them demonstrated that if you spit on your hands you could hold a big black carpenter bee in them without getting stung. The talk was about how, the year before, a petition to have Judy and her daughters expelled for loose morals had been circulated through the town, but nothing had come of it. The Spanish word was *fácil*.

When she asked about the mechanic, Judy's first reaction was to clear her throat. Nobody said anything more.

"Oh, my," Wendy said finally.

"What kind of a car do you have again?"

When Wendy told her, her English-speaking boyfriend whistled. "*Mierda de Dios.*"

Wendy arched her back, feeling his eyes on her breasts. "I was sure the old lady could make it. I know her pretty well. Anyway, so what can you guys tell me about this . . . ah . . . ?"

They all looked at each other. Finally, Judy said, "Listen. All we can tell you is just hearsay. You should really talk to someone he's done work for, a guy they call Pancho Clamato. Clamato is a good citizen, even if he drinks too much. He won't pull his punches."

Several margaritas later Wendy retired to bed. A yellowed paperback copy of Faulkner's *Sanctuary* lay on her bedside table, and she leafed through it in growing horror and fascination. Why was it there . . . to amuse the guests? Sometime after midnight she put the book down, turned out the light, and lay there listening to a faint thudding in her ears. Definitely one margarita too many. She hugged herself and shivered in the dark and heard the church bells ring at least once before she fell asleep.

The early morning was reassuringly crystalline—cool and still, the distant ocean calm as a lake. Pancho Clamato, blond, lanky, and dried out as a prune, was sitting in a rocking chair on the porch of his house in the Barrio San Ignacio across the valley from the town when she walked up on the dusty road. He was reading a magazine and a jug sat within easy reach. A brick two-story building that looked like an abandoned school loomed across the road, and from somewhere in back of it she could hear a contented, oddly human mooing.

A large beige dog with black undershot jaws got up from the porch and moved toward her. "Name's Devil," Clamato called. "Wouldn't hurt a fly."

She walked through a gap in the pole fence into the dirt yard and stopped next to the porch. "What's in the jug?"

"Vodka. With a little clamato."

"Then you must be who I'm looking for."

"Uh-oh. Are you an attorney?" He looked up at the roosting buzzards in the taco palms behind the house, put down the magazine—*The Surfer's Journal*—and showed a set of large yellow teeth that looked like old piano keys. "On second thought, you couldn't be an attorney. You're too good looking."

She sighed. "I'm just a damsel in distress."

When he learned about her car and how old it was, he literally scratched his head. Parts were going to be a problem; in his case there had been another defunct old Land Cruiser around to cannibalize. Plus, he had to admit a Mercedes was a little different than a Toyota, although of course an engine is an engine.

She thought she could get her Hell's Angel mechanic in Del Rey to round up the parts and air-freight them down.

"That could take more than a month." Clamato looked amused. "Why don't you have him fly down with the parts? Then he can do the work himself."

"Wow. You must think I'm rich."

Clamato rocked back in his chair and grinned. "Let's put it this way. If you're not rich, you have no business bringing a car like that down here."

"Touché." She raised her eyebrows at him.

"There's only one good mechanic in this town, and I wouldn't touch him with a ten-foot pole."

"Why not?"

"Because he's a scorpion, that's why. You know the story about the scorpion and the eagle?"

"I think so. Where the scorpion asks the eagle to fly him across the river and they both drown? The eagle asks why did you bite me, and the scorpion says because it's my nature?"

"Exactly. But this scorpion is a great swimmer. He didn't even need the ride."

"Does this scorpion have green eyes?"

He looked at her with concern and shook his head. "Oh, Jesus."

"I stayed at Judy's last night. She said I should talk to you about him. She actually gave you as a reference."

Clamato laughed so hard he almost fell out of his chair. Haw shit, this was probably the first time anyone had ever given him as a reference for anything. But yeah. He took her around the other side of the house and gestured at his old black-and-yellow Land Cruiser, a 1975 station wagon model that a friend had just abandoned in his yard three years ago. The mechanic had gotten it running again, no problems ever since.

The oddly human mooing sound was growing closer. Finally, a big man with a broad grin and completely empty eyes appeared outside Clamato's gate, raised a hand, and bellowed. Clamato bellowed back, went inside, and came out with a Hershey bar. "Hunh. Must be nine. I thought it was earlier."

She watched as he walked to the gate and handed over the Hershey bar while the man mooed loudly and clapped him on the shoulder. The man walked away unwrapping the chocolate, and the mooing sound slowly faded into the background. "Well, that's *Jefe*," Clamato said back in his chair. "The boss, that's what they call him. This is a great town for nicknames."

"This place is right out of Faulkner, isn't it?"

"Yeah." He poured and chuckled. "Ever read *Sanctuary*?"

"Wow." She shook her head in amazement. "As a matter of fact, I was reading it last night. Over at Judy's."

"She have a copy? I'm not surprised. Anyway, you should read it carefully if you're planning to stick around."

"Do I have any other options? Other than just abandoning my car?"

"Maybe not."

"So tell me about this mechanic. What's his name, to start with?"

"Marco Blanco is what they call him. But his real name is Mark White. Here. Sit back and drink your drink, and Pancho Clamato will tell you a story."

Mark White's father was an Irish American adventurer from San Diego who'd built one of the first big watering holes in Cabo. This was before the Baja road, and rich gringos would fly in with private planes for fishing and partying. It was a huge success, and his bookkeeper was a smart, handsome woman from Paraíso. Before too long she was pregnant, then they were engaged to be married, then Mark White's father was bought out by the Hilton chain and went back alone to San Diego a rich man. He married into La Jolla society and had two other sons.

The summer Mark turned sixteen he called his father and asked if he could visit. Well, okay. His father must have been feeling guilty because he even arranged the visa and paid for the ticket. His wife was not happy but had known about the child and told her own children that their father had been married before. Mark's half-brothers were two years and four years younger than he was, going to a fancy La Jolla private school with computer camp and soccer league in the summer.

Mark's English was terrible, so his father sent him to the only language school he could find. The other students were mainly children of Mexican immigrants and illegal aliens, or were immigrants and aliens themselves. In a month he was speaking passable English, and in two he was fluent, with an accent practically indistinguishable from his half-brothers'. The school had even found him a mechanic's job, which he'd taken to supplement his small allowance. His father was impressed enough to invite Mark to spend the rest of the year in La Jolla and enroll in the local high school. He acknowledged legal paternity and got him a US passport.

But his wife disapproved of the mechanic's job (even though it was an upscale, imported-car garage), and when Robert, her oldest son, began to hang around there after school she asked Mark to quit. If he wanted to work, she could find him a job in a real estate office where she had friends.

"What would I be doing?" he asked.

"Why, office work." She smiled. "You'd learn how to operate a computer, for one thing."

Mark's two half-brothers spent most of their free time hunched over computers. They seemed lost to the real world, although he thought there was hope for the older one.

So he said he'd rather stay at the garage, and, surprisingly, his father backed him up. "The boy's a really good wrench. I've talked to his boss," he told his wife.

At the garage, Mark learned about Windansea Beach and the Pumphouse Gang. He'd surfed occasionally in Paraíso, where the waves could get huge and hollow like the north shore of Hawaii, and when he tried the break on a borrowed board he found he was able to hold his own and then some. He made a few friends and got respect. After a while, the surf crowd at the high school picked him up. They thought he was cool, with his dark Mexican skin and green eyes. And they started calling him Marco Blanco.

Mark's stepmother became his bitter enemy, though he didn't discover the extent of it until later. "He's fallen in with a really low set," she told his father. "Drugs, alcohol, you name it, they do it. Robert worships him. Look how he's started to spend time at that . . . garage. It's just a matter of time before Robert gets into surfing."

"Surfing's not the end of the world," his father said. "I used to do it myself."

"It's different now. Don't you read the papers? One of them was just charged with being the biggest smuggler of marijuana in the world. There's a whole gang called the Brotherhood of Eternal Love. Why, they're making millions selling drugs to our kids." She suggested strongly that Robert spend less time with his stepbrother, and Robert did. Gradually, under his mother's influence, he began to look at Mark with disapproval. Her campaign made even his father distance himself. Family meals became four against one.

In the spring, Mark came home from the garage to find a Latino cop standing at the door of the La Jolla house. "Hi, Mark," the cop said in a casual tone. "I'm just a friend of the family. Frank's the name."

"Hi," Mark said. "You're Mexican, right?"

"US citizen," the cop said. "Since five years old. Listen, your stepmom is a little worried about some things."

"What things?" The cop's badge read *Gonzalez*.

"Well, she's afraid people are taking advantage of you."

"What are you talking about? How are people taking advantage of me?"

"I dunno. Maybe something that happened a while back? She said you wouldn't mind if I took a look in your room. That okay?"

Mark stared. "I guess so. Sure."

"Well, let's take a look then, okay?" Gonzalez stood back and motioned him through the door.

Up in his room, Gonzalez went carelessly through his desk and bureau, whistling the tune from a Mexican *corrido*. Then he opened the closet door, reached way back on the shelf, and, still whistling, pulled down a medium-sized cardboard box. "Mind if I open this?"

"I've never seen that before. It must have been in there before I came."

Gonzalez's whistle changed to a long falling note when he opened the box. He reached in and pulled out a plastic bag of reddish weed. "About a pound, I'd say." He opened it and sniffed. "Damn good Mexican red. Probably worth a couple thousand on the street."

Mark shook his head to clear it. "*Jesus*. I told you I've never seen that before."

"You mean Billy Martin didn't ask you to drive down to Ensenada and pick this up? *Ya que estás Mexicano?*"

Billy Martin was a leather craftsman and older surfer who hung out with the Pumphouse Gang. "Billy Martin has never said a goddamn word to me."

"But you know who he is, right?"

"Sure, I know who he is."

"Did you know he was working with Sam Cook?" Cook was the smuggler Mark's stepmother had read about, recently sentenced to ten years.

"I don't know, and I don't care. It has nothing to do with me. But I know why that stuff was planted in my closet."

The cop held up both hands. "*Callete, mijo*. Now stop right there. Can you prove it was planted?"

"Of course, I can't."

"*Entonces, no me hagas tonterías*." Gonzalez smiled and drummed his fingers on the cardboard. "Look, we're only trying to help you stay out of real trouble."

The deal was, no charges would be filed if Mark went back to Mexico and never entered the US again.

He headed back to Paraíso in an ancient Chevy pickup he'd rebuilt from the ground up, and a few months later he opened his garage. Clamato said he'd had quite a few *novias* over the years, all of them *gringas* and all of them unhappy. "He likes to pull their wings off and watch them crawl," Clamato said. "It's part of his revenge on the world."

"Wow. And how do you know all this?"

"I used to surf Windansea myself back in the fifties. I keep in touch. 'Course, he doesn't know that." Clamato raised the jug and drank. "In *Sanctuary*? This guy Popeye? I don't think old Bill just made him up. He's the real thing."

"You're saying he's like Marco? But Marco's just a mechanic, no?"

"And Al Capone just owned a bar in Chicago."

"You mean he's—"

"And more, baby. People have died."

The mechanic seemingly hadn't moved since she saw him last, still at the workbench, still fiddling with a carburetor or something. Reassuring yet unnerving. Work went on, but was there any progress? She waved at him when he looked up, then walked to the Mercedes. Dust was already beginning to settle over it, and she traced a slow question mark with her forefinger on the front fender.

"What does that mean?" He was behind her.

She slowly turned, wondering how much her black bra showed through the borrowed white blouse. "It sounds like you're the only man in Baja Sur who can fix my car. But I don't even know your name." Bit of innocent deception to make her feel in control.

"They call me Marco Blanco around here. And yours?"

"My name is Wendy." Her voice sounded oddly formal. "Wendy Davis."

"And where are you from, Wendy?"

"North County. Encinitas."

"Encinitas? No way."

"Are you calling me a liar, Marco? That's not a very promising beginning."

"I just meant you're not *from* Encinitas, even if you live there now. I know people from Encinitas. But you're from the East someplace, right?"

"Well, I was born in Philadelphia, and I guess I grew up there. How did you know?"

"Just a way of acting." He paused. "You said 'beginning'?"

"Well, yeah. You're going to work on my engine, aren't you?"

"If you want me to."

"So what's the first step . . . in this process?"

He tossed his head. "I take the engine down, see what the damage is. And I give you an estimate. Then you order the parts, if you want to go ahead."

"When can you start?"

He grinned. Aw shucks. "Well, I already started. Took off the hoses and connections. She's ready to come out."

She's ready to come out. What if she didn't want that? She had other options, no?

"If you want, I can reconnect them," he said smoothly. "Wouldn't take more than half an hour. I was just trying to save you time."

She watched while he got things ready: unbolting the mounts and the transmission, setting up a wheeled tripod with a chain lift over the open hood, attaching a chain bridle to the engine. Then, moving smoothly and efficiently and sometimes whistling a snatch of tune, he pulled on the chain ratchet to the lift and the engine slowly rose out of the car.

The damage wasn't as bad as it could have been. The pistons, rings, and cylinder walls were all in pretty good shape because the problem had been detected early. But yes, like he'd thought, the crankshaft and bearings were badly worn. She could get away with just replacing them, although now that the engine was out and apart he'd recommend a total rebuild.

"You must think I'm rich," she said for the second time in two days.

He turned away. "I'll give you a list of the parts we're going to need, and I'll work up my estimate. How'd you like Judy's?"

"Fine."

He shook his head. "They're crazy over there, you know that, don't you. And they charge too much. Look, my mother's got a little *palapa* she rents out up on the hill on the other side of the valley above Pancho Clamato's. Want me to find out if it's vacant?"

"No, that's all right."

"It's only thirty dollars a week. Plus I can probably get you a discount if I'm working on your car."

"Well, okay. Ask her." She opened the trunk of the Mercedes and pulled out her bag. "Meanwhile, I'll take this over to Judy's."

"Put it in the truck and I'll drive you." Marco grinned. "It's way too hot to drag that heavy thing through the streets."

When she called her Hell's Angel mechanic from the town's only public phone to order the parts, he offered to fly them down himself for nothing. And he offered to stay and do the work for exactly what the other mechanic would ask (not more than $2,500, he figured), plus pay for his own room and board. "I been caretaking that old bus for a long time, Wendy." She always had trouble fitting his mild voice to his 250-pound body. "If it was ruined, why . . ." He paused. "I've never been south of the border, y'know. I'm due for a goddamn vacation."

She was touched, very, but she really couldn't let him go to all that trouble. What about tools? What about a place to work? The mechanic here seemed very . . . ah . . . *capable.*

The Hell's Angel laughed. "A capable Mexican mechanic is like a hen with teeth."

"He's got good teeth." She laughed self-consciously. "And he speaks perfect English. Must have spent time in the US. Plus people say he's the best mechanic in the whole state."

"Okay," the Hell's Angel said. "So you like him, hunh?"

"Hey! I've only just met him."

He chuckled. "Look, it's going to take me a week or two to round up the parts. Can you deal with that?"

"Of course, I can. You know you're saving my life."

"Just drive carefully, Wendy," the Hell's Angel said. "Call me if there's any trouble. Call me anyway in a week. Want me to go over to your house every once in a while to pick up the mail and stuff?"

"Greg, that would be so *great*." She realized she'd hardly ever used his name.

Her friend Dave didn't want to give up his room at the luxurious Twin Dolphins in Cabo for a two-hour bus ride and a funky bed-and-breakfast. "I'll come if you need me, for sure. But you know I've only got five days. I'm really sorry about the car, but hey, don't say I didn't warn you."

"I won't." She tried to keep the relief out of her voice. "Have a great time. I'll see you back home in a month or so."

She canceled with much more regret a shoot for *National Geographic Adventure* on women competing in the Molokai Channel paddleboard race. She knew the Molokai Channel, thirty-two miles of spectacularly rough, windy open ocean. A plum assignment even though it was her first for them, and who knew if they'd ever give her another?

Finally, her book editor, a hearty but evasive former sportswriter for the London *Times*, who wouldn't tell her how many copies were in the first printing. But he did say *Publishers Weekly* had given it a "very positive" advance review. "I like it, Wendy. 'The photographer's off in the wilds of Mexico and cannot be reached at the moment.' How *can* you be reached, by the way? The old cleft stick?"

"Well, there's email. There's a hookup here. Hotmail's easy."

"Hotmail's everywhere, isn't it?" He sounded distant. "Well, if there's anything urgent I'll let you know. Keep in touch, will you? We won't tell your public about the car."

The telephone operator accepted her money grumpily, and she walked out into brilliant sunshine. A light northwest breeze was just easing in, and the fronds on the taco palms vibrated gently. The beach was about a mile away, down dusty lanes among the irrigated farm fields. Judy had told her the route, but swimming was dangerous. The water was deep right up to the sand, and big ocean waves came in unimpeded. It was called Playa de los Muertos because several people had drowned there.

The sand crunched merrily under Wendy's sandals. Quail and white-winged doves called from the big mango trees and taco palms beside the fields. A farmer bent over his hoe straightened up to watch her, and she found herself singing her favorite walking song, "On the Sunny Side of the Street." The road ended in huge dunes, high enough to give a great view of the green valley, the little town with its white church tower up on the south bank, and the jagged mountains hazy in the distance.

The huge ocean beach ended in sharp hills to the south and stretched to infinity to the north. Not a soul in sight. A platoon of pelicans surfed the air currents on the wave faces, which Wendy figured might be six feet at most and easily swimmable. She'd brought a towel from the inn to lie on but no bathing suit. Does a tree falling in the forest make a sound if no one is around to hear it? She luxuriously pulled off her clothes, waded into the frothing white soup, and dove into a wave face. Out beyond the break, she jackknifed and swam for the bottom, eyes open to the spangled blue.

Just before sunset, Marco drove her up to his mother's *palapa* in his truck. It was high on the hillside, higher than most of the other houses.

Very basic, one room, a palm-thatched roof and walls of woven sticks, no glass in the windows. A one-burner propane gas ring, a propane camping refrigerator, kerosene lamps, a tiny bathroom with a sink, shower, and toilet. Electrical service hadn't gotten that far up the hill, but water wasn't a problem because the town storage tank was right behind the house. They'd run their own line into it.

She tested the bed: a foam pad on a wooden platform with an old brass headboard for decoration. "Did you ask your mother about a discount?"

Marco motioned her out into the sandy little yard, protected by a big green cactus, a waist-high fence of woven sticks, and a small flame tree in full red bloom. The sun was beginning to dip into the sea, losing its roundness and becoming more like a flaming orange helium balloon. Chimes carried from the cinder-block church across the valley. "Lived here myself until I built my own place. It's kind of scenic, isn't it?"

"It is." She walked to the fence and gazed out at the view. "So where is your place?"

"Next to the shop. You saw it. Much more convenient."

"Convenient?" She tilted her head. "You're not married, I guess."

"Just waiting for the right girl." He was fiddling with a loose stick in the fence. "My mother said yeah, she'd give you the place for twenty US a week, since I'm working on your car."

"When could I move in?"

"Tomorrow."

No, wait. It was all too fast, too perfect. Maybe she should talk to Judy about it?

You better act fast when you make a decision. It might be the wrong one. Her brother used to say that. She watched the sun disappear, half-expecting to see the omen of a green flash, but it didn't happen.

"Hey, I worked up an estimate." The aw-shucks grin.

It was very high, $3,000, but of course she'd already ordered the parts. And after she accepted the estimate, deciding on the *palapa* wasn't too hard.

Nature Takes Its Course

Investigations at my erstwhile boarding school ruled against arson, but the school was as unenthusiastic about having me back as I was about going. I begged to be sent to the local public high, but thanks to our father's English fetish for boarding schools I ended up at a second-rate outfit in the Colorado Rockies. Six thousand feet above sea level, nature finally took its course: I grew five inches, my voice changed, I made the climbing team and the honor roll. But Colorado always seemed to me like a papier-mâché stage set that you could poke a hole through and nothing would be on the other side. My sister wasn't there to make it real: that was the problem, looking back. I don't mean *physically* there, of course.

She'd been trundled off to an elite, verdant girls' prep overlooking the Potomac River in the Washington suburbs. It had a name for being both social and very academic: there were teas and dances, graduates went off to top colleges and married boys who were slated for white-shoe law firms, the most prestigious banks, the diplomatic corps, and the CIA.

After a month or two, my sister was put on probation for roller-skating nude through the library. She made matters worse in the spring by taking up white-water kayaking in the Potomac, down the cliff from her school, in place of afternoon tea with the headmistress. The kayaking was definitely not sanctioned by the school—she'd become a kind of mascot for a group of young government men who did it to let off steam after hours.

"We are a little at a loss what to make of Wendy," the headmistress wrote our parents (I found the letter after our father's death, going through boxes in the attic). "While we admire her spirit and feel she might be rather an addition to the School, we obviously can't allow her to take undue risks while under our supervision. So we are forced to place her on bounds, and I must tell you that if she persists in her present activity we will have no alternative but to send her home."

This was followed by a letter from our father (carbons in the folder) asking for more details.

The next letter was unabashedly on CIA letterhead:

Dear Mr. Davis,

I hope you'll forgive me if I'm out of line. I just feel you should know that your daughter Wendy is a very, very talented young athlete, one of the most talented I've ever personally known. A small group of us white-water fanatics are training now on the Potomac with the hope and expectation that kayaking will be allowed as an Olympic event in the next Games. We have the highest safety standards, the best equipment, and are all former collegiate and/or Olympic competitors in one field or another. We'd be honored to include Wendy in our group, not only as by far the youngest, but also as the sole female. We would of course take full responsibility for her safety and well-being. Sir, would you and Mrs. Davis consider signing a release so the school will allow her to participate?

However, no such release was in the folder. There was a last letter from the headmistress reporting Wendy was in the hospital having almost drowned on Great Falls (no one in her group had ever dared it, but she'd taken an early-morning shot alone), and was slated to

43

undergo a series of psychological tests designed to identify her "conflict points, which very often had to do with a girl's home life." After review, these results would be forwarded, along with the school's recommendations. As far as I know, our parents never visited her while she was in the hospital, and they never told me a thing. Later, they explained they hadn't wanted to "bother" me at my new school.

I'd written her many times from out in Colorado, chatty, lighthearted, superficial notes, not like the ones from the other school. She never answered, and when I came home for the summer she'd already been shipped to England. Our father had convinced our mother that the best thing would be to spend a year far away from her "conflict points," boarding with keen sailing friends of his in Hampshire.

But there was some kind of major blowout when our parents went over to see her for Christmas (I stayed with a classmate in the Texas Panhandle), and my sister was put in a place called Briarcliffe, a fancy mental hospital in the Connecticut woods. I was not allowed to visit when I came home the next June after graduation, and phone calls were forbidden. Our father described her as "just needing a bit of peace and quiet." Our mother refused to talk about her at all.

So I hijacked the little Husky for the second time. The hospital was only a couple of hours' drive. Like before, I hid in the trees around the main building and waited for her to appear, surprised there were no fences to keep them in.

I waited for almost two hours, but she never showed. Plenty of other people wandered around or sat on benches and chairs. I thought my sister was probably confined to her room behind thick wire screens, maybe even in a straitjacket. Finally, I marched in the door and demanded to see her.

To my amazement, the nurse smiled, told me to sit down in the waiting room, and someone would tell her I was here. She was just finishing "a session." The waiting room seemed very like our living room at home, right down to the musty smell of the blue velvet armchairs. I sat as far from the door as possible so my sister wouldn't take me by surprise. I could feel my legs shaking. I hadn't seen her for more than two years.

The person who appeared in the doorway was a young woman in full flower—Gigi herself. Black cocktail sheath, high heels, pearls, coiffed brunette hair, lipstick, makeup discreetly applied. I could smell Chanel No. 5 as she kissed both my cheeks, and I could hear the light rasp of her stockings as she sat opposite me and arranged her legs. Her slightly lopsided, secret smile was new, too. She was still strong and wiry, the same racehorse legs, the muscles bunching in her upper arms and bare shoulders, but it only made her more stunning. And her square, clear blue eyes (that looked as if they had chunks of broken glass in them) were also the same. The same as mine.

We chatted about this and that in a bizarrely grown-up way, as if the waiting room that looked so much like our living room had turned us into our parents, and I finally asked her when she was due to come home.

"Never." With her new smile.

"What? Hey, you look wonderful. I guess you decided to be a girl after all."

"You do too. I guess you decided to be a boy."

"As our father would say, nature took its course." Peter and Wendy redux. Could I still feel the old split? Or rather, the old connection? "Hey, they said you couldn't have visitors. Or phone calls."

"Did *he* say that?"

"No, Mummy."

"And you believed her? That's always been your problem, Peter. But I'm glad you came to see me. I really am."

"Listen, you look good. You look *happy*. I was worried, believe it or not. You never answered any of my letters."

"I *am* happy. I guess all I needed was a good mental hospital." She had a mysterious new laugh that fitted with her smile. "I'm sorry about not writing."

"Well. I . . . *missed* you."

"I missed you too." She smoothed her hair back. "Do you like this dress?"

"Well, yeah . . . it's very . . ." I was going to say "sophisticated" but decided not to.

"For my sixteenth birthday. And the stockings." She giggled. "The underwear too. It's all from Lord and Taylor in New York. And the shoes."

"What about the pearls?" I was trying to picture the Lord and Taylor underwear.

"Cartier, but of cawsss."

"So they came up and took you shopping? Lucky you. They never did anything like that for *me*."

"Over my dead body." She angled forward in her chair. "I told Mummy to keep away, I didn't want to see her, I didn't want to hear from her." I watched a thick vein pulsing in her throat. "I told her I'd kill myself if she came."

I couldn't say a word. Now she had the same look as when I was cutting her hair in the abandoned barn. And I felt the same strange, involuntary shutter come down in my mind. *No one home. Cannot process.*

"They had *nothing* to do with it." She slowly relaxed. "Nothing. Nada. Hey, I've been taking Spanish lessons. I really am going to make it to Mexico, you know. Want to go with me?"

"Definitely," I said quickly.

"But you're going to college, aren't you? That's wonderful. Where is it?"

I cleared my throat. "Little way south of San Francisco."

"Perfect. Ten thousand miles from home. It must be on the way to Mexico. I'll pass through on my way and pick you up."

"I'll be waiting," I said. "So who'd you go shopping with, then?"

"What?"

"Who bought you all the birthday goodies?"

"Ah." I don't think I'd ever seen her blush before. "Wouldn't you like to know."

46

"One of those kayakers, right?"

"Maybe, maybe not."

"Someone from here?"

She tilted her head and thought. She had big news, and she never had been good at keeping a secret, especially from yours truly. She wanted to tell so badly it was almost forcing its way out of her mouth. A deep breath: "Promise not to breathe a word?"

"Of course, I promise."

"Cross your heart and hope to die?"

I crossed my heart. "I hope to die if I breathe a word."

She exhaled, eyes shining. "Okay. You're my brother so you should know. His name is . . . *Carl*. There, I've said it."

"Okay . . . but who's Carl?"

"Well, if it weren't for him, I'd still be . . . you know."

"You mean . . . he's your *therapist*?"

She nodded eagerly. "A lot more than that."

"Holy shit, Wendy. How old is he?"

"Don't you see? It doesn't *matter*. I'm happy, and I'm not crazy anymore." With girlish wonderment. "He's helped me become a *woman*."

"Wendy. You're only sixteen."

"I'm grown up now. Can't you see?"

I looked away. In another second I'd be crying. I didn't want her to look grown up. I wanted my sister back. "Look. I want to tell you something," I heard myself croak. "I'm sorry for what happened. It was all my fault."

"What? What are you talking about?" For the first time she looked scared.

"In the car. I turned us in, remember? Maybe we could have made it. I've thought about it a million times."

"Oh *that*." She laughed in relief. "I was plenty pissed for a while, all right. But then I realized you did the right thing. The whole thing was nuts, wasn't it? What were we thinking?"

We smiled carefully at each other from opposite banks of a fast, cold river.

On the way out past the reception desk, something made me stop. Then I went on. Then at the door I turned back. The receptionist was on the phone, and I stood there while she told someone that Dr. Reiger would be available for consultation at 10:30 a.m. the next day.

"Excuse me," I said when she hung up. "Would you happen to have a facility brochure, by any chance?"

"Of course." She smiled, reached under the counter, and handed me an expensive heavy matte cream-colored folder inscribed with the place's name in cursive black lettering as if for an invitation. I opened it back in the Hillman. Dr. Karl Reiger was Briarcliffe's new director. He'd come from Austria.

Volver

It was an open-air dance floor with Van Goghish stars overhead. The girls sat together at tables, giggling, and the guys stood along the wall, looking them over, like high school dances in gringolandia. The little band played mostly one-two one-two ranchero numbers, but every once in a while they'd throw in a waltz. Pancho Clamato didn't know the step, so he and Wendy—in her most demure outfit, a sleeveless, skirted white cotton dress—would sit those out.

Then she saw the pushcart man, still in the same white baggy *campesino* clothes and cowboy hat, watching her sadly from the stag line. She smiled and nodded to him. "He's got great honey," she said to Clamato. "I bought two bottles when I first got here. He said his name was Augustin something."

"They call him Felipe Reyes. From the old radio show," Clamato said. "*Felipe Reyes, amigo del pueblo.* The Mexican Lone Ranger. He rides into town, kills the bad guys, rescues the girl, and rides off into the sunset. I told you this place is famous for its nicknames. There's Jefe the town retard, Felipe the Lone Ranger, and El Farolito the lighthouse, a blind guy with a guitar. Maybe you've seen him. Anyway, they mostly have a twist."

"More than a *twist.* So Felipe Reyes is actually Don Quixote?"

Pancho Clamato snapped his fingers. "*Precisamente.* Instead of a windmill he takes on a D-9 Cat. Drives the sucker into the ocean because the surfers tell him it was leveling ground for a new whorehouse."

"What was it really doing?"

"Hotel." Clamato laughed. "Right on the break. They never found another D-9, so the thing was never built, see, so Felipe saved the break instead of saving the town's morals like he thought. Felipe Reyes, *amigo del surfo*. Hey, Isabel."

A sturdy Mexican woman with long, tangled black hair threw her arms around him, kissed his neck, and stared past him at Wendy. "Clamato never comes here before. What you do to him? Put on a spell?"

"Wendy, Isabel. Isabel, Wendy," Clamato said. "The town *artista*. Just to make things *complete*."

"We were talking about nicknames," Wendy said.

"*Díos mío.*" Isabel rolled her eyes. "I hate to think what mine is."

"Want me to tell you?" Clamato asked.

"*Claro que nunca.*" She smiled at Wendy. "Wait till you get one."

"She already has one," Clamato said. "Record time. Only took a week."

"I have a nickname? Okay, you *have* to tell me."

"Doña Mercedes. Not bad, hunh?"

"That depends," Wendy said. "What's the twist?"

"Ah! So it's *you*," Isabel said. "Marco Blanco's new project. *Claro*, I mean the car."

"Is that a good thing?" Wendy asked.

"He take pride in his work," Isabel said carefully. "This I know."

"Well, good. Are you from here too?"

"Mexico City. *Una chilanga*. But I'm here almost a year. A good place to work. What do you do?"

"I'm a photographer. And you paint?"

"Some. A little performance stuff. Little of this, little of that, you know? Come by sometime, I show you. How long you'll be here, *querida*?"

"Until the car's fixed, at least."

Isabel shot a glance at Clamato. "*Bueno*, Mercedes. Clamato shows you where I live, right down the street. You can come tomorrow if you want. Around *mediodía*, okay?" She wove her way gracefully through the tables and sat down with the fat telephone operator and a striking young girl Wendy had noticed earlier in the phone office. With the next ranchero number, Isabel and the telephone operator got up to dance.

"So now I'm Mercedes," Wendy said. "What's the twist again?"

"There's not always a twist," Clamato said. "Look at mine. So how's Marco doing, anyway?"

"Still waiting for the parts. But he took the block to La Paz today to have the cylinders honed and the valves ground."

"Isn't that him over there?" Clamato nodded toward the bar behind her. She could recognize Marco from the back, in clean jeans and a white dress shirt with the sleeves turned back on his forearms, saying something to the guy next to him, standing hipshot, one elbow on the bar, one long-fingered hand around the neck of a Pacifico. The easy bend of the back from the narrow hips to the solid shoulders.

She and Clamato hopped around to a little number called "Camerón Pelado" and then sat down when the band struck up a slow waltz. She saw a white blur in the corner of her eye—it was Felipe Reyes asking Clamato for permission to dance with her. Clamato grinned and waved his hand, and she stood up and led the way back onto the dance floor. Felipe touched his hat gravely when she turned to face him, smiled, and held out her hands.

The number was "Volver," a great old flaming Latin love song, slow and stately. He held her at arm's length, and they started to twirl, a real waltz step like she'd learned in dancing class. Where did he learn to dance like that? She closed her eyes to feel it, and when she opened them again she saw they were dancing alone. Everyone else had left the floor.

Marco, still at the bar, had turned to watch. As they twirled, she looked over Felipe's shoulder, saw the mechanic smile, lean over, and say something into his friend's ear, the friend nodding and smiling back. She danced more extravagantly, swinging her legs out, holding

Felipe close and sometimes resting her cheek on his shoulder. Seeing if she could wipe the smirk from Marco's face and thinking in fact that she succeeded about halfway with the reckless excitement of a girl at her first major prom. Floating and swirling in three-quarter time: *I dare you.*

Felipe was looking at the sky and didn't seem to notice, and when the song ended, the band just looked at each other, grinned, and started over again.

Y volver, volver, volver
En tus brazos otra vez
Estaría donde estés
Yo sé perder
Yo sé perder
Quiero volver
Volver, volver . . .

When the music finally stopped, people were whistling, cheering, and carrying on as if they were Fred Astaire and Ginger Rogers. Was the entire crowd shitfaced? Marco had folded his arms, staring, and she staring back. *I dare you. Do your worst.*

Then a drunk fisherman began to weave his way across the empty floor toward her. The fisherman had lost three fingers on his right hand in a boating accident, and she later learned his nickname was El Capitán Garfio. Captain Hook to her Wendy.

Felipe held his ground as the fisherman tried to push past. Suddenly, they were grappling, then they were rolling on the dance floor. Someone tried to pull them apart, and someone else slugged him. The band struck up another ranchero number, and after the first few beats, almost in time with the music, a wave of drunken men broke over them, serenaded by screaming women.

Clamato pulled her clear while the mélée took over, yelling something in her ear when the cops showed up, four of them. Three went to break up the fight, and the other, heavy set with gray hair, and probably the senior officer, came over to Wendy and Clamato.

He was smiling as he asked her name. He wrote it down on a pad of paper, asked if she was American, and wrote down the answer to that. He asked how long she'd been there and wrote down those answers, asked where she was staying, and wrote that down, too. He was smiling the whole time.

"*Entonces.*" He was looking at Clamato. "*Con quien anda?*"

"*Yo soy soltera,*" Wendy said. Since arriving here, her Spanish had picked up considerably.

"*Soltera pero no solterona,*" the cop said. Single, but not an old maid.

"*Anda conmigo,*" Clamato said.

"*Pues, mejor que la sacas.*" He never stopped smiling.

"*Gracias,*" Clamato said carefully, turning to Wendy. "He wants us to get out of here."

"No. He told you to take me out," Wendy said, and turned to the cop. "*Estamos en punto de salir.*"

The other three cops had gotten Felipe back on his feet and cleared out the drunks. With a smile, one of them handed Felipe his crushed hat, which he put on. She could see he was looking their way from under the brim.

It felt like she was walking down the aisle. When she got to Felipe, she lifted her skirt and curtsied, the way she'd been taught in dancing class. Felipe doffed his hat with a perfect flourish and bowed back—she couldn't remember ever having been bowed to before. She put out her hand, and he kissed the back of it. Marco was nowhere in sight.

Her Own Worst Enemy

I was staying with a friend from school in Easthampton a week or so after my Briarcliffe visit when Trish, my father's secretary, called. "Peter, your mother's been in a car accident. She's in the hospital. Maybe you ought to come home."

"Wow. Is it serious?"

"I don't think so. But maybe you should come anyway."

It didn't sound serious, but you never knew in our family. Nothing was clear with us, except the hatred that sizzled between my sister and our mother. I took the next train to New York, cabbed from Grand Central to Pennsylvania Station, and was lucky enough to catch the express. When I got to the house at eight, Hannah, the cook, said my father had gone to a dinner party but would be back early.

I called the hospital, but the nurse told me my mother was too tired to talk, didn't want visitors, and that I should come next morning. Hannah fixed lamb chops, okra, and baby potatoes, and afterward I sat in the living room waiting for my father, looking through old family photo albums and feeling like everyone in them was a stranger. I crashed a little after midnight and didn't get up when I heard his car in the drive.

On our way to the hospital the next morning, my father told me the details: car totaled, five broken ribs, broken collarbone, broken hip, multiple contusions. A hell of a lot more serious than I'd been led to believe. I didn't even ask why he hadn't called me himself. I already knew why. It was business as usual, and as usual I just sat there and took it, feeling hollower than ever.

In *Rebel Without a Cause*, one of my favorite movies, there's a scene I sometimes think about when I think of my father. James Dean, the confused teenager, is on his knees, arms around his father's waist, howling, "Please, Dad, tell me what to do." His father is doing the dishes in a woman's floral bibbed apron, looking completely nonplussed. He's not a bad guy, just out of his depth.

I think about my father too when I see photos of Queen Elizabeth and Prince Philip. My father and the prince, consorts, kept men, were way too handsome for their own good. So they'd been collected. The queen and my mother looked very much alike into the bargain, the same regal frumpiness masking their power.

Mummy had been coming back from the country in her Saab with a load of fresh corn. There was no stoplight where her little road crossed the four-lane Westchester Pike; she picked the wrong moment to pull out and was hit squarely on the driver's side by an eighteen-wheel car-carrier going about sixty. "The road was straight. The visibility was good. She just picked the wrong moment, that's all." My father sounded like a sleepwalker. "You should see the car. It's a miracle she survived. You know, I asked what I could do for her last night and she said, '*Nothing,* just go to the dinner party and tell me about it.' She'd been looking forward to it so much." He sighed and looked at me as if seeing me for the first time. "She'd let me do *nothing.* You know, she's always been her own worst enemy."

In the hospital, my mother was hooked up to a respirator, and her eyes were closed. An electrocardiogram showed her heartbeat in graceful green curves of light that snaked across a black screen. The nurse said she'd "taken a turn" around dawn, and that the doctor would be in shortly.

I couldn't remember anything the doctor said while he opened one of his mother's eyes and shone a light into it. The pupil didn't change size. "It looks very dry," my father said in a shaky voice, and the doctor abstractedly lubricated the eye with a few drops of water.

"Hadn't we better call Wendy?" I asked.

My father was staring at the electrocardiogram.

"Papa?"

He turned, gave me a polite smile, and raised his eyebrows.

"Wendy," I said. "Shouldn't she be here?"

My father cleared his throat. The only other sound was the clicking and wheezing of the respirator. He turned back to the electrocardiogram.

"I'll go and call her," I said. "I'll be back in a minute."

The nurse showed me to a pay phone, but I didn't have enough change. I charged the call to the home number, Midway 2–0816, and heard Hannah accepting. Then the woman at Briarcliffe said my sister couldn't come to the phone.

"What? This is an emergency! I have to talk to her."

"Who is this, please?"

"This is her *brother*. Her mother has just been in a car accident. She's—"

The woman put me on hold. After what seemed like hours a man's voice said in a German accent: "This is Doctor Reiger." There was a long silence after I explained what had happened. Then Reiger asked if my father was available.

"He's at the . . . bedside."

"Quite so. I'm very sorry." Another long silence. "Under the circumstances, I don't think it would be beneficial for your sister to hear this information now. She's . . . ah . . . she's in a fragile condition and in fact tomorrow she's scheduled to be transferred."

"Transferred? Where to?"

"To a more inclusive facility."

"A more inclusive facility? What are you talking about?"

"A facility that is better able to meet her needs. Your mother and I discussed this several days ago when she visited here. . . . These were her wishes. Your father will know the details, of course."

"He never told me about any of this."

Reiger didn't say anything.

"What's going on, anyway?" My voice suddenly cracked.

"I think you know what is going on," Reiger said after a short time. "After all, your mother acted because of what you told her, did she not? After your own visit? Please accept my heartfelt condolences, but I must go." The line clicked and went dead.

Because of what I told her? Numbly, I hung up the phone and marched back down the long white hall to the intensive care unit. At my mother's bedside my father and I watched the green curves on the electrocardiogram flatten out to a straight line. I realized I'd never seen him cry before, then realized I was crying myself. How very strange and sad: one minute the line was jumping and the next it was flat. I could almost feel the fatal pressure on the accelerator against my own foot. And suddenly I knew she'd done it on purpose.

Your father will know the details, Reiger had assured me in his Dr. Strangelove accent. But now we were crying together. I thought of putting my arm around his shoulders. I wish I had, but such a gesture wasn't in our family repertoire.

The time was never right to ask about the details. Three months after our mother's death, our father remarried, to an old family friend. My sister came to the wedding with an attendant on a day's leave from her new facility, wearing a loose black wool dress that seemed very similar to the one she'd chosen for me in the Sears Roebuck. She wouldn't even look at me, much less talk. Her face was closed, and if I'd passed her on the street I might not have recognized her. She could have been anywhere from sixteen to thirty-five.

Hot Sake

And here was Ellen on the phone twenty years later, telling me in her rapid-fire New York voice that my sister's book had just hit the stands at Barnes & Noble, a not-too-bad display on one of the front tables. So far it had only been reviewed in the trade press: a rave in *Publishers Weekly* and a bash in *Kirkus*: "Wendy Davis tries valiantly to combine Arbus and Warhol through the entire spectrum of photographed sports, including her own work. This would be difficult, perhaps impossible, even if she had the talent."

But it was early on the stands, a good thing to be on time for the major reviews. "Thanks," I said to Ellen. "I'll run over and get a copy. How's it look?"

"Well, garish. The cover is that Clay-Liston shot, you know? With Clay crouching over the body, showing his teeth? But in really, really hot pink and purple, with blue stars."

"Catches the eye, right?"

"You don't have to defend her. She's not even speaking to you. How long has it been?"

"Ten years. We tried seeing a shrink together, then blooie. Anyway, she doesn't need me to defend her. So, are we still on for tonight?"

"Unless you've made other plans."

"I've got a new manuscript to get through. See you at the Blue Ribbon at seven?"

"Okay, my sweet." She blew a kiss into the phone. "I'll try to survive on my own until then. I kind of liked the cover, by the way. You know me, I've always liked garish."

At lunchtime I walked from my office to Union Square and circled warily around the Barnes & Noble display tables, heart beating as if I were about to see my sister in the flesh. There she'd be, with her slight crooked smile and her wide shoulders, watching me out of my own eyes. It would be like looking into a mirror for the first time in ten years.

But where was the book? Could Ellen have been putting me on? Only the New Discoveries table left, and of course that's where it was, a low stack of four copies, the top one not even raised. Automatically, I removed the prop from a neighboring book and used it for one of hers. *In Sport.* The title in dark blue italic lettering over the hot pinks, purples, and electric blues of Clay-Liston. The standard quality coffee-table production, but slighter than most. Nervously I flipped it over to see the author photo, but there was none. As if she knew I was going to look for it. The brief bio read: *Wendy Davis is a sports photographer and artist whose work has appeared in most major national sports magazines. Her art is included in the permanent collection of the San Diego Museum of Art and has been shown at the Gardos Gallery in Los Angeles, among others. She lives in Encinitas, California, and drives a 1956 Mercedes cabriolet.*

In the first section, a discriminating collection of the great sports photos of the past—Babe Ruth pointing his bat, Billie Jean King at the moment of victory over Bobby Riggs, Dempsey KO-ing Firpo, Jesse Owens taking a hurdle at the Berlin Games, Toni Sailer on the grand slalom course in Kitzbühel, Bernard Moitessier at sea in the roaring forties, the 1956 Yale Olympic crew after their triumphant finish in Melbourne—retouched and augmented as in Warhol's portraits of Jackie Kennedy, Marilyn Monroe, and Chairman Mao. The subject matter was so extreme that they didn't seem derivative. Some of them worked, some of them didn't. But at least (I thought) they were all audacious.

The second section featured her own shots, some retouched, some natural, and my heart sank. She *was* trying to be the Arbus of sport—portraits of anguish, marginal characters verging on the freakish, big names caught off-balance—and she was not quite bringing it off. She hadn't found her own way.

Leaving the propped-up copy on the table, I carried the others to the checkout line and told the girl that the stock had been sold out. It was the least I could do.

A wooden trencher of New York's best sushi arrived, and Ellen poured our cups full of hot sake. We'd reached the stage in our relationship where she was beginning to ask about its direction. Where was it all *headed*? Why does it have to *head* anywhere, I'd answer. Aren't we having fun with it the way it is? We weren't living together, but sometimes I'd spend the night at her place on West 12th Street, sometimes she'd spend the night at my loft. Sex was comfortable—if it didn't work out, she'd laugh and talk about training wheels. She loved finding new restaurants and watching obscure movies, and she'd once flown alone to Bali to see the fields because of a line in a Sting song about gazing on fields of barley. Maybe I *would* end up marrying her. I could think of worse things.

Before Ellen there'd been Alaia, a hippie-dippy folk singer from Vermont who sang like Lucinda Williams. Then Barbara, a raging inferno of intellect and neuroses who'd been to Yale and done graduate work in English at Berkeley. And French Céline, a high-fashion ad stylist so picky and critical I finally put her on a plane back to Paris. There were others. Sometimes I had trouble remembering them all, though I seemed to have no trouble remembering their breasts. Their nipples . . . the delicious range of shapes, sizes, and colors, each pair completely unique, like snowflakes. The good-byes were always dramatic, much more than the hellos. You could write a pretty good article about all the good-byes.

I lost my virginity in my junior year of college, living in a group house in a bad section of Palo Alto. It took no great effort on my part. She was the sister of one of my housemates and the former girlfriend of another, very smart and funny, overweight and Jewish. Endearingly called her bras "miracles of engineering." Her nipples were unremarkable. We both knew it was just a fling, casual and unthreatening.

After a few weeks of sleeping with her, I visited a university counselor. "I'm kind of worried about my sex life."

The lady counselor, somewhere in her forties, looked politely interested. How many times had she heard this line before? "And why is that? Aren't you getting any?"

"Well, yes, but . . ."

"You mean, you don't enjoy it?"

"Sure I *enjoy* it. But . . ."

The lady leaned forward with a little smile. I had her attention. "But . . . what?"

"It just doesn't seem to be as great as I'd been led to believe."

The lady laughed as if this were the funniest thing she'd ever heard. Then she gently put her hand on my knee and said with great friendliness, "Well, join the club, Peter. You have absolutely nothing to worry about."

I left her office feeling very confused. Losing my virginity had certainly not been my first sexual experience. But there was no way to compare it with what had gone before.

Céline and I would make love for hours. During one of these endless sessions she caught me looking at my watch and blew up. "You check the time when you're making love with *me*?" she shrieked. "That's it, it's all over. You don't understand what life is about. You're nothing but a sitz-bath American."

As my "gay bachelor years" in the Big Apple slipped slowly by, there was one feeling I couldn't shake. Céline once called me a "black hole" (she pronounced it "owl"), typical French hyperbole, but there was a kernel of truth in it. There was an emptiness somewhere inside me, a hollow place, and as far as I knew there was only one person who could fill it.

"So I bought your sister's book," Ellen was saying. "Wow. Has she always been that, ah . . ."

I cocked my head, raised my eyebrows, and gave her my best shit-eating smile.

"Hey! I do believe you're jealous."

This seemed to be the time to tell Ellen about what had happened at Briarcliffe and afterward, something I'd been putting off. She looked wide-eyed over her cup of sake. "My God, Peter. She put her life in your hands. I hope you . . ."

I didn't say anything. I might have looked down at my plate. I might have looked guilty, even though I wasn't, as in the fire at school. It was all part of a syndrome. My sister had always given me the benefit of the doubt.

"Oh, Peter." She set down the sake, open-mouthed. "How could you have?"

My face began to burn. All wrong. She was on the wrong side and there was probably no turning back. Maybe I'd known that all along. "Ellen. Wait a minute. I didn't tell a soul. What do you think I am?"

"You told your beloved mother. Didn't you? And you didn't even *know* what was happening. All you knew was that he'd taken her shopping for her birthday. After she'd told her parents to fuck off. Girls that age get crushes, Peter. They just lose it. They're off on cloud nine, in a different world. Your mother should have known that, even if you were too fucking *dumb*."

"Ellen, for Christ's sake."

"What did she do? God, you goyim."

"Goyim? Goddamn it, you have a goy name yourself because your father was ashamed of his real one." My hands were shaking, my thumbs twitching back and forth across my fingertips—pill rolling, someone had called it. A syndrome from my mother's side of the family.

She turned her head from side to side slowly and tolerantly. "Okay, big surprise. So now we know what you really think about my family. Let's get back to what your mother did with your . . . *information*. Something awful, wasn't it?"

"What she did is beside the point, Ellen. *I . . . did . . . not . . . betray . . . my . . . sister.*"

"You really believe that, don't you, you arrogant asshole? You just can't see it, can you? That makes it even worse." Her lips pulled back from her teeth, and her black eyes blazed.

I slammed my fist down as hard as I could on the table and watched her flinch and raise her hands as if she expected me to hit *her*. People at the other booths had stopped talking and were staring at us. It made me want to really give them their money's worth.

"Take it back, Ellen. You can't say that to me."

"I can say anything I goddamn well want to anybody. But I sure as hell am not going to tell *you* any secrets."

"Keep your fucking secrets. Now take it back, or I'll do something I'll *really feel sorry about*." The thing was on rails now. The rubberneckers were not going to be disappointed.

"Hah! *You*? Feel sorry? When was the last time?"

"I'm sorry I ever told you that story. It was too important. You got it all wrong."

Her eyes narrowed. "What does that mean, Peter? Can't you stand to hear the truth?"

"Bullshit. I told you the *truth*. But you wouldn't know it if it bit you on the ass. Somebody pays you and you write it up: *Always Maxipads are the answer to your prayers.*"

Her eyes and teeth were the last things I saw before the world went red. I yelled and tried to get to my feet, but a table corner caught my leg and then I was on the floor, hands to my face. Some liquid ran over my lips and I licked them involuntarily. Hot sake.

Someone poured a pitcher of cold water over my head, and I heard a Japanese voice telling me to open my eyes. Water poured into them when I did, and I screwed them closed again. Someone put a cold face towel on my forehead and mopped the rest of my face with another. There were murmuring voices all around.

Finally, the Japanese voice again. "You want 911, sir?"

"You tell me. Can hot sake hurt the eyes?"

"Not think so, sir."

I slowly sat up and held out my hand. "Can you give me another face towel?"

When I felt it in my palm, I dabbed my eyes with it and tried opening them. Through a pink haze, I could see that indeed a number of rubberneckers were standing around, but Ellen was nowhere in view.

Another one down. I finished the sushi alone.

Fanning the Flames

Back in my loft on Crosby Street on the outskirts of Soho, I placed a call to my sister's best friend Claire, recently divorced from her mountain-climbing husband and living in Livingston, Montana. I knew Claire from childhood. She'd been in my sister's class in grade school and often came over to play. She was the prettiest of my sister's buddies and had a childish crush on me that I found kind of flattering.

She'd called me after our mother was killed, but instead of ranting and raving about my alleged betrayal (assuming Wendy had told her by then), she said she was sorry for me and burst into tears.

Twelve years later, at our father's funeral (he'd died of pancreatic cancer and Claire had come, as she put it, as Wendy's "chaperone"), she talked my sister and me into a week of joint sessions with a shrink friend of hers in Jackson Hole, where she was then living as a newlywed.

Wendy was back on her feet by then. It might not have been I who betrayed her but I had to admit that, from the cold viewpoint of history, blowing the whistle on Reiger had not turned out too badly. Rockland State Psychiatric Hospital, where she was transferred from Briarcliffe, had been good for her. Her chief therapist this time around had been a no-nonsense woman, and she'd known where she stood at all times. In a few months she'd been re-accepted at her old school on the Potomac. She'd graduated with honors and spent a couple of years at the MIT film school. When our father died she was living in Encinitas, a beach town north of San Diego, making a start as a freelance sports photographer.

All she'd wanted from our father's estate had been the Mercedes. She planned to start driving it west right after the funeral. It was early spring, still raw, just a tinge of green on some of the trees. After the coffin had been covered, the three of us—Claire, my sister, and I—found ourselves standing alone on green grass among gravestones, me in a dark blue suit, the girls identically dressed in black wool sheaths with sleeves. Claire's blond hair pulled back in a ponytail, my sister's brunette cropped exactly the way I'd cut it in the barn many years before. I'd seen her a few times since the blowout—a Christmas or two, and at our sick father's bedside—but the time was never right for a "discussion." I barely dared to look at her for fear she'd vanish in front of my eyes.

And what was I going to say? I knew she'd never believe me. Sometimes I didn't even believe myself.

"All right, you guys," we heard Claire say. "This has been going on long enough, don't you think? And don't you dare ask what I'm talking about."

My sister and I just stood there looking at all the familiar family names on the gravestones. Our parents were having their final party, and as usual we weren't invited.

"Peter here has just turned thirty," Claire told Wendy. "A new decade has just gotten under way. Your loving parents are now history. I suggest you swing through Jackson on your drive west and meet your brother on neutral territory. Just for five days. An hour together in the morning with a very capable friend of mine, then an afternoon of mountain climbing with yours truly, if you can keep up. What do you say?"

"All right," Wendy said conversationally, not looking at me. "If the car makes it."

"Peter?"

I didn't trust my voice, so I just nodded.

The sessions were a disaster: we only made it through three of them, and the issue of my "betrayal" never even came up. We never got beyond our mother and how differently we saw her. Like before, my old protective shutters clanged down, but my sister would only talk in generalities anyway. What exactly had been done to her? She wouldn't say. Of course, there were things I wouldn't talk about either.

The shrink's office had a big picture window with a breathtaking view of the Tetons, but our mother came in and took it over. Made it hers, like the eight-hundred-pound gorilla.

After that, Claire and I stayed in touch with a couple of phone calls a year, and I knew she was still in close touch with my sister, but the info she doled out was strictly bare bones, just enough to let me know my sister was still alive. She'd forward my letters and email, but wouldn't give out addresses. God knows, I tried.

"Haven't heard from you in a while," Claire said coolly and a little indistinctly. "What's up?" It was dinnertime in Livingston, and I could imagine her chewing on a tofu and bean sprout sandwich.

"Just got rid of another girlfriend. We got to arguing about Wendy, and she threw a cup of hot sake in my face. It's lucky I can still see."

Claire giggled. "You'll be okay. Did you love her?"

"God, no. Probably all for the best."

"What was the argument?"

"Oh, you know. The usual. I went over what had happened at Briarcliffe and she said I betrayed her. Isn't that what everyone thinks?"

A long silence. "You mean, isn't that what *I* think? Peter, I'm not going to touch that with a ten-foot pole. That isn't why you called, is it, I hope? What else is new?"

I was *that* close to hanging up, and actually counted to ten before I answered. Amazingly, it worked. "Well, Wendy's book just hit the stands here, among other things. Have you seen it?"

"Amazon's still listing it as not out yet, and the local bookshop won't have it in for weeks. But I did hear about the *Kirkus* review. So what do you think, big bro?" The words "big bro" had a nicely calibrated ironic edge. Claire had always been good at that.

"I think I'd like to go and cane the reviewer. Except they're too chickenshit to sign them. The book is brilliant, of course."

"Of course," Claire said, still chewing. "Why don't you drop her a line and tell her?"

"I thought I would. Is she still in Encinitas?"

"Actually, she's in Mexico for a while. But she'll come back sooner or later, and when she does, your letter will be waiting for her."

Mexico! My God, so she finally made it. Without me. I suddenly felt close to tears, as if I were a child again. Peter and Wendy! How far do people ever get from their childhoods, anyway?

We weren't children anymore, but she'd held on to the dream we'd shared . . . a flight to Neverland that I'd bollixed because I couldn't deal with what she was trying to tell me. Well, now she'd gotten there. She'd kept the faith.

And what had she found? Was it as amazing as we'd imagined it would be? Or did she need me to complete the picture?

Of course, Claire knew about our long-ago escapade, but she didn't mention it. I didn't want to dredge it up and all that went with it, so I kept my voice as even as possible. "She never answers my letters. I'm not sure she even reads them."

"Oh, she reads them, Peter. Of that you can be sure."

"What does she say about them?"

"Peter, I don't want to get into this. Just write her the letter. Who knows, maybe it'll do some good. The book is really important to her."

If it was so important to her (trying to keep it casual), why was she in Mexico just when it was coming out? No book signings? No author tours? Claire didn't know, or didn't want to say. Since the Jackson Hole sessions, my conversations with her were all kind of the same, a friendly but rueful sparring. "Have you heard from her at all?"

"I *did* get an email a few days ago." I could hear the clattering of dishes in the sink. "A bit worrisome, I have to say."

One of the few times she'd let her guard down. "What was worrisome about it?" I knew I sounded too eager.

"Peter, forget I said that, okay? I wasn't thinking."

"Listen, can you forward it to me? You don't have to say anything more, just push a button. You can erase the address."

A short silence. "I'm really sorry, Peter." She sighed. "But you know her. If she found out, she'd never forgive me."

We listened to each other breathing. "So do you think she'll ever forgive *me*, Claire? For something I didn't do?" Not a new question, but there did seem to be an opening.

"I love your sister, Peter. She's one of my best friends in all the world. Maybe time will take care of the problem."

"Jesus." I giggled compulsively. "That's what she used to say about our *mother*."

I could hear her sigh.

"Do you think ten years is a long enough time?" I went on. "Frankly, I've just about given up. You gave it your best shot, and I'm eternally grateful, but those sessions were a complete rat-fuck, you'll have to admit. I'll never forget her face when we went our separate ways . . . Talk about stone. Hey, remember that time I tracked her down in Encinitas and she called the cops?"

"Reported you as a stalker? Yeah, I remember." A long silence, then almost in a whisper. "Don't give up, Peter. Last year was the millennium, don't forget. It's a whole new *century*."

Claire always thought in macro terms. It was kind of endearing. After I hung up, I rubbed my ear, which felt tender from the pressure of the phone.

Because It's His Nature

From the little yard of her *palapa* she could hear the dance music continuing across the valley. The sky looked like pinholed black velvet with an inconceivable source of light on the other side. Every once in a while, a pickup would clatter up the hill, radio blasting *norteño*, and fade away into the desert. Dogs barked, some near, some far. Her skin felt thinner and more sensitive; even the light breeze gave her goose bumps. There was night jasmine blooming not too far away.

She went inside, lit the kerosene lamp, took her notebook off the shelf, and lay on the bed, propping the notebook on her thighs. Her first entry since she got here. What was the date? Mid-June would have to do.

Every morning a gimlet-sharp laser of white-hot sunlight penetrates a chink in the palo de arco siding of my house facing the street, bouncing off my coffee cup and setting dust motes dancing. One morning the light goes out. I tiptoe over and peer through to see why: there's an eye peering back at me.

Whose eye was it? Was it our mother's? Was it the eye of God? I looked into this eye until I felt myself disappearing. It never blinked. I've never felt so . . . naked . . . as I do now. And of course there's a man involved. A dangerous man. The eye was probably his.

How that excites me!

The clattering of yet another pickup faded out on the street near the *palapa*, and a cab door opened and slammed closed. Footsteps scrunching up the sandy walk, a knock on the door.

"Who is it?" She kept her voice flat, knowing the answer. *I dare you.*

"It's me." The door opened, and a white-shirted figure glimmered. "How are you doing? Are you okay?"

"I'll survive, thanks. No broken bones."

He closed the door quietly and moved into the room, face still in shadow. "Those dances can get rowdy."

"They can indeed. Are they always like that?"

"Well, this was a little special." His teeth shone in the lamplight. "They haven't seen a performance like you gave them for a while."

"Felipe's amazing. He must dance all the time."

"Takes two. Not many girls here can really waltz. None of them can."

"So where did *he* learn?"

"Not here. He's from the mainland somewhere. Where did *you* learn?"

"Back in Philadelphia. Miss Potter's dancing class. My mother made me go."

He tossed his head and pouted. "Nobody ever made *me* go to dancing class."

"You're lucky."

"Bullshit."

"Well, it's not hard." She got up from the bed and went through the step. "Back-side-together. Front-side-together. One-two-three. One-two-three. *Volver, volver, volver. . .*" Holding out her hands. "Come on, try it."

"Nah. I'm not a dancer."

"Then why did you go to the dance?"

He shrugged.

"Don't tell me you're only a mechanic. I might start feeling sorry for you."

He didn't say anything.

"So," she said after a while. "How was the trip to La Paz? Did you get my poor old engine block to the shop all right?"

He took a step closer and reached out his hand. She took it, he pulled her in and set his closed teeth on the side of her neck under her hair. Opened them slightly and took a fold of her skin between them. When she pulled away, he put his other hand around her jaw and tilted it up. He was only a couple of inches taller and not much heavier.

She crossed her free arm so that the forearm was against his own neck and pushed. He raised his hand with hers in it high over their heads, moved his other hand from her jaw to her hip, and horsed her into a twirl. She finished the twirl with a light karate kick but he caught her ankle and threw her off-balance onto the bed, her white dress around her thighs, arms bent, hands open, palms up on either side of her body.

She watched as he unbuckled his belt, unzipped his pants, and dropped them. No underwear . . . that would have spoiled it. When he moved on top of her, bracing himself with his hands on her forearms, she raised a knee toward his crotch and held it till the weight of his body pushed it flat. *Do your worst.*

They were lying face to face, chest to chest, groin to groin, knee to knee. His breath on her forehead, his hands tight on her forearms. He pushed his upper body up and away and she could see the lantern-light flicker on his expressionless face, eyes in shadow.

Was it play? She clamped her knees together with all her strength but felt his knee working its way between them. She set her teeth in his right forearm, looked up into his face, and began to bite down.

As her legs opened, her teeth closed. That was how this worked. Blood pounding in her veins and blood seeping between her lips into her mouth. Her teeth breaking through the skin as her legs spread wider and wider.

He pushed easily inside her as her body melted and her strong, sharp teeth sank into him. When he could go no deeper, he stopped and she stopped too, swallowing blood and watching him smile. Right on the edge.

Then a slow, startling thrust forced her mouth open. She twisted back, hands still pinioned. His lips came down and his long tongue filled her mouth. She locked her legs around him, closed her eyes, and strained against it. Each thrust pushed her farther down. She was breathing blood, dissolving, and then suddenly she was gone in an echo of his laugh.

Hey, Peter, remember when I got my period that time in the car? My second? I've had two hundred and sixty-four more since then. Never missed one. A girl has to keep count, right?

And now that your name has come up, can I ask you a question? Do you think our mother killed herself?

Kate

In early spring I'd gotten a call from my old college roommate, who held a doctorate in physics but was teaching high school math in Mendocino. His daughter, sixteen going on seventeen, had been caught shoplifting for the third time. He was threatened with losing custody to his ex-wife, and his daughter would have to move to Boston.

"Do you guys ever have sixteen-year-old summer interns?" my old roommate had asked. "My sister and her husband live up on 86th Street on the West Side. She could stay with them. Listen, the kid's fucking brilliant, tests off the scale, but she's gotta get out of here for a while."

"What's she interested in?"

"Interested? *Obsessed* is more like it. She wants to be a goddamn writer."

"Wow," I'd said. "She really is crazy, hunh?"

A short silence. "I think she's good, but what do I know. I can send you some of her stuff if you want."

Her stuff was at least college-level, with some surprisingly original twists and turns. Enough to hold one's attention, or hold mine anyway. She didn't force it, either. It wasn't overdone. And it seemed to be all her own.

That's how smoldering, nutty Kate had gotten a little space in the corner of my office until her school started again in mid-September. Her job was to read unsolicited manuscripts. I didn't tell her, but the odds of getting one published were more than a thousand to one. She wrote gushing letters of encouragement to some of the authors, and at first I wondered what they'd do if they knew who was writing them. But then I decided that they needed all the encouragement they could get.

God, she's a walking cliché, I'd think as I watched her drift rather gracefully around the office. Tall, pimply, and spectrally thin. Padded bras, some rounded, some pointed (pointed ones favored toward the end of the week). Dirty-blond shoulder-length hair, black tee shirts, jeans, and pink Keds that she never tied. Steel-rimmed glasses. The only item lacking was heavy metal on her teeth. Well, at least the publisher got a kick out of her—she was a whiz at backgammon, and he'd been dropping by to play with her some late afternoons.

Back at work this Monday she seemed more twitchy and excited than usual, or so it seemed—I was on the phone to ICM, turning down one of their highly touted new writers. She kept looking at me, biting her lips, fiddling with her pen. When I finally got off the phone, she jumped to her feet and practically danced to my desk. She was carrying a bulky manila envelope.

"You've gotta read this. It's *wonderful.* I stayed up all night Saturday, could *not* put it *down.*"

I smiled and sat back, the ICM agent's gravelly voice echoing in my ear: *You're missing the opportunity of a lifetime, Peter. This book could save your miserable has-been ass.* "What makes this so different from all the others you wanted me to read? Listen, Kate, enthusiasm's great but you have to learn to be much more discriminating. This is a rough business. Almost nobody makes it."

"*You* made it. You discovered a fantastic new writer and made this place a fortune. He was on the best-seller list for how long?"

"Year and a half." I had to grin. "But that was a while back, and you're only as good as your latest book. Nothing looms on the horizon. That was ICM on the phone, incidentally. I just passed on yet another of their submissions. And they're one of the best shops in town."

"This is different. It's really good, I'm *telling* you. If you don't like it, well maybe I shouldn't be working here. I mean, maybe there's no future for me in this business."

I picked up the manila envelope and looked at the return address: a post office box in Steuben, Maine. God, another regional writer? Well, at least it was a woman. And the handwriting in blue roller point was intriguingly unconventional slanted lines.

When I put the envelope back on the desk, she picked it up, pulled out the manuscript, and selected a single page from the middle. "Totally arbitrary page. Just read one paragraph. Isn't that what you told *me* to do?"

"Kate, I've got a meeting with the golden boy in ten minutes. I'm probably going to get fired."

"*God*, why are you always so pessimistic. They'd never fire you, you're the best they've got in this dump. By far." She shook the page in my face. "One paragraph. It'll take ten *seconds*."

I took the page impatiently and dropped my eyes to a longish middle paragraph. It was better than I expected, a lot better, a clean simple style with no wasted words and a poignant aftertaste. I read it again, then the paragraphs before and after it, and handed it back. "Give me the first page." She had it in my hand almost before I stopped talking. "Okay," I said finally. "I hardly ever read manuscripts during the week, as you know, but just as a favor to you I'll read it tonight." A smile and a nod. "You're right. It does seem good."

She clasped her hands over her heart and smiled back, her eyes shining behind her glasses. "You're sweet." Leaning over my desk to kiss me on the forehead. The shaven-headed hip publisher was scarily hearty in the meeting, but I told him I might be onto something.

"Where did you *find* this?" A few days later, the publisher tapped the manuscript with his pen. "I was reading it in the bathtub until three ayem. My skin almost fell off."

"Kate found it."

"Ah, the brilliant Kate. So it was in the slush pile?"

"So it would seem."

"Who is this woman? Does anyone know anything about her?"

"She lives in Steuben, Maine. I checked all the sources: she's never published a word before."

"So we don't know how old she is, whether she's married or single, where she went to college, what she does for a living, nothing?"

"Nada. Wasn't it T. S. Eliot who said the author doesn't matter?"

"Don't get literary on me. Have you talked to her?"

"No."

"Well, my God, she's probably sent this all over the place. We've got to call her."

"I did try information. She's not listed."

"Unpublished number?"

"No number at all."

"Where is Steuben, for God's sake?"

"On the coast, north of Mount Desert. *Way* out there."

"How the hell do you get there?"

"Fly to Bangor and rent a car."

"Well, Peter, go with God, and congratulations. You're our star. Feel her out. I don't know, maybe fifty grand to start with, and if she doesn't take it, call me."

"I'm way ahead of you," I said. "Got a flight booked for tomorrow."

"Oh, take me with you," Kate implored when I told her about the green light. Eyes huge, hand on my arm. "If you don't, I'll never forgive you."

Where had I heard those words before? "Kate, this is a business trip, not some kind of junket. Plus if golden boy found out, we'd both be fired. You're *sixteen*."

"So what? Is there an age limit on business trips? I could pass for twenty and you know it, if I had the right clothes. Plus I found this woman, didn't I? Doesn't that entitle me to *anything*?" Next minute she'd be in tears. "I could be a big help to you. I know this woman like I know her book."

The right clothes. That would have to be my job. In the SoHo Bloomingdales after work, Kate modeled a series of dresses, coming out of the fitting room with that shine in her eyes, doing a long-legged twirl for my inspection. I'd never seen her bare legs before.

Finally she appeared in a black cocktail sheath, stopped short, and just stood there watching my face. I knew I'd gone pale: the dress could have been the same one my sister had worn so proudly that day in Briarcliffe.

"What's the matter?" A little smile.

"Kate, for Christ's sake, this is not a cocktail party we're going to."

"That woman would like this dress. I tell you I know her."

"Forget it." I clapped my hands. "Okay, I think we've seen enough. We're getting the beige one."

"The *beige* one? Omigod, that's so retro it's off the scale. I'd rather *die* than wear that."

I shook my head. "Okay. The gray business one then. With the pleats. Très chic."

"Shit. That's for a little Wall Street secretary. It's *mousy*."

"It's understated, Kate. It doesn't come up and scream in your face, but it's pure silk and expensive as hell. Don't forget who's paying for all this."

"Okay, okay." She flounced off to the fitting room, swaying her hips. Over her shoulder: "Don't blame *me* if she doesn't sign." In the shoe department I bought her a pair of low black heels. Très chic and très cher. She didn't even look at the price tag.

She was wearing the gray silk dress and the heels the next morning when we met at LaGuardia for the nine o'clock shuttle to Boston with a connection to Bangor. I was in a Glen plaid suit, one of my father's that I'd had re-tailored (waist let out, chest taken in). The contract was in my brown leather briefcase. The shuttle was packed with other business people, and I hoped we passed inspection. Of course, I could be a father taking his daughter on a college tour.

In our seats, she smoothed the dress over her knees and I could see she was wearing stockings. Or pantyhose. I'd avoided the department they sold those in, so she must have had some of her own. "So what's the plan, boss?"

"I offer her big bucks, and she signs."

"How much?"

"Too early to say."

"But what are you going to start at?"

"Please leave that to me, okay? You'll be there. You'll find out when the time comes."

"Aw shucks, boss, I don't get a say in this?" She was grinning.

"Your job is to sit there and look brilliant. And businesslike. I'm really going out on a limb for you. For God's sake, don't blow it."

"Thanks, boss." She patted my knee. "Don't worry. I won't let you down."

By the time we got to Ellsworth in the rented Ford Focus, wisps of fog were hanging in the tops of the big white pines and cars coming toward us from the east had their lights on. Visibility near Steuben was so low I almost missed the sign. Buildings loomed, and when I stopped we could hear a foghorn somewhere close by. The neon sign for a clam house turned the atmosphere red.

In the post office, I showed the lady clerk the manuscript's manila envelope. "I'm an editor from New York, and this is my assistant. We wanted to take this back to her in person. Can you tell me where she lives?"

The clerk's eyes got big. "Oh! I was here when she sent those off."

"She sent a lot of them?"

"Oh yes! Twenty or thirty at least. Some of them have come back already, but you're the first to actually *bring* one in person."

"Really." I glanced at Kate. "Does she live far away?"

"'Bout fifteen miles out past Corea. Boyfriend's a lobsterman. Oh, won't she be excited! We could call her, but they don't even have a phone."

"Can you tell me how to get there?"

"Well, sure." She paused. "Don't you want to wait till this lifts? I've never seen it so thick, and there are some tricky turns. Got lost myself out there more than once."

"When is it likely to lift?"

"Fog like this?" She checked her watch. "Well, it's past three now. Not going to lift today. Could even get thicker come nightfall."

"Can you draw us a map? We'll take it slow and easy."

It was like driving through cotton wool. The gray road was the same color as the fog, and without the dividing line to follow I might have driven off into the spruce woods even with the headlights. We found a turn that might have been on the map, then another. Kate had tuned in Blue Hill Radio, a hippie station that was playing Dylan's "Not Dark Yet." Give me a break. Once in a long while, another car would loom toward us like a will-o-the-wisp. Nobody was going faster than ten miles an hour, but the sound of the passing cars seemed deafening.

The gray road curved left, right, and back again until I'd lost all sense of direction. Sometimes the dark shadow of spruces gave way to a lighter gray and we could smell salt water and seaweed. After a while, we clattered across a wooden trestle bridge.

"That on the map?"

"No, and I think we should have come to another turnoff by now."

"Shit. Guess we better turn around."

On the map, the turnoff we missed would be on the right but the first one we came to went left. "Maybe that's it. Goddamn it, you'd think there'd be a sign."

"Yeah. I remember that one, but I don't remember seeing any other one for miles."

The turnoff was narrower than the road we'd been on, just wide enough for one car. We seemed to be crossing a salt marsh: no trees and the smell of mud on both sides. We were creeping along at five miles an hour—either the light was fading or the fog was thickening or both. Then we were on gravel, a bad sign, but the road was too narrow to turn around. The gravel gave way to dirt, and the dirt became a two-track.

I stopped the car and got out. The fog was so dense I was damp in a few seconds. The roof light cozily lit up the inside of the car, and Blue Hill Radio was playing Dave Matthews. "Turn that off a minute, will you?" I said. "I want to see if I can hear anything."

The foghorn sounded farther away than before. Between its faint moos I could hear the clank of a bell buoy. It sounded almost next to us. The fog hissed and curled in the headlights and began to bead on my hair and eyebrows. Fifty feet up the road I felt as if I were in outer space.

Back inside, with the window rolled up, the light still on, and Kate watching me inscrutably.

"Our options at this point are very simple." I tried a grin. "We either try to back out, or we go forward and hope for a turning place."

"It's an awfully long way to back out," she said. "Isn't it?"

"It is. And with every foot we go forward it's even longer. Suppose there's nothing up there."

"*God*, there you go again. Don't be such a *pessimist*. This road has got to lead somewhere. Otherwise it wouldn't be here, right?"

"When you get to be my age you'll understand that roads don't necessarily go places. Actually, my mother taught me that when I was even younger than you."

"She was a pessimist too, hunh?"

"No, she was a romantic. A hopeless romantic."

"I get it. The glamour of the road versus the predictability of the arrival. The trip qua end in itself, and all that Kerouac nonsense."

"Whatever it is, it's not pessimistic. And you're not old enough to call it nonsense."

She didn't say anything, and I put the car in gear. "Okay, fuck it. We'll go on then."

The grass beside the road grew taller, and the tires began to squelch through puddles. Every once in a while the high center between the tracks scraped against the chassis. There was no backing out now, and I was afraid that if we stopped in this mud we'd never get started again. We went a little faster.

When the car finally high-centered for good and the wheels began to spin, I took it out of gear and sat back almost in relief. "Shit. What would Kerouac do now?"

When she didn't say anything, I turned on the roof light and saw she was crying. "I'm so sorry, Peter. I fucked it up good, didn't I?"

"Not your fault. It was my decision."

"Oh God, I should never have come." Snuffling miserably like a little girl.

The fog curled in the headlights, and I shut them off. After a few minutes I cut the engine and extinguished the roof light. The light outside was gray, like a gray dawn except it was now only a little after five in the evening according to the dashboard clock. With a sob she threw her arms around my neck and pressed her wet face against my chest.

At first I was tense with remembered parallels . . . the fog, the little car, the girl next to me. But gradually I relaxed, put my arm around her, and began to whisper comforting words as I patted her back. It was still not too late for someone to come along.

Even if they didn't, the front seats of the Ford folded way back to sleep in. The temperature was comfortable. The fog would lift in the morning. I could put brush under the tires and rock them off the high center. Backing out in daylight would be a piece of cake.

The dashboard clock read ten past seven. Brilliant halogen lights cut through the dusk and fog behind the Ford and blasted through the rear window. A big truck engine burbled around men's voices, raced and burbled. Two doors slammed, one after the other, and a flashlight shone into my face. Laughter from one side of the car and whistles from the other. "Well, now. So what hev we here?" A tap on my window. "Lose your way, bub?"

I rolled down my window. "Yeah, we got lost in the fog. Then we couldn't turn around."

"Well, shit, y'almost made her. Beach is right up close. You could hev turned around thayuh."

"Ayuh. But he probly didn't *want* to turn around. Didja bub?"

"The car's stuck," I said. "It's high-centered."

"This a rental, ain't it? Y'should hev rented a real cah stead of one them compac pieces a shit."

"But lookit how them seats go back. Now that's a right handy feature, ain't it?"

"Hey, man, take it easy," I said out my window, although the man who said it was on the other side of the car, looking in at Kate. She took her glasses from the glove compartment and sleepily put them on.

"Where you frem, Bahstn?" The man outside my window was dressed in a green plaid wool shirt, jeans, and construction boots. His face was invisible behind the flashlight.

"Can you take that light out of our faces?"

The beam moved to Kate's chest (the pointy bra), down to her knees, and back again. "You folks been to a pahty or somethin?"

"Noah, they were *hevin* a pahty."

I tried to push my door open, but the man outside was in the way. The man put his hands on the top of the door and opened it wider while I got out. The man had dark, curly hair like mine, pale skin, and was about my height. The truck engine burbled quietly behind the headlights, and the fog swirled. "Your friend has a few manners to learn," I told him.

"Hey, Edgah," the man said in a conversational voice.

"Ayuh?"

"Says your momuh fell down on the job wicked bad. Didn't learn you how to act in p'lite compny."

Edgar walked around to our side of the car. He was shorter but stockier, in a blue wool watch cap that showed red hair in the back. "What I been tellin' you all these yeahs?" the first man said.

"*He* should talk," Edgar said to me. "Just he's bettalookin."

We could hear the passenger door open, and Kate got out and walked barefoot and tousled around the back of the car in the truck's blazing blue headlights. The skirt of the gray silk dress was wrinkled, and the hem rode up. Nobody said anything for a little while, and then Edgar whistled. "*Uh*-oh. Warren, I hev to say I'm a little shawcked."

Warren didn't say anything.

"Guess this fella never heard the song," Edgar said. "*Fif-teen, six-teen, seven-teen . . .*" He stopped and grinned. "What's that, bub? You know?"

Kate looked fragile and scared, a little girl inside her grown-up dress.

"*That's jay-ul baaayt.*"

I felt my left fist connect cleanly with Edgar's right cheek and my right connect cleanly with his chin. Edgar went down. I'd moved so fast I hadn't had time to think, but now I thought *wow*! Strong arms went around my arms and body from behind, and I watched Edgar getting slowly to his feet, shaking his head.

Edgar walked up to me with a serious, intent expression, set himself, and aimed a punch at my stomach. I heard a girl scream, and I thought, *Shit!* My stomach imploded, air bellowed out of my lungs, something smashed into my front teeth and then clubbed down on the back of my head.

The first thing I did when they got me back on my feet was feel my teeth. By some miracle they were still there. I wiggled them gently at first, then harder, but they were still firm. I looked at Kate's horrified face and smiled. Warren reached me a pint bottle of Jack Daniels—I took a swig, washed it around inside my mouth, and swallowed it. I took another. There was a kind of hush, as if they all expected me to collapse again, but I stayed on my feet. The back of my Glen plaid suit felt wet and muddy.

Then Warren was helping me into the cab of the truck. Kate climbed in beside me and Warren went around and got into the driver's seat while Edgar jumped onto the truck bed behind and tapped on the rear window. The big engine roared, and we started moving slowly backward as the Ford faded into the fog. We were on our way to Warren's place: his girlfriend was a nurse who could tend to my cuts and bruises, give us some food, and we could spend the night on the couch and in the spare room.

Hours or minutes passed, and we were pulling into a foggy driveway with the little house looming in the headlights. The front door opened, and a long-haired woman in a sleeveless teal fleece over a black turtleneck and jeans came out onto the stoop and slowly put one hand on her hip.

The woman's clear gray eyes moved from me to Kate and back again while Warren explained how he and Edgar had been checking the marsh road to West Beach for deer and had found us stuck.

"Floundering in the mud?" She had a little smile, but she didn't have a Downeast accent. There was something about the way she said "floundering," a kind of gentle irony, that caught my ear.

"Do you write, by any chance?" I asked.

I made the trip back to New York in jeans and a striped snap-button cowboy shirt borrowed from Warren. The signed contract specifying an advance on sales of fifty thousand dollars to the writer and world rights to the publisher was in my briefcase—she'd been so embarrassed that her boyfriend had beat me up, she would have signed anything. She had ironed the gray silk dress, and Kate looked fresh as a jonquil sitting beside me in the Legal Seafood branch at Logan Airport, waiting for the shuttle. I had ordered Champagne and oysters, Perrier for Kate.

When the Champagne arrived, I lifted my glass: "Here's to you. And to Edgar. Without the two of you, this whole thing would never have worked out."

"No, no. *You* made it happen." She put her hand on mine. "You did. I was so proud. You were like . . . I don't know, I don't want to be trite. *You came to my rescue.*"

We didn't get back to Manhattan till around 9 p.m., what with one thing and another. When I told the driver to stop first at Kate's aunt's address on West 86th Street, she said faintly, "Please can I come home with you?"

The light in the backseat of the cab was too dim to see her face properly. "What?" Had I known this was coming?

She just laid the side of her head against my shoulder. "Please. Don't I deserve it?"

She had no idea how close I was to my inner sixteen-year-old, who would have said fine, come home, we'll curl up together. Like I might have said to my sister.

I had to wrench myself away from him. "You deserve a lot. But a girl your age does not go to an older man's apartment and spend the night."

"Who'd know? I'll call my aunt and tell her we were delayed, had to spend the night in Boston. Please?"

"Out of the question," I said in my totally phony grown-up's voice. Though it didn't sound so phony anymore.

Buena Suerte

So tell me, are you pregnant?" Marco grinned. They were in his truck, driving to the customs house in La Paz where she had to sign for the engine parts, which had finally arrived a month and a half after they'd been ordered. Early August . . . how time flew!

"Heaven forbid." Wendy had just gotten back from a surf surfari to the East Cape with Clamato and one of his old surf-hero buddies. Clamato had told her she was a natural, picked it up faster than any woman he'd ever seen, but the main idea had been to get away from Marco for a while. "Why do you ask? Is it supposed to be funny?"

"I don't know. Maybe you look different or something."

"The surf was *mierda*. Clamato has some friends in Los Frailes. We hung out with them a lot. And ate. I guess I put on some pounds."

He reached out and squeezed her nearest breast. "Looks like it all went into one place." He had a crescent-shaped red scar on his forearm.

The squeeze was painful, and she pulled his hand away. "Marco, I've done a lot of thinking while I was gone, you know? Mostly about you. Us, that is."

"*Ay caramba.*" Marco gave a falsetto howl.

August was the rainy season, and the brown desert was now lush and green. Leaves had burst out of the scrub, fruit out of the cactus, huge yellow flowers out of the big cardons. She watched it through the open window as the truck clattered along. The sun was bursting through the damp air.

"Well?" Marco asked. "What have you come up with?"

"I've been thinking about the basis for our . . . ah . . . mutual attraction, you know?"

"Mutual attraction. Is that what it is?"

"Well, what else would you call it?"

"I don't know. It's *your* language. You can pick the words better than me."

"Okay, try Spanish. I can speak it pretty good now."

Marco grinned. "What about *lujuria*?"

"Well, there's not much luxury involved, is there?"

"*Lujuria* doesn't mean luxurious."

"What does it mean then?"

"Look it up," Marco said. "In your little yellow Cassell's. But anyway, what were you going to say? About the basis?"

She took a deep breath and crossed her arms. "You are an angry man, Marco Blanco."

"What?" The truck swerved slightly. "Angry? I have everything I want, and I'm doing exactly what I want to do. Why would I be angry?"

"I don't know why. But you are. Wouldn't you say so?"

"If I *am* angry, does it scare you?" He tossed his head. "You're starting to get scared, is that it?"

She uncrossed her arms and touched his scar. "Yes, I'm scared. But not of what you think."

"You're not scared of me?"

She rubbed the scar gently. "No, Marco. I'm scared of whatever it is between us. See, I'm an angry woman."

He whistled and nodded. "*Claro que si.*"

"But I'm tired of being angry. I don't think I want to be angry any more. You know?"

"You *are* pregnant, aren't you?"

"In your dreams, maybe. No, I think it started after I finished the book. Maybe that's why I came here, to kind of rejig my life. You know I have a brother?"

He shook his head.

"Yeah. We tried to run away to Mexico together when we were kids. I haven't talked to him for at least ten years."

"Are you angry at him?"

"It's a long story. But yeah . . . at least I was." She threw her head back and sighed. "I'm *tired* of it. Marco, I think we should give it a rest."

The truck clattered on in silence. "Another thing," she went on. "I haven't worked since I got here, and my book's not doing as well as I thought, so my cash flow's a little shaky. Isabel said I could camp out in her spare room, and I think I'm going to take her up on it."

He turned and glared. "Isabel! That *pinche tortillera*. So now it's you and her, is that it?"

"Of course not. Don't be crazy. It's just a free room."

"Jesus!" Raising his hand in the air, fingers stiff and extended. "Hey, if you're broke, how are you going to pay for the car?"

"Don't worry. The car's been figured into this."

Chopping the wheel with the edge of that hand. "You know what? I've done a lot of work already on that fucking *chingadero*, and what have I been paid? Nothing. *Nada. Ni un pinche peso.*"

"I can see what I can scrape up right now. How much do you want?"

"How much do I want? Well, since you and I are just business now, I want the whole thing up front. The whole five thousand."

"*Five thousand?* We agreed on three, Marco. That's what I set aside."

"Show me where that's written down. It'd cost you six to have this done in the states. Easy. Ask your mechanic up there."

"I will. He offered to fly down and do the work himself for three. I think I'll ask him to do that very thing."

"The hell you will. That car's in my shop. Nobody is going to touch it until I get paid."

The truck's movement was making her nauseated. And she was tired, so tired she felt like crying. God!

"Why are you doing this to me, Marco?" she asked faintly.

The customs house was closed when they got there and wouldn't reopen till late afternoon. She told Marco she had some shopping to do and headed for the nearest *farmacia* where she bought a pregnancy home test kit. She strolled with the rest of the tourists along the *malecón* carrying the kit in an opaque plastic bag, hoping she wouldn't run into anybody she knew and thinking she should throw it in the nearest garbage can. *Buena Suerte*, the pink box said. Good Luck. That was the brand name.

She came to a restaurant before she came to a garbage can—a pleasant open-air place across the *malecón* from the harbor with elderly waiters in white shirts and black pants and a mostly Mexican clientele eating large afternoon meals. She got a table, ordered the *sopa de mariscos* and a glass of Santo Tomás chardonnay, and went to the ladies' room.

The ladies' room was large and clean, with three metal stalls. Sitting inside one, she took out the kit and read the Spanish directions: hold the wick in the urine stream for five seconds, read the results in the little window after three minutes. One pink line, not pregnant. Two, pregnant. The Spanish word was *embarazada*.

"What a joke," she thought, holding the slim white wand between her legs. After two pink lines showed up in the window, she threw the whole ensemble into the wastebasket near the door on her way out.

Halfway through her bowl of soup, she found herself wondering if she'd really read it right. Was *embarazada* one line or two? Had she waited for the right amount of time? She went back into the ladies room and took the wastebasket inside a stall with her.

Yes, the stuff was still there. The two pink lines in the window seemed more thick and solid than before. The pink box featured two illustrations of the window, with each result labeled in blue letters. The word under the illustration with two pink lines was unmistakably *embarazada*. She wrapped the wand in the opaque plastic baggie and took it back to the table. *Buena suerte.*

Now the soup was cold. She stirred it listlessly, finished her glass of wine, and waved for another. She'd missed her last period, but she'd been surfing hard in the hot sun. That had probably done it. Wasn't she due to get one soon? When she got back she'd check her calendar.

Why didn't she keep track of things more closely? That first time in June, where had she been on the goddamn calendar then? And the other times? The pill was horrible. She'd never used it, and planning any other kind of birth control had been out of the question. She touched the breast Marco had squeezed. Yes, it was sensitive, but then they always were just before her period. It was coming, just as Miss B had assured her it would, for the next forty years. *My heart and my door are closed to you.*

The sun was setting by the time they'd found the right man at the customs house, gotten through all the paperwork, paid the fees, and loaded the box of parts into the truck. Marco said there was a place outside of town on the way back that had good food, music, even a dance floor if they felt in the mood.

"I have to say I don't really feel in the mood," Wendy said. She'd checked the wand one more time before throwing it away for good. No change.

"No problem," Marco said. "I'm not much of a dancer anyway. As you know. But it's a friendly place. I go there a lot. They make a good enchilada."

They turned down a wide dirt road through the desert scrub, potholed with heavy traffic. There were rustic hitching rails in front of three large buildings and a few cars. They stopped at the middle one, Mi Ranchito, in large lit-up letters.

It was a huge dim cavernous space like one of the old New York discos, tables on a raised platform around the dance floor, a stage with microphones and loudspeakers. Men were sitting at some of the tables, and girls were standing around dressed in gringo-style clothes like short cutoffs and tight tee shirts. The lighting was reddish.

A large woman came up and talked to Marco in Spanish so fast Wendy couldn't follow. They were like old friends. She led them to one of the tables, sat down with them, and leaned over at Wendy. "The music playing right now very soon," she said in English. "'*Volver!*' You know?"

"Yes, I do."

"You dance good, he tell me. You—"

Wendy pointed at Marco. "But not him. He doesn't dance at all."

"*Híjole!*" She slapped Marco on the hand. "*Que mentiroso.*"

"Do you have a menu?"

"Menu?"

"I hear you have great enchiladas."

The woman laughed and laughed. "Enchiladas! *Ay, Dios.*" She waved at the girls lined up against the wall. "There they are, *mija!* Which flavor you want? The mango?"

Marco leaned over and said something to her, pointing to one of the girls. The woman smiled and nodded. "Excuse, *mi amor,* okay?" She went over and said something to the girl.

"What is this place, anyway?" Wendy said. As if she didn't know.

Marco just smiled and nodded. The musicians came on, and when they struck up the number the girl he'd pointed at came over to their table. They went to the dance floor together and did a pretty good waltz, Mexican style. They were the only couple on the floor.

When it was over, the girl came back to the table with him, and he introduced her as Miel. "Miel and I are in business too. Like you and me. We have a small transaction to see about, maybe fifteen minutes. Wait for me, okay?"

She pretended to watch the band after Marco followed Miel out of the room, but she could feel the eyes. Girls giggling behind their hands, heavyset middle-aged men tapping their toes and pretending to be looking at something just behind her.

So this was the worst humiliation he could come up with. On short notice, of course. Before, she would have been angry, but now she was truly scared. She should never have broken off with him until she'd gotten her precious car back. Just a week. Couldn't she have put up with him for just another week?

Red hot struggle, blood, bruises, harsh panting in the dark. She'd wanted it before. She'd sought it out. She shivered and looked around the huge dim hall, and all the eyes looked back with interest and amusement.

"Ay Dios!" Isabel's eyes got big. "So when was supposed to be your *regla*?" They were sitting cross-legged opposite each other on the floor of Isabel's little white spare room in back of her studio. A *campesino*-style canvas cot was the only piece of furniture.

"About three weeks ago. Maybe more. But my *reglas* have never been very regular." She'd decided not to mention the pregnancy test.

"No, no, *querida*. I can see the difference."

Wendy put her hand on her stomach. "You mean I'm *showing*? Impossible. I've just put on a little weight."

Isabel touched one of her own breasts. "How do they feel?"

"Big. Sore. Like I'm about to get it."

Isabel reached out her hand. "May I? I have some experience here."

"Just be careful, okay?"

She felt the same breast that Marco had squeezed, and Wendy couldn't help flinching. "What?"

Shaking her head slowly. "You don' feel sick?"

"Not really. Just a little tired."

"And Marco?"

"Well . . . he did ask. I told him no, naturally."

"So that thing in the *ranchito* had nothing to do with this?"

"No. He was just pissed because I told him I wouldn't sleep with him anymore."

"You think he's gonna finish your car?"

"He wants five thousand US up front, when we agreed on three."

"You have five thousand to pay?"

"Yes, but—"

"Don' argue with him. Give him half now quick. Is a lot of money for him. Then you fly home for a week, if that's what you wanna do, you know? Pay him the rest when you come back and he finished."

"Wow. You make it sound so simple. But I can't just leave my car. I just can't. I can't *abandon* the poor thing. Anyway, it should be finished in a week or so, and I'll have gotten my period by then." She ran her hand over her breast. "I'm telling you, I can feel it coming. It was just all that surfing that threw it off."

Isabel looked at her carefully. "You love your car, no, Doña Mercedes?"

"I do. We've been through a lot together, she and I. You have no idea."

"Her? In Spanish a car is *him*, Mercedes."

Wendy laughed. "You and Clamato are the only ones who ever call me that. I think you guys made it up. So what happens if Marco won't play along?"

Isabel put her chin in her hand, raised her eyebrows, and grinned ruefully. "Well, there's always the *policía*."

PART TWO

Fresh Start

It felt like a back-to-school day. Clear, crisp, and windless. Still warm, but not that lazy summer warmth. The school year would be unblemished, full of promise. Maybe this would be the year I'd get straight As and make the varsity hockey team. Why not? Anything seemed possible.

Eight thirty a.m. I'd taken a cup of coffee up on the roof to savor the day before going to work. Work was good, thanks to Kate, and there were other hopeful projects in the pipeline. A lunch date with golden boy loomed pleasantly in the near future. Even blocky, drab New York looked good: eastward, the solid line of incoming traffic on the Williamsburg Bridge inched along with stately, colorful purpose; farther south, the golden lady on top of the Municipal Building glowed numinously. The World Trade towers, less than a mile away, stood out with a blue intensity usually seen only in the high peaks. The sun was delicious on my face. I'd put in fifteen years to get here, and it felt like I'd only just arrived.

Across Broome Street, framed in a large loft window, I could see a young woman with dark hair and a white nightgown watering plants with a long-spouted copper can. She felt my eyes, looked up, hesitated, then lifted her hand in a little wave: too nice a day not to. I waved back, watched her finish watering and leave the room. It was a bare white room with an old maple floor and a few large pieces of art on the walls. She was single, I was sure of it. And so was I.

So yes. This could be the year for a new start. Romance, a real romance that would fill the hollowness, could be waiting just across the street. At the other end of the phone. A perfumed room. A sweet presence. The Big Apple! Even the sound of a big jet, swooping low over the city from the north where a building blocked my view, probably full of eager commuters from Boston, was part of it.

Half an hour later I was lying on the floor of my loft, holding my knees tight to my chest to ease my spasming back. Channel 7 News showed the two World Trade Center towers smoking scenically into the deep blue sky, backed up by speculation ranging from pilot error to all-out war. When I still had been on my feet the TV could be confirmed by the view out my window, but seeing the fireball of the second plane's impact had sent red and blue currents of electric pain shooting from my head into my lower spine, and from then on I lay on the floor and watched only the TV screen. There was no footage of the first hit—maybe no one but I had seen the big jet disappear into the tower, leaving an unbelievably small hole.

I dragged myself to the window when the announcer screamed, but it was too late to witness the fall. The sight of a single smoking tower where there should have been two was the worst thing. Was I going insane? I knelt at the window, gripping the sill with both hands, not taking my eyes from the remaining tower for the next half hour until it too soundlessly disappeared in a seismic brown-textured cloud highlighted by a fluttering snow of Xerox paper.

Kate. Hadn't I begged her, since the regular messenger service was booked, to pick up a crucial contract from an agent's office down there in the Wall Street area before coming to work?

I levered myself gradually to a bent-over stand and shuffled to the phone. A machine answered her extension at the office. Nothing happened at all when I dialed her cell phone. Another machine answered for the switchboard operator. I called Kate's machine again: "Kate, it's me. I'm here at the loft. Call me immediately." I couldn't hang up, even when the machine beeped the end of the recording.

The brown cloud out my window floated gently over the New York harbor southeast toward Brooklyn. With both towers gone, it was somehow less scary, less as if your mind were playing awful tricks. If you worked at it, you could almost think the towers never had been there in the first place. But the streets outside were screaming with sirens, and the first few survivors, covered with white dust, disheveled and bleeding, were beginning to straggle past, up Lafayette Street. The words *rescue, emergency room*, and *body bags* came from the TV.

"You sent her down there. You *find* her," Kate's aunt Mary sobbed at me when I called the West 86th Street apartment. Kate had left at eight thirty to be there when the agent's office opened at nine. The first tower had fallen at about ten. The office was on Rector Street, but how far it was from the towers I had no idea. Yet another machine when I dialed the number. My own cell phone registered no service.

Find her? I could barely move. People were dying, it could be war, and my back had gone out. I started to laugh. There were only two people in the world who would be able to laugh with me, I knew that, and one was somewhere in Mexico and hadn't talked to me in ten years.

I had some pills left over from the last time my back had gone out—Valium for relaxing the spasmed muscles and codeine for the pain—so I swallowed a big dose and lay back down on the floor in front of the TV, cradling the phone. A reporter interviewed a survivor who was raving about flying men. A transmission from one of the planes indicated it had been hijacked by Arabs. The towers fell over and over in instant replay, and people fleeing the billowing cloud couldn't have been filmed better by Spielberg. None of the terrified, powdered, bleeding faces on the screen were Kate's.

Gradually, as the Valium and codeine took hold, I began to think maybe staying here was for the best. I could never have found her out there in the screaming crowds shown on the TV screen. My home phone still seemed to work—I should be here when she called, and she was bound to call sooner or later. People were calling other people up and down Crosby Street. I could hear phones ringing in all different keys and volumes, but nobody seemed to be answering. The lack of connection made me think of my sister: she'd never call, never in a million years. But then she was in Mexico. She probably hadn't heard yet.

As time passed (I checked my watch every once in a while—it was passing very quickly), the sound of traffic, sirens, and shouting grew less, but the ringing phones seemed louder. One of the TV reporters had come up with a story about a man trapped in the wreckage who was calling out on a cell phone (how did *his* happen to work?), begging for rescue while his air ran out and a steel girder slowly pressed down on him. Why didn't anyone answer the phones? A cordon had been set up on 14th Street, sealing off lower Manhattan. Was I the only person left in the area?

I didn't want to use my phone in case a crucial call might be on its way to me, but then I remembered I had call waiting. I couldn't get to my address book, so I dialed information in Livingston, Montana, and asked for Claire Barstow. Miraculously, her number was listed.

And there she was, sounding breathless. "My God, Peter, I've been trying to call for hours, but the circuits have all been busy. Are you all right? Holy *shit*."

"You won't believe this. My back went out. I'm lying here on the floor stoned out of my mind on Valium and codeine."

"You're kidding. Your *back's* out? When did that happen?"

"When the second plane hit. I saw the first one, too. I can see everything from here, but I can't stand up."

Claire didn't say anything.

"You still there? Claire? Are you still there?"

"Yes, I'm here. I'm just trying to picture you."

"I'm flat on my fucking back. Meanwhile, the *world* is coming to an end."

When she started to laugh, I was outraged. Then I remembered I'd been laughing myself. A phrase came into my head: *gales of laughter.* Claire's laughter was like that. Fresh gales . . . Christ, I was stoned.

Finally, she calmed down. "God, I'm sorry, but it feels better when I laugh. Maybe I'm hysterical. Did you hear about the *Pentagon*?"

"Yeah."

"And the one that went down in *Pennsylvania*?"

"Yeah."

"Your sister called, you know. That's one of the reasons I've been trying to reach you. She wanted to know how you were."

I went into a shallow glide. "She did?"

"I wouldn't lie to you, Peter. She called a couple of times, in fact."

"Amazing."

"Yes."

"Well. Tell her I was thinking about her too. But don't tell her about my back, okay?"

"Oh, Peter, I'm sorry I laughed. It must be awful to be lying there helpless in the middle of all this. It was just your tone of *voice* that set me off." She giggled. Tone of *voice*. It was exactly how my sister would have said it.

"What about it? What about my tone of *voice*?"

"Don't get mad, Peter. I wish you were here. I wish both Wendy and you were here. God, what's going to happen next?"

While I wondered about that, I heard the call waiting beep. "Claire, I've got to go. That could be my assistant. I'll get back to you. Sorry." I pressed the flash button before she could answer.

A strange woman's voice. "Is this Peter Davis?" The woman in the loft next door? But how? No, she was calling from Bellevue Psych Emergency. Were they coming for me?

Someone had been brought in. A girl. She'd given them my name.

The drugs had worked well enough for me to start hobbling toward Bellevue thirty blocks north. Many people assumed I'd been hurt in the crash and kept offering things like water and fruit. I declined them with a red face and a limp smile. Above 14th Street there was still some traffic, and finally a black taxi driver pulled alongside and in a Caribbean accent asked where I was trying to go. At the word

"Bellevue," the driver got out, helped me into the cab, and we were there in fifteen minutes through practically empty streets. No charge. The driver helped me out again and roared away.

The psych emergency waiting room, when I finally found it, featured a large TV in front of which were clustered two uniformed guards and a few people in street clothes. Patients? One of the guards turned to me. "Sir, this is psych," he said gently. "I can take you over to shock-trauma. It's not too far."

Kate and a fireman had been brought in together, and so far they were the only crash casualties admitted to the ward. A lady doctor in green scrubs opened the locked door and led me down a long, pale green corridor—she didn't crack a smile when I explained why I was bent over at a forty-five-degree angle. "They're both in a state of pretty extreme disorientation," she said of Kate and the fireman. "Apparently, they went through something terrible together, we're not sure what. Are you family?"

"A family friend, she's interning in my office. They can't tell you?"

"Well, they're not talking. Neither of them has said a word since they came in. . . . Well, Kate did give us your name. The rescue people said they were just wandering down there in a daze with their arms around each other when they were picked up."

"Are they still together?"

"No, the fireman's sitting in the common room, and Kate's lying down in one of the, ah, rest areas."

"Oh, she's asleep?"

"No."

The small room was lit by a single recessed bulb in the ceiling. Kate was a lump under the blanket on the farthest of the two cots, face up, eyes open, hair straggling on the pillow. I pulled one of the two straight-backed wooden chairs nearer her and sat with a sigh. "Jesus, Kate, I'm so sorry."

I sat there for a long time, but she never moved. Air hissed in a vent, and there was a faint pulse of machinery. Everything was cottony from the drugs. . . . like warm fog. Thicker and thicker, deeper and deeper.

I was in my bed in the big old, sad Philadelphia house. Sweaty and scared after a nightmare, and for some reason my bedside light didn't work. Ditto the wall switch. I might have been about seven. Or eight. I had no idea of the time.

I got out of bed and crept into the hall. My sister's bathroom was the first door on the left, and it was open, the lights inside combusting through a thick, impenetrable cloud of steam. There was no sound, no voices.

I'd never in my life been into her bathroom, but sometimes the door would be open as I walked by and I could see an old claw-footed tub and a toilet (same as mine) and a large white-painted wooden table. The table was waist high, as big as a sideboard, with a pull-out section in the top, and a vertical row of drawers halfway down one end. When my sister was still in diapers, whoever changed them must have used this table.

I stood for a long time at the open door, still half asleep. First I was outside the steam cloud, then I was part of it. Did it come out into the hall, or did I step through the doorway? The cloud muffled and swirled, warm and damp, and seemed very familiar: thoughts pushing their way to the surface, roiling, changing shape, receding and being replaced by others. Somewhere ahead of me was light, and I was making my way toward it. Light and two human shapes, one bending over the large white table, one lying on it.

I've lived this scene over and over, but it never comes clear.

The voice whispering my name was Kate's. I could see now that she'd turned her head toward me on the pillow. She was saying something too softly to hear. I got off my chair and knelt down close to the bed, but still I couldn't make it out. My hand reached out and lightly stroked her forehead. "Don't worry," I heard myself say. "Nothing more is going to happen. It's all over. I'm here now." When her own hand came up and clutched my forearm, I realized I was really speaking to someone else.

Acrid yellow smoke had been choking lower Manhattan for three days before the publisher's PR maven was able to wangle seats on a San Francisco flight out of Newark for Kate and myself. After taking her from Bellevue to her aunt's, I'd hobbled down to the nearest blood donor station, but the lines were around the block and I couldn't stand up that long. (Hospital emergency rooms, geared up for a flood of survivors, were almost empty. A Saudi terrorist named Osama bin Laden was reported to have been the organizer. Mayor Giuliani waded impressively through the smoke and debris and abandoned political rhetoric for halting simple words.) I'd wheeled the TV nearer to my bed and waited for intermittent phone service so I could talk to Kate's father, her aunt, and Claire Barstow. Kate herself still was not talking. The fireman she'd come in with had checked himself out and disappeared. The phone listed under his name rang without answering; a Bellevue shrink theorized he might have returned to Ground Zero. Meanwhile, all my meals were take-out Chinese delivered by smiling bicyclists. The attack hadn't slowed them down at all.

Kate, in dark glasses, jeans, and a navy pea jacket, was waiting for me on the sidewalk in front of her aunt's apartment building in the late afternoon; the smoke up here was much less intense, almost unnoticeable. She put her duffel in the trunk of the taxi and climbed in without a word.

"Your dad's going to meet us at the airport," I said. "He says he's got rooms at the Mark Hopkins."

"For you too?" Her voice sounded creaky.

"I've got a flight to Bozeman at six ayem."

"What are you going to do until then?"

"I guess I'll just lie on the floor. It's actually better for my back than being in bed. It's only about four hours anyway."

"Bozeman, Montana? Why Bozeman?"

"My sister's best friend lives near there."

"Your sister's best friend? Why aren't you seeing your *sister*?"

"I plan to. This is the first step."

"What are you talking about?" The dark glasses swiveled toward me.

"My sister and I have been kind of estranged. We, uh, haven't spoken for the last ten years."

"Jesus. Why not?"

"Well . . . she blames me for something I didn't do. Among other things."

"Wow. Must have been something pretty bad."

"It was. Please don't ask me about it."

"So why don't you tell her the truth?"

"Wouldn't do any good. She believes what she believes."

"So it's her fault, hunh?"

"I didn't say that at all."

"What if she doesn't *want* to see you?"

"I hope to Christ she will."

The glasses swiveled frontward. "Well, I hope so too." Her tone was bitter and ironic: a whole new way of talking. "What about your precious *job*?"

"Golden boy's letting me have two weeks paid leave, after we signed that woman in Maine." I nudged her gently. "You'll be getting a fat bonus yourself. Your dad will be very proud."

Silence.

***

The airplane had rows of two seats on one side of the aisle, three on the other. We got the two-seated side, close to the galley in the rear: a good place to be, I thought, if hijackers took over the cockpit. Also, you'd be more likely to survive a crash there. Kate kept her dark glasses on. It was a five-hour nonstop flight. The plane was full, and many people seemed to have noisy babies.

"So," Kate said finally, "you're going to see your sister because of Osama bin Laden?"

Jesus! Was she right? I had to think a minute. "Let's put it this way: because of him I decided to take matters into my own hands instead of sitting around feeling sorry for myself. Kind of a now-or-never deal." A hollow chuckle. "Plus I heard she's in Mexico, and I've always wanted to go there. I hope her friend tells me she's near a beach."

"Well, hooray for Osama. How come you didn't try to fix it before he came along?"

I just shook my head. I couldn't face going into what happened at the sessions in Jackson Hole. I wasn't even sure what had happened in them myself. Just that a poisonous issue had been brought out, laid on the table between us, and left unresolved, assuming that there *was* any way to resolve it. Plus it wasn't really an issue. It was our mother.

Kate opened up a *Vanity Fair* she'd bought at the airport and riffled through the pages without taking her dark glasses off. "Tell me more about your sister, will you?"

"Take off those glasses and I will. Do you want to make yourself blind?"

"I wish I *was* blind. Anyway, they're my new disguise. I'm traveling incognito."

"Why?"

"I've seen too much." She was camping now. In a noir flick. On stage. "I know too much. People want me dead."

"What . . . ah . . . what have you seen?"

She took off the glasses and stared at me out of eyes that definitely did look like they'd seen too much—the old thousand-yard stare. "I'll never tell. But *they* don't know that." Her laugh was like a small explosion. "Okay, the glasses are off. Now tell me about your precious sister." Picking at a feathery patch of the flesh beside her thumbnail.

It was important to say exactly the right thing. Keep it intellectual? "Well . . . her favorite philosopher is Kierkegaard."

"Kierkegaard? Nobody reads him anymore."

"Wendy does."

"Her name is *Wendy*? Peter and Wendy, that's pretty poignant, all right."

"Our mother's idea. She was an incurable romantic, as I told you."

"Or maybe she just wanted to keep you from growing up." Kate tore a glossy bathing suit ad out of the *Vanity Fair* and threw it under her seat.

"Ah. You're very perceptive."

"You bet I am. Maybe what I need is a lobotomy."

I turned my laugh into a cough. "Please stop picking your thumb. Look, now it's bleeding." When I put my hand over them, her fingers felt like ice. I squeezed gently and, I hoped, reassuringly. It was my job to warm them up.

"So, what did your sister see in Kierkegaard?" she asked after a while.

"Let's see if I can remember the quote she liked. Something like 'The point of life is to make yourself weary of living.'"

"Actually, what he wrote was, 'Life's destiny is to be brought to the highest degree of weariness with life.' My father had a copy of it lying around."

"And you read it? How old were you?"

"About twelve. I'd read anything back in those days."

Back in those days. About four years ago, to be exact. I realized I was still holding her hand and took my own hand back.

"Do you love her?" Kate asked coldly. "She sounds kind of interesting."

"Of course I do."

"Can she fly?"

"Only in my dreams."

"What if you saw her jump from a burning building and hit the ground right in front of you? Do you think she'd bounce? Or just kind of go *splat*?"

"I don't know," I said softly.

She stared at me for a few beats, then put her glasses back on and opened the *Vanity Fair* to a piece about David Bowie. "Do you think you'd try to catch her?" she asked after a while.

My old college roommate was waiting for us wanly at the exit of the disembarkation ramp (allowed, I guessed, since Kate was a minor—I'd had to get both parents' signed permission for all her flights). She tried to walk past him, but he bundled her into his arms and stared at me over the top of her head. I hadn't seen him since we graduated, but he looked almost exactly the same.

"Christ, I'm sorry, Dwight," I told him.

"Well, we know who to blame." He tried a grin. "At least she's here now. At least you both got out okay."

Kate wriggled out of his arms. "Daddy, can you get me a Snickers? They didn't serve any food on the plane."

We headed to a news shop, and she peeled the wrapper off the candy bar and ate it with both hands, like a child. "I guess we better head down to the baggage claim," her father said nervously. "Peter, I can't thank you enough for all you've done."

"Don't thank me. Kate's got the talent. She was the star of the shop." Shooting a shit-eating grin Kate's way. "By the way, golden boy said to tell you you'll be welcome back next summer, and he'll give you a glowing college recommendation. Where are you thinking of applying? Stanford, like your dad?"

She wiped her nose. "College is a bit redundant, don't you think?"

"Come on, Kate," her father said. "Your bag will be the last one left. Give Peter a kiss good-bye."

She didn't raise her face to me, so I kissed the top of her head and gave her an awkward pat on the back. "So . . . see you next summer, okay?" My voice echoed as if through an empty theater.

"Good luck with your sister." She cut her eyes up suddenly. "*I'd* believe your story, whatever it is. For all *that's* worth."

Thin Air

After she'd called Claire for the third time, Wendy decided she needed a long swim. So far, her record was forty-five minutes. She was going to beat that now. Ocean swimming was her new sport. Lying on a surfboard was beginning to feel strange. Not uncomfortable exactly, just not centered. She'd started to take her camera out to the break—next best thing to doing it herself. She was shooting in black and white, which gave an intriguing edge to the wipeouts.

The Mercedes still wasn't finished, though almost a month had passed since the parts arrived. Marco made surly excuses that she had no way of verifying. Time had turned funny. It didn't seem to move anymore, like in a dream. If she really tried, she could calculate that it was early September. But she'd almost rather not.

Last week Isabel had taken her to a *bruja* who lived in the Barrio Las Flores, back in the valley, a neighborhood of old-timers. The *bruja*'s small house was almost engulfed by a huge bougainvillea, and she herself was under five feet, with large, slightly bulging deep gold eyes like a lemur. She lived alone, although Isabel said there was sometimes a little black dog around. "You never see them together, her and her dog. You know why?" Wendy said she didn't. "Because she *is* the dog. You never see her in town, but you see the dog watching and listening. The dog can go anywhere, and it sees things that a person cannot."

"The dog's about this high, sharp ears, short tail, curly hair?"

"*Precisamente.*"

"It goes through my garbage a couple of times a week."

"It does more than go through your garbage, *querida*. She knows all about you now."

"Holy shit. People must be terrified of this woman."

"No, no. She's . . . *de la gente.* Sometimes they go to her for help, advice, like that. Like visiting the little father. She doesn't do bad things. But, for example, if someone put a curse on you, she can take it off."

Everything was very *calm* in the *bruja*'s house; that was what struck her. Nothing unexpected. Of course she was pregnant, no sense in denying it any longer. "What should I do, *doña*?" she asked.

It was early evening and the room was lit by one kerosene lantern. She felt the *bruja*'s tiny hand on her arm. "When the time comes, you will know that too."

So she was waiting for a sign when Isabel came running up the road with news from New York. Then Isabel's arms were around her, wild hair tickling her face, Isabel's strong musky smell, the solid width of her back. Wendy buried her face in the warm curve of neck and shoulder under the hair, closed her eyes, and wondered if she was going to faint.

She knew from Claire that her brother was living downtown. Without being asked, Claire had also supplied his address and phone number.

"Oh God," she whispered into Isabel's hair. "Let him be all right." They were kids again, driving the Husky to Mexico, her giggling at the way he looked behind the wheel in his new blue wool Sears Roebuck dress. Him tossing his head, lifting his left hand from the wheel to settle his red beret, and turning to grin at her.

What had happened since then? Well, he'd betrayed her. Hadn't their mother confirmed this on her last visit to Briarcliffe? What was it she'd said exactly: *Never trust your brother?* Oddly, this was the sole piece of motherly advice she'd ever taken seriously.

Never trust your brother. Her mother had showed her teeth when she'd said that, and her face had been red. She'd been sitting opposite Wendy in one of the blue velvet armchairs in the Briarcliffe parlor—so like the ones in their house in Philadelphia—and had leaned forward to touch Wendy's knee, but her daughter had shrunk away as if from a branding iron.

In the Jackson Hole shrink's office her mother had reappeared. Teeth. Red face. She tried to tell her brother what she'd said, but it was no use. He couldn't hear. He wouldn't believe her. He quite obviously thought she was nuts.

Isabel held her hand on the walk across the valley to the phone office. Like two schoolgirls. The office was packed with gringos, trying to call their loved ones, and one of them reported that the lines to New York were clogged and nonfunctional. Was it a sign? So Wendy called Claire instead and never mentioned that she'd been trying to call her brother. At the time, Claire herself had no news. It took two more calls for Wendy to find out how he was.

Her swim didn't turn out as she'd planned. Afterward, alone in the house with a bottle of wine, she decided she'd write it up in her journal as a letter to her brother—next best thing to talking to him. Isabel was out to dinner, and she hadn't felt like joining her. Evenings tended to be queasy. Her belly popped and roiled, and sometimes she knelt at the toilet waiting but nothing ever seemed to come up. She ate *galletas* and drank mineral water and felt kind of surrounded from inside.

Dear Peter—

On the evening in question (I spent most of the day in the telephone office trying to get news from your city), the waves were hypnotically big. A chubasco *coming in, or something. I sat* and watched them for a while and noticed that they came more or less in sets of twelve. The ninth wave was usually the biggest. Then they tapered off, and between sets for a few minutes it was pretty calm. If I timed it perfectly and swam as hard as I could, I could make it out beyond the break before the next set began.

Well, I could either sit there and stew about New York or give it a shot, correcto? The first wave of the next set was beginning to feather up when I got there, but I decided to swim over instead of ducking under. Felt like I was never going to stop rising, and when I got to the top with that last little push as it almost grabbed me and threw me back onto the sand, I positively howled with glee.

Way up in the air, I looked back to watch the monster crash on the beach, and guess what? There beside my little pile of clothes was this postcard Mexican in a baggy white campesino outfit like the ones you see in Diego Rivera murals from the thirties, a straw cowboy hat, and huaraches.

This man was not unknown to me. Not long after I arrived in this place, I had the incredible experience of waltzing with him. After the music stopped, he bowed and I kissed his hand in front of all the village! He can waltz like a knight of olde, and in fact his nickname here is Felipe Reyes, after a kind of Mexican Lone Ranger. But there's a quixotic twist. . . . This man wants to do good deeds, save damsels in distress etc., but nothing ever works out the way he plans. A veray parfait gentle knight erroring. Take me, for example (please take me). He wants me to be his Dulcinea, but instead . . . Would you say I'm pure as the driven snow? No? Well, he thinks I'm perfect in every way. It's kind of gratifying. You might even say he worships me. Your sinful, nutty sister! It gives me something to live up to.

Never one to discourage worshippers, I waved and shouted again out there in the waves. Big mistake. He thought I was *drowning and needed rescue (not farfetched: no Mexican ever swims off this beach).*

Luckily, it was a small set, and by the time he'd made the decision to keep his clothes on during the rescue (this took a minute or two), it was calm enough for him to get out through the waves like I had. And I'll have to admit that in this clear water I worried about my own lack of clothing.

"I'm all right," I called before he got too close. "I'm all right. Don't worry."

I could see his mouth open to answer, a little wave wash into it, him coughing, thrashing. And I suddenly realized that he could barely swim!

By the time I got to where he was, he'd gone down. The water was so clear I could see him easily, hanging there about ten feet above the bottom. I dove down, grabbed him across the chest (tip o' the hat to Joe McQuillen's lifesaving lessons at the Bar Harbor Club), and got him back to the surface where, thank God, he started to cough.

"Don't move," I said. "I have you. Just stay calm. It's all right."

I did have him. His back was pressed against my breasts, my arm was across his chest, and my hand was hooked in his armpit. Every once in a while our thighs would brush. We had to wait out there for quite a while for exactly the right moment between sets, rising and falling and rocking back and forth in that warm, silky water. Then we started in, using McQuillen's patented scissor kick and sidestroke.

The beach was only about fifteen feet away when a big one began to make up out beyond the break, first obscuring the horizon, then rising up into the sky with a kind of breathing sound until you could see silver Sierra mackerel chasing schools of silver minnows in it, backlit by the peach-colored sun.

There was no chance anymore of making it out onto the beach. "We have to go under this wave," I told him. It feathered up to about fifteen feet and began very, very slowly to curl. I put my hands on his shoulders and pushed down, but his feet were planted firmly on the sand. So I put my arms around him instead and we watched that breathtakingly beautiful lip come floating down toward us.

Luckily, it fell just short, and instead of smashing us into the bottom, the recoil bounced us up and we were flying through the air in a cloud of spray, enjoying the arc (at least I was) like Toad after the car crash in the Wind in the Willows, *beginning to think it could go on forever when we landed on the sand, him underneath me. The flying water covered us, rolled us up the beach and left us high and dry.*

I remembered I was without clothing at about the same time he came fully to his senses. He struggled to sit up, ripped off his soaking shirt, and held it out to me with his head turned away. I put it on and thanked him for saving my life.

"It was nothing," he said. "Are you all right?"

"Oh yes. I'm fine."

"Well then . . . good-bye."

Before I could think of anything else to say, he'd gotten to his feet. The air was full of peach-colored spume, and the sun was just a finger or so above the horizon. Everything was glowing very numinously. As I watched him walk (rather unsteadily, but nude from the waist up) away into that huge perspective, I found myself thinking thoughts I don't think I've ever had before. Maybe I should add that I'm a wee bit pregnant and trying to decide what to do.

Yes, pregnant! What do you think our mother would say? What words of motherly advice? Was she ever pregnant with us? Did she actually want us? Or did she just stumble over us in the garden?

Just kidding. Of course she wanted you, at least.

You know what? Felipe is going to cure me of these kinds of thoughts. Have you ever been worshipped? It's a nice feeling, and I'm going to try not to let it turn me on too much in spite of my raging hormones.

She was writing this on her cot in the tiny spare room, the bottle of mineral water and carton of *galletas* on the floor within reach, when she heard the front door quietly open and close. "Isabel?"

No answer. She felt the hair on the nape of her neck begin to rise. Her window was high and almost too small to squeeze through, but it might be possible. She was on her feet, hands on the sash, when Marco's chuckle sounded from the hall. "Isabel's at the Zaguan, having *caldo de pulpo* with Anna. I just passed them."

She could see from his face, when it appeared in the doorway, that he had found some blow. Not surprising. Blow was all over town these days since a 727 full of it had gotten stuck in the mud of the dry lake north of town where they'd been offloading for years. Just small prop planes up to now, but then they'd gotten greedy and tried the Air France 727. It was just too heavy. After transferring the blow into state police trucks, they'd started cutting up the mired jet with police arc welders and burying the remains with police earth movers, but someone had tipped off the press. A week later, the entire local contingent of *judiciales* had been transferred to another part of the country.

"Anyway"—Marco's eyes were glittery and his smile was crooked—"I heard you spent the whole day at the phone office. Thought I'd drop by and see if everything's okay." He licked his lips, sniffled, and wiped his nose. "I'd say I was sorry about what happened in New York, but I'm really not. The fucking gringos finally got what they deserved."

Wendy crossed her arms.

"They've been asking for it for years, you know. And now they finally got it. Hope your brother's okay, though."

"He is," Wendy said carefully. "Thank you for coming by. It was very thoughtful of you."

Marco went to the bottle of wine and picked it up. "*Caláfia*. I thought you'd be drinking Chilean."

"Well, things are a little tight. I've got an engine rebuild to pay for. It must be just about finished, isn't it? I would have come by today, but . . ."

He took a long, gurgling swallow. "Every time I get close, something else comes up. It's the pissiest job I ever took on."

She couldn't stop a yawn. "What's wrong now?"

"Goddamn valves. The shop in La Paz fucked up. I got to have them reground."

"I didn't know the valves were involved. I thought it was just the crankshaft."

"Anytime you take the head off, the valves should be reground. Your Hell's Angel buddy could tell you that."

"How long will it take to regrind them?"

"About a week. Why, is there someplace you have to be?"

"You know there is, Marco. I should have been back weeks ago."

"What? Don't you like it here?" He spat on the floor and licked his lips. "I bet you miss me. That's probably it. You're horny as hell." Eyes on her breasts.

"Far from it."

"I think Isabel is feeding you too many *tortillas de harina*. Every time I see you, you look bigger." He cupped his chest with both hands and grinned.

"Marco, it's been a long day. I don't want to be rude, but I really have to get some—"

He reached out, grabbed the neck of her tee shirt, and yanked back as hard as he could. There was a ripping sound and the piece of cloth came away in his hand. The red bra she was wearing was actually Isabel's, a no-nonsense number from one of Mexico City's top corsetiers. She'd borrowed it because hers barely fit anymore. Lucky, she thought. Very lucky. Something forced its way into her throat. Was she about to burst into laughter?

Marco's voice stopped her. Soft, husky, and urgent. "*Ay Mamac-ita.*" His green eyes glittered behind half-mast lids. She had heard another story recently. He'd killed a man after a bar fight by dragging his unconscious body under the wheels of a parked truck. Leaving him to be crushed but not actually doing the deed himself. "*Las dos leches. No podría probarlos?* For old times sake? I'll be gentle, don't worry. I mean, after all . . ."

She had picked up the wine bottle from the floor where he'd left it and was preparing to defend herself as well as possible when Isabel showed up with a clack of heels.

For minutes or hours, nobody said a word. Then Marco sniffled and laughed. The sound gave Wendy goose bumps.

"Three's a crowd," he said softly and huskily. If he'd been a panther, his tail would be twitching and his ears would be flat. *If called by a panther, don't anther.* "Or maybe three's company."

The two women stood frozen as he took the wine bottle from Wendy's hand, had another long pull, and set it on the floor. "*Oye, chicas!*" Pulling a film canister and a Bic pen top from his pocket, removing the canister's lid. "*Cien por ciento. Directo de Colombia.*" Offering it to Isabel. "*Mi amor, un regalito del fondo de mi corazón.*"

Isabel kept her face averted. *Never look them in the eyes.* She dropped her gaze to the floor and bent her neck slightly in submission. She was a different woman. Watching her, Wendy was terrified.

Marco dug the concave spike of the pen top into the canister, held the little white pile to his own nostril, and sniffed sharply. Once more on the other side. He growled softly and ran the black plastic spike down Isabel's averted cheek, under her chin and across her throat. "*Bueno, mi amor. Hasta pronto.*"

He returned the equipment to his pocket and turned to Wendy. "And you, *mamacita.* Do you still dance?"

She couldn't help looking at him. Just for an instant. His panther eyes. His wet mouth. Then he bowed. *"Entonces*, may I have this one? It's a waltz. I think you know it."

He put his right hand on her waist and took her own right hand in his left. Purring, raspily, a snatch of tune. Stepping forward with his left foot—front, side, together—and she found herself following him through the opening stanza of *"Volver*," around and around the room.

Finally, he let her go with a twirl and stood there facing them. Breathing a little hard. Watching them with merciless eyes. Wendy saw that Isabel's lips were quivering.

She stepped forward, curtsied, and held out her hand for Marco to kiss.

"The way he was looking at us," Isabel said after they heard the front door close, "I was sure we were gone. What did he say when he left?"

"I could see you were sure. That's what scared me more than anything. I couldn't hear what he said." Wendy chose a black tee shirt from the closet and quickly pulled it on. She *had* heard.

"You did exactly the right thing, *querida*. But how did you—?"

"Pure instinct. I was so scared I just stopped thinking." She ran a hand absently over her belly. "God, what a day. Too bad he didn't leave some blow."

Isabel snorted. "And there you are in my bra the whole time."

"Actually, it made me feel like Wonder Woman. It's a power item."

"Gringos. You're amazing. But *dios mío*, suppose I hadn't come back early."

Yes. Suppose.

"Listen, you think he, ahm—?" Isabel waved her hand across her own belly.

"He never brought it up. Why? You can't see anything, can you? Just that my boobs are a little bigger. Not even that much."

"My bra fits you pretty good, *querida*. And I'm a full D."

"He thinks you're fattening me up. Feeding me wheat tortillas and pork."

"*Que palomilla!*" Isabel squeezed her upper arm, then stroked it worriedly. "Listen, I know him better than you. I tell you we're very very lucky. Plus he can get away with anything. You know his mother married a big judge?"

They sat on the porch, sipping beers and letting off pressure. Being lucky felt good, and maybe it was more than luck. Whatever it was, you felt alive and tingly. "I don't want to sleep alone tonight, though," Isabel said. "I bet you don't either."

It seemed very natural to climb into Isabel's double bed together, lying like two spoons, both in tee shirts and underpants, Wendy in front. Isabel's sheets carried her musky smell, and her warmth was cozy as a blanket.

"Were you really scared?" Isabel asked after she turned out the bedside lamp. "You didn't look it. I was impressed, very. You looked strong. Well, *claro*, you *are* strong. What were you going to do with that bottle?"

"I had no idea. It was just the only thing around."

"You could have broken the bottom off and then jammed him in his face."

"Wow! That's pretty intense." Wendy tried to imagine the act and couldn't.

"Intense, you call it? You gringos don't know, you have no idea. Blood!" She touched Wendy's neck lightly with the tips of her fingers. "You don't feel it."

"Ah, but I do. That's where you're wrong. My heart's still beating a mile a minute." Wendy put her own fingertips over Isabel's and gently moved them over the big artery. "Feel it now?"

"Ah," Isabel breathed. *"Aquí está."*

A pickup rattled up the dirt road. "Do you think it's a bad little creature inside me? Like its father?"

"No, *querida*. I think they all start the same."

"Have you ever been . . . you know, *embarazada*?"

"No, never."

"Do you think you ever will?"

Isabel didn't answer. "I tell you one thing," she said finally. "You look better now than I ever see you."

"Ha! You told me that before."

"*Sí, claro*. But now more than before." She laughed softly. *"Estás muy verde*, chica."

"Green? You think I'm turning *green*?" Wendy rolled onto her back and looked over. "What *can* you be talking about?"

Isabel smoothed the hair from her face and laughed again. *"Dios mío*. It's just a way of talking. Shall we try to go to sleep?"

"Let me tell *you* one thing first." Wendy propped herself up on an elbow. "I feel very close to you right now."

"And I to you."

"What do you think I should do? Truly."

"I can't tell you that, *querida*. But whatever you decide, I will be there to help you."

Wendy bent down and kissed her forehead. "What would I do without you? I'd be fucked."

She could see Isabel's face in the headlights through the window as another pickup clattered down in the opposite direction. Her eyes were closed.

She woke sometime later to the hissing of the night wind in the taco palms behind the house. They were lying like spoons again, Isabel's arm loosely over her, breathing heavy and regular. Very cozy, like when she'd slept with her brother in the Husky near the big river. And she'd gotten her period. She stretched and shifted slightly, and Isabel's hand drifted onto her tender breast.

Drawing a sharp breath and shifting again. Jesus! But the hand (she's asleep for God's sake) stayed where it was, and as time passed there was no way to stop her nipple from hardening uncomfortably.

Isabel's window showed one impossibly bright star. Or maybe a planet, since it didn't twinkle. Glowing with a quiet intensity. Star light, star bright, first star I've seen tonight. Wish I may, wish I might, have the wish I wish tonight.

Her nipple was aching, and the ache was spreading through her entire body. Should she roll away? Or remove the hand? But all she could do was lie there paralyzed like the girl who trod on a loaf in Anderson's *Fairy Tales*. Unable to move while wingless flies crawled over her with an unbearable tickling.

She wanted the hand to move. Anything to relieve the slowly spreading ache. The nipple felt huge and dark. She heard herself sigh, but Isabel's breathing continued just the same.

As if by her own will, she felt the hand move slightly, and sighed again. It felt like her own hand.

A little freaky at first, but slowly she got the hang of it. The real trick was not to be too eager. The hand was tantalizingly slow, but in the end it did mostly what she wanted it to. It knew what was right, actually better than she did.

The star out the window glowed more brightly. She was floating, then flying. Up off the bed, out the window, through the dark air past the hissing palms. The lights of the village below fading away as the star grew closer. Second star on the right, then straight on till morning.

Claire in Montana

The Bozeman airport looked like a ranch lodge, with soaring raftered Douglas fir ceilings, and granite abutments. A tall female figure was waving as I limped out of the boarding tunnel, and I waved back hopefully, even joyfully.

When I kissed Claire's cheek, I could smell expensive perfume. Jeans, green and black tooled cowboy boots, and a white dress shirt. Thick oak-blond hair pulled back and tied with a black velvet ribbon à la équestrienne. "You look like a debutante that's gone native," I told her.

"Well, that's what I am." Her grin was less confident than I remembered, but her nostril wings flared bravely. "God, it's good to see you, big bro. How long has it been, anyway?"

I'd forgotten how downy her cheeks were; I hadn't seen her since she'd come to New York maybe five years earlier with her then-husband on a climbing equipment junket paid for by Patagonia. "A coon's age. At least. But you look exactly the same. The life out here must agree with you."

"I've only been here for a few months. I let Tom have the place in Jackson. Don't care if I never see it again. How long does a *coon* live?" Narrowing her light gray eyes. Skier's eyes, someone had called them.

"That would depend on the *coon*." I tossed my head and tried a grin myself. "So it was bad, hunh?"

She pushed a stray lock of hair from her forehead: blunt strong fingers, trimmed clear nails, wedding ring the only jewelry. "Well, it was a Svengali deal right from the start. He wanted to turn me into the world's top female climber. He wasn't my husband, he was my fucking *trainer*. Plus he was never that smart, you know?"

"He was a hell of a climber. Remember that time the three of us went up the Grand? A couple of years after the, uh . . ."

"After those rat-fuck sessions? And I had you dangling over a two-thousand-foot drop? Yeah, I remember. I remember thinking what if I let you *go*."

"After you had me sleep alone in that cave with the rats? The worst night of my life. I was *praying* to be let go."

Claire laughed and patted my shoulder. "Poor you."

"The night before that you made me sleep in my car. You said, don't leave the door open; the bears might get you. You gave me this little sleeping bag that only reached my waist. You called it an *elephant's* foot."

"Payback time," Claire said, nostril wings fluttering.

"Payback for *what*?"

"Let's not go there. You know Wendy called me three times after the attack, trying to find out how you were?"

"Yeah, you told me on the phone. Don't you remember? You said only a couple of times, though."

Claire's old Toyota Land Cruiser smelled of hay, and in fact there was a bale of it in the back. For the horse, she explained as we chugged over the high pass between Bozeman and Livingston. Mountains loomed all around us, separated by vast perspectives.

"Do you keep a horse these days?"

"Not yet. But I'm looking. Meanwhile, I like the smell of hay. Sometimes I'll take a little nibble."

I was charmed. How long had it been since I'd smelled hay? I reached back, pulled a few stalks from the bale, and held them to my nose. "All I've been smelling for the last few days is yellow smoke. The city says it's okay, but everyone knows it's fucking up their lungs big time."

"Poor Kate. Poor everyone. What do you think happened to her?"

"I think she was standing there and some woman hit the ground right in front of her. They call them *jumpers*. Nobody seems to know how many there were."

"My God." Claire turned to face me. "Everything's different now, isn't it? You feel so *stupid* out here under the good old spacious skies."

"The amber waves of grain. Whoa!"

She swerved back onto the highway. "The fucking purple mountain *majesty*."

"The goddamn fruited *plain*."

Oh God, it felt good to laugh. We built it up together, reinforcing each other, tears running, faces bursting. Whenever one would slow down, the other would start up again. A heart attack was right around the corner, and it wouldn't be a bad way to go. We covered miles and miles that way.

Claire finally wiped away her tears and sniffled. "I ought to feel more patriotic now, but I don't. I just feel sad and kind of old hat. I guess it's the end of the twentieth century. Like World War I ended the nineteenth. We're all just supernumerary now, one foot in the grave."

"Kate says that the twenty-first is going to be all about religion. I think I agree with her. You can see it happening everywhere you look."

She slapped my knee. "You and I better get some, old hoss. Before it's too late. Actually I *did* go to church on the eleventh. Right after your sister called for the third time. Isn't that pathetic?"

"What did you pray for?"

"Oh, nothing. That never works. I guess I just wanted to be near people. I was thinking of *you*, flat on your back in your loft. Which I've never seen. When do you have to go back?"

"Well." I sniffed the stalk of hay and put it in my mouth. "That's one of the things I need to talk to you about."

"It's not much." She stopped the Land Cruiser in front of a little clap-board Cape Cod on a quiet side street lined with cottonwoods just beginning to yellow. "But maybe it's home."

"It *looks* homey," was all I could think of to say.

"Just renting by the month for now." She hoisted my bag and helped me out of the Land Cruiser. My back had frozen in a sit-down position. "How long is this going to last, anyway?"

"What? The back?"

She raised her dark eyebrows and nodded.

"Actually, if I move around, it's a lot better. Sitting is the worst."

"Good. I've got some country I want to show you."

There was one bedroom, a living room–kitchen with light oak flooring, and a tiny bathroom. I'd be sleeping on the pull-out sofa.

"You know what I'd like more than anything right now?"

"If it's within my power, you shall have it." With an ever-so-slight blush?

"A nap. I'm wiped out."

"Ah. I was just going to say. I've got some errands to run, and I'll pick up some lunch stuff. What do you like?"

I grinned. "Tofu and bean sprouts would be just great."

Lying on the pull-out sofa, looking out the window at cottonwood leaves trembling in a light breeze. A slant of light projecting itself in a thick band on the floor. A housefly buzzing in the bedroom, sound-ing like a voice. Mind a white blank with shapes moving somewhere behind the whiteness.

The tofu and bean sprout sandwich was on a plate on the floor beside the pull-out sofa, along with a note: "Didn't want to wake you. Cold wine in the fridge. Back around 5. XXOO P.S. Since when did you go vegan?"

My watch read four. Christ! I'd slept forever. I swung my legs to the floor and prepared to lever myself to standing but lay back down instead. The leaves on the cottonwoods had turned dark gold, and a car swished slowly by in the street. I picked up the sandwich and took a bite. It tasted better than I expected.

As I lay there chewing, I began to realize that I felt very comfortable. My back seemed better, and I was refreshed and alert after the nap, but that was just part of it. I was in the right place at the right time—a feeling I'd only had a few times before, and it had never lasted very long. Oddly enough, one of the times had been in the Briarcliffe parlor, sitting in the blue velvet armchair, watching my sister walk through the door.

I took out the knowledge that she'd called and turned it over and over in my mind, like a crow will fondle a shiny bead.

The cadaverous wine steward looked like Hank Williams. After he'd filled our glasses, Claire raised hers. "Well. Better days, as my father used to say."

"Better days. To absent friends and family. To *anyone* who's absent."

"To you know who. Who cares about you more than you know."

"Hey." I clinked my glass on hers. "Maybe I care about *her* more than *she* knows."

"Maybe you do. That'd be nice. Is that one of the things you need to talk to me about?" She tilted her head back to drink, and I watched her Adam's apple bob.

"Yes."

"Well. Go on. Talk."

"I want to go see her. Will you tell me where she is?"

A little measuring smile. "You've changed. You know that?"

"Everybody changes."

"No, they don't. You said I hadn't changed at all. I don't think I *have* changed all that much. But you have, my sweet."

"How so?"

129

"Well, you're here, aren't you? That's a change. You've decided you want another shot at seeing her in spite of . . . everything. How come?"

So I told her more about Kate, how she reminded me of my sister, what had happened in the car in the fog, and how close it seemed to our earlier flight. And I told her about listening to the phones ringing up and down Crosby Street after the buildings fell, ringing and ringing with no one answering. I told her how I'd felt on hearing my sister had called from Mexico to find out if I was okay. After ten years of silence. "Jesus. Look what it took. Haw—not really, but there *was* a little whisper."

"You guys were headed there when you ran away that time, right?"

"Yes, we were. And I fucked it up. I fucked up a lot of things."

"Well, at least you admit it. . . . That's another change. And now she's finally made it. How does that make you feel?"

I wanted to get this right. "I feel left behind. I should be there too."

"Aha. But didn't you ever try to get there yourself?"

"Closest I could come was Costa Rica in the Peace Corps. They didn't have a program in Mexico, but I didn't know that when I applied."

"I knew you went down there, but I never knew what you did."

"I was helping to set up a national park on the Osa Peninsula. I spent two years in the *jungle*."

"The *jungle*!" The nostrils. Now she was humoring me. "And how did you like that?"

I clapped my hands. "There were more jaguars than humans. I loved every minute of it."

"Yet afterward you came back to the Big Apple and got a job with the *Paris Review*. You've been in the city ever since, am I right?"

"Look. I try to get outdoors as much as I can. Half of me still thinks I should have stayed in the *jungle*."

"Even after your successes in publishing?" She looked absently around the room, finished off her wine. "Mexico's been uh . . . not exactly what your sister expected. Don't ask me the details. I really don't know them, and I wouldn't tell you if I did."

"Just tell me if she's in trouble, okay?"

Claire poured her wineglass full again and took a large swallow. "I think she *is* kind of in trouble. But don't you dare breathe a word."

"You can trust me, *mi amor*."

"I hope so. Now, I'd like you to tell *me* something."

"If it's within my power, you shall hear it."

"Why is Wendy so sure it was you who ratted to her mother while she was in Briarcliffe?"

"Huh. You never asked me that one before. I guess she figured I was the only one who knew, other than herself and Reiger. Reiger thought it was me, too. He said so when I called him from the hospital just before our mother died. Sure, it was a logical assumption, but . . ."

"But what?"

"Well, shit. There must have been someone else. Didn't that ever cross anyone's mind?"

Claire leaned toward me a bit portentously—the bearer of important news—her dark blue wraparound dress showing a tasteful bit of cleavage and the edges of a black bra. "Did you know your mother *told* her it was you?"

"*What?*"

"That's what Wendy said. When your mother came to Briarcliffe just before her car wreck. She told her, '*Never trust your brother.*'"

"You're kidding."

Claire lifted her chin slightly to confirm what she'd said. Her expression was neutral but not closed off. Eventually she lifted a hand to her hair, absently smoothed it back, and I could see the glint of her wedding ring. Why was she still wearing it?

"Jesus," I was saying. "Why would my mother lie about a thing like *that*? It just doesn't . . ."

She was shaking her head slowly. "Doesn't sound like her? I think you can only tolerate *your* version, but maybe you're learning. Okay. I'll tell you what I'll do. I'll ask your sister if she'd like to see you. And I'll tell her I think she should. Three times lucky, right?"

"Thank you." I reached over and touched her hand, lying palm down on the table.

But then Claire was looking over my shoulder and smiling. She took her hand back. Turning, I could see the owner of the restaurant approaching with another man in tow. "Want to make an introduction," the owner said to Claire. "This here's Tim Collins. Best writer in the great state of Montana."

The writer looked disconcertingly young and vigorous for a man pushing sixty. Maybe he mixed human blood into his George Dickel. Sculpted nose riding above a long, humorous upper lip. Swirl of thick, Appaloosa-gray hair, noble chin, and large, crazy blue eyes.

He pulled out a chair and sat on it backward. "You look like a horsewoman. Am I right?"

Sweeping her hair back. "What gave me away?"

He cocked his head and opened his mouth.

"Don't answer that. Please?" She gestured my way. "Like you to meet Peter, from New York City."

"Uh-oh," the writer said and looked at me for the first time. "Poor old New Yawk. Wow! So Dubya's really going to get his war?"

"Possibly." But the possibility hadn't actually occurred to me until now.

"What a fuckin' nightmare. But if I know the Big Apple the tiniest bit, there's at least one thing there that's doin' okay."

I took a swallow of wine. "I'll bite."

"Chinese takeout."

"You're right, of course." Feeling my face redden.

"We'll all be part Chinese in a hundred years," the writer went on. "So don't worry about it."

"Okay," I said.

"Will there be Chinese cowboys?" Claire asked. The writer was dressed in jeans and a striped snap-button Western shirt.

"There are Chinese cowboys as we speak," he said. "Mostly from Sacramento. They're good too. Good hands. So tell me: what are *you* ridin'?"

"Nothing at the moment. But yeah, I used to ride a little. Back East."

"English saddle, huh? Betcha have a good seat."

"One of the best."

"Just bought a new cuttin' horse. A mare, from Oklahoma. You should come out sometime and meet her."

"I'd love to. Could I ride her?"

"Well, she's crazy as a bedbug. All she thinks about is cow."

"I've always been good with mares."

"This one's more like a freakin' mountain lion. She'll get down and *hunt*."

"I'd love to pick up on some of that. You a header or a heeler?"

"Aw shucks." The writer grinned. "Can't really call myself a heeler, but that's where I try to put it."

"You rodeo?"

"Just little chickenshit deals. Got one coming up next week in Gardiner, if you're interested."

"Great! Maybe I'll come flesh out the peanut gallery."

"Flesh out th—? Sheeit, don't waste it there. Come back in the pens and give us a hand! We need all the help we can get."

"Be right back." I pushed back my chair and headed for the men's room.

Alone in front of the urinal, I tried to figure out why I was so pissed off. Chinese takeout! The writer had just been trying to keep it light. He *was* light. He had just been doing his thing. Claire had been playing up to it, for sure, but why shouldn't she? As far as I knew the writer was between wives or girls, and she was unattached and loved his work. And she loved horses.

Made in heaven.

But I felt I'd been watching bad soap opera, and Claire was better than that. Now she was free of one asshole, I didn't want to see her glommed by another.

It wasn't my business. But still, I didn't feel like going back to the table. The men's room was located close to the main entrance, and before I knew it I was out on the sidewalk, pushing my way through a chilly wind. Maybe I *had* changed. A while back, I probably would have returned to the table and gotten into a fight. . . . They always seemed to happen in restaurants.

My idea was to walk back to her place, but after a few wrong turns I realized that would be impossible. Wasn't this town famous for its bars? The Liberty Bar actually had swinging doors, and when I pushed through them several heads turned to check me out.

"Where you from, stranger?" a Jeff Bridges knockoff asked in an echoing voice after I'd sat on a stool. Was it vaudeville?

When I answered truthfully, it was as if someone had dropped a glass. New York! The big room went silent, dim faces peered. Then the Jeff Bridges guy put his arm around me. "You need a drink, friend." He waved to the bartender. "What'll it be?"

After the first couple, I lost count. Nor would anyone accept my money. A small army of Jeff Bridges gathered warmly around me, and their faces were the last things I remembered seeing until Claire opened the door of the Land Cruiser to wake me from the hay in back.

Water drummed against a shower curtain and a tendril of steam issued from beneath the bathroom door. When the door finally opened, Claire, in a white bathrobe, combusted outward through a blinding cloud. I closed my eyes, and shortly felt the pull-out couch sag with her weight.

"Peter? You awake?" Waggling my foot. "Peter?"

"Yo. Whoa."

"Wake up, slugabed. We're due out at Tim's ranch in an hour."

"What? You're kidding." She was sitting cross-legged, drying her hair with a pink towel. "What time is it?"

"It's nine ayem mountain time. And luckily for you I *am* kidding."

"Christ. Thank God. Don't scare me like that, it's bad for my back."

"He *did* invite us, though. Thought we'd like to meet Peggy."

"The crazy mare? No thanks."

"Well, I told him you probably wouldn't because of your back."

"My back is quite a bit better, thanks. But you're right, I could have a relapse."

She giggled. "I thought your job was to *woo* writers."

"Haw. He was too busy wooing *you*."

"Well, I'm still wearing a wedding ring, if you haven't noticed. Keeps the flies away. And why would you care anyway?"

"I just didn't like the way you were playing up to it. You're better than that."

Claire's eyes frosted over, and she uncoiled from the sofa. "You know, I sent your sister an email before you woke up. I'd take it back if I could. You haven't changed at all."

She disappeared into her bedroom. I myself couldn't believe I'd said it; I'd sounded like my father. "What the hell did you think you were doing last night?" she called through the doorway. "When are you going to grow *up*?"

The door slammed. I pulled on some khakis and stood near it. "Claire, Jesus. I just care, that's all. You know what? You and my sister are the only people in the world I can really *laugh* with."

No answer.

"How about you?" I asked.

"What?" In a muffled voice, probably pulling something over her head.

"How many people in the world can *you* really laugh with?"

"Not that many."

"Don't you think that's important?"

The door opened, and she stepped out wearing a dark blue turtle-neck sweater and beige corduroy Levis. "Yeah, it's important. I forgot to get milk yesterday. I'll just run down to the corner."

A few minutes after she'd left, the phone rang. Probably the writer. I could let the machine get it, or I could pick up and let the writer know I was on the premises.

But it was a woman's voice, one I knew very well. "Is . . . Claire there?"

"Wendy?"

Silence.

"Hello? Wendy?"

The line clicked and went dead. I was still holding the phone when Claire got back.

She hadn't told my sister I was on the scene, she explained rue-fully. "I thought it would just complicate things."

"Jesus Christ. What do we do now?"

"Wait for her to call back."

"She's not going to. I know it."

"We'll give it an hour. Then I've got to go put in some time at the gallery."

"So you can't call her?"

"Nope. There's only one public phone where she is."

"But you can send email?"

"She's gotta go to a restaurant to get it."

"Well, can you send her another?"

"Peter, I think I've said all I can via email. Or all I want to. If she doesn't call back, she doesn't call back. It was too bad you picked up the phone, but maybe it was meant to happen that way."

She fixed a breakfast of fresh-squeezed orange juice, Hawai-ian papaya, scrambled eggs and serrano peppers, sourdough toast, and espresso. We watched the big clock over the sink work its way through the minutes.

When the hour had ticked by, I said: "Claire. I have to go anyway. *Please.*"

She just watched me.

I struggled on. "Look. Last night I had kind of an epiphany. Our mother wanted to drive a wedge between us. She was *jealous.* That must have been why she told Wendy I'd ratted. She's kept us apart for so long, Claire. Don't let it be for the rest of our lives."

Claire's clear gray eyes seemed to be looking into my soul. She might have seen my theory was only the best I could come up with, and I prayed she'd give me the benefit of the doubt.

PART THREE

Big Day

She'd only said one sentence into the phone before hanging up, but when she came out of the little booth everybody in the telephone office seemed to be watching her with unusual interest. She was wearing one of Isabel's loose white peasant shifts, hair pulled tightly back in a rubber band, feeling tired, bloated, and frumpy, not interesting at all. Blushing as she smiled and nodded her way out, thinking, *They must all know . . . No, impossible, don't be paranoid.* Her jeans still fit, she'd tried them on that morning, but the shift was more comfortable in the unusual muggy heat and she liked its Isabel smell.

She'd known her brother's voice as soon as he'd answered, and she should have hung up then. Why hadn't she? His voice hadn't changed at all, and apparently hers hadn't either. But what was he doing at Claire's? Claire hadn't mentioned him in her email.

The World Trade Center attack had happened five days ago. Maybe he'd gone out there because of that. But then why had Claire sent her the email asking her to call?

Suppose it was sex! Wouldn't that be just like him, to steal her best friend and confidante? Sex and war, perfect fit. *Never trust your brother.*

That was it! They were *fucking* each other, and Claire had been going to tell her, but her brother had screwed it up by answering the phone.

On the other hand, maybe she'd told him about the email and he had been waiting for her call. Maybe Claire had been setting her up.

The midmorning heat was suffocating. She walked slowly to the little plaza in front of the church and sat on a bench under a laurel tree out of the buzzing sun. Cumulus clouds towered explosively over the valley, and her brain felt charged with static. Exquisite irony! Just when she'd started to forgive her brother and actually feel tender toward him, he gloms her best friend and her best friend betrays her. Claire most probably had told Peter she'd called three times to find out how he was. What else had she told him?

Claire knew about the Mercedes breakdown, the thing with Marco Blanco, but not about the pregnancy. Right? Or had she confided too much? Today was a Sunday and the Internet café was closed, so she couldn't check what she'd said in her earlier emails. But she remembered hinting at something after her visit to the *bruja*, something about a decision she was going to have to make very soon. If only she could remember her exact words.

Pancho Clamato's black-and-yellow Toyota station wagon, with his old Velzy longboard up on the roof rack, eased around the corner from Juanita's market and slid to a stop across the plaza from her bench. Clamato leaned out and waved her over. He'd moved out of the Barrio San Ignacio to his own house near the baseball stadium, and she hadn't seen him since well before the attack. His wizened face was as excited as a kid's. "What the hell are you doing sitting around in the park? Don't you know this is the biggest day since January 15, 1982?"

Big day! The towering clouds, the distant cannonade of surf, her brother's voice on the phone. They seemed to fit together: maybe it was all part of the sign she'd been waiting for. "Thanks, Pancho." She leaned down and kissed his cheek. "You going out? Can I get a ride?"

Clamato had already gone out once, at dawn, and had come back to get a towrope: the huge waves had forced so much water into the *estero* that the raised two-track past the break was covered and hard to see. A Mexican kid had borrowed Bo Hansen's jeep to bring beer and food from town and had gone off the track into the water. The jeep was stuck, and the water was rising, but when the panicked kid came running back for help the surfers told him it would have to wait—the surf was a once-in-a-lifetime deal. The kid's eyes goggled; he couldn't believe it. Clamato finally went for the rope as a favor to Bo Hansen's father, an old friend from Windansea.

"Fifteen-foot sets, measuring Hawaiian style." Clamato slowly looked her up and down. "That means twenty-five on the faces. You're going to get some shots today, baby. Cover material for sure."

She walked around the car and got in beside him.

"I hear Marco's been giving you a hard time. He's out there today. Had the privilege of getting cut off by him myself, in fact. But he's good in the big stuff, I'll say that for him. Long as you keep out of his way. Curren wants to kill him."

"Pat Curren? The guy who rode Waimea for the first time?"

"The same. He's about seventy now. Marco snaked the wave of the day from him."

They picked up Wendy's camera gear from Isabel's (old Nikon F2 with motor drive, 500mm lens, tripod, and twenty rolls of thirty-six-exposure Kodak PLUS-X; she wouldn't be caught dead using digital) and rode out through the green, flowering desert. From a rise about a mile from the break, they could see the ruler-straight ridges marching in from the horizon under a glassy surface, and the break itself was shrouded in spume. A big storm was brewing off Cabo Corrientes, about seven hundred miles south, sending beautiful, regular wave pulses out in every direction.

They negotiated the flooded *estero*, past the mired jeep, past the palm grove around Garth Murphy's ranch. Clamato got out to engage the hubs, and they hauled through deep sand ruts to the small village of tents and four-wheel-drive camping rigs in the dry wash short of the break. A crowd had gathered on the sand, silhouetted against a wild backdrop of swirling creamy soup. Nobody turned as they walked up, and Wendy unfolded the tripod and screwed the camera into place. Amazingly, she had the field to herself—there were no other cameras.

Between sets. The surfers were specks almost at the horizon, sitting on their boards waiting for the next one. She could count only four, and Clamato reeled off their names: Doyle with the red gun, Curran with the natural, Murphy on bright green, Marco Blanco with the red nose and the black suit. All veterans.

She poked Clamato in the ribs. "You going out again?"

"Gotta go save the jeep. You?"

"Think I could handle it?"

He gave her a half-smile. "No problem. If you were in shape."

"Say no more. I haven't surfed in weeks."

"It *shows*," Clamato said, smiling a bit crookedly, turning back to the ocean. "*Ho* shit."

"Outside," someone yelled, and the four surfers swiveled their boards and scratched for the horizon, up the dark blue face of the first wave like tiny black water striders on a rapid. They all made it, and then the wave feathered, curled, and peeled off in a perfect double-overhead tube. Clamato groaned. "God, I hate to see an empty wave."

The second wave was bigger, but all four of the surfers made it again. Marco Blanco and Garth Murphy were establishing a lead.

The third wave was about the same size as the second. "Doyle's going for it," Clamato said, and Wendy zeroed the camera in to see Doyle sit back, swing his board toward shore, let the peak lift under him, take a couple of strokes, and pop to his feet in a low crouch.

"Get this," Clamato said. "Backdooring at twenty feet. Don't see that too much. Around here, anyway."

Still crouching, Doyle shot straight down the long blue face like a downhill racer. The peak was to his right, and when he reached the flat he cut sharply toward it, trimmed forward, and tucked again as the moving face pulled him up onto it. Easy and fluid, as in a toy wave at Malibu. "Classic Doyle."

Wendy pressed the shutter button and the motor drive began to click off exposures as the peak feathered and curled ahead of the speeding figure, then a backwash off the beach from the previous wave made it jack. Eye to the eyepiece, camera clicking. "He's not going to make it. Pull out. Pull *out*."

"Too late. He could straighten out and prone it in, but he's not going to. That's Doyle."

Doyle trimmed straight down the line as the peak closed over him and he disappeared in a white explosion. Some of the girls screamed, and Wendy released the shutter button. The wall of churning soup was almost as high as the wave, bright and beautiful in the sun.

Doyle's red board surfaced first, and finally his black head some distance away. "Broke his leash." Doyle stroked toward his board as the next wave feathered and broke and another thick wall of soup rumbled down on him. He reached the board just ahead of it, pulled himself on, and disappeared again.

Glimpses of the red board could be seen in the frothing soup, and when it finally rushed up the beach and sucked back, the board with Doyle anchoring it stayed high and dry on the sand. Then Doyle was on all fours, heaving and retching. "He's your friend. Aren't you going to go help him?" It seemed to go on and on.

"He's okay," Clamato said. "I was with him for a while last night at Shut-up Frank's. He's operating with a hangover and four hours of sleep. Just getting rid of the poisons."

Clamato left with Doyle and the Mexican kid to pull the jeep out of the water and then take Doyle to the Centro de Salud to get his foot sewed up: the board's sharp skeg had sliced it to the bone. Wendy sat by herself near the camera, hugging her knees and watching Marco Blanco on the waves. A big day. Big Sunday. Portentous, yes, but still . . . maybe things already had gone too far. Maybe it was too late.

If only Isabel were here to give her advice, support, and love, but Isabel was in Mexico City for a few days delivering a batch of paintings to her dealer.

She smoothed Isabel's shift over her knees, sniffed it, and felt a ripple of warmth lap over her skin. Her nipples smarted. Sex with Isabel was everything that sex with Marco had not been: tender, gentle, full of understanding and sweet anticipation. Pregnancy aside. Or maybe not aside. That thought was a little prickly. But even the prickle was tender.

Curren and Murphy came in, and four other old-timers went out, so now there were five. She could always tell when Marco was up because of his style, though she didn't shoot him. He fought the wave instead of going with it like the others, which made for some dramatic encounters but wasn't pretty to watch. He was getting more rides, picking up the smaller inside waves as well as the big ones outside, never getting caught. Since she'd been watching his etiquette had seemed acceptable, though there had been some grumbling on the beach about the Curren episode.

Not far away from her, a handsome black-haired kid about seventeen was being zipped into his spring suit by an older man who looked like his father. "Look, Tommy," the older man was saying, "you're great on the thruster, but I wouldn't use it today."

"I used it that big day at Trestles. It worked fine, Dad, you gotta admit."

"Nobody better that day than you. People still tell me about that tube. But those were twelve feet, these are twenty. Some of them, anyway. Everyone out there now is on a gun."

"It was fifteen at Trestles," Tommy said. "Everyone said so."

"Whatever. This is bigger. And this is a Pipeline wave, no margin. Trestles will always forgive you. Look, that gun of Garth's? The Bean? It would be perfect for you today."

"The Bean's a great board, Dad. I know you shaped it, but . . ."

The older man cocked his head.

"It's just not my style, Dad. You know? My board'll work for me." He slapped his father on the shoulder and grinned. "I'm gonna make you proud."

The kid's board was under six feet, a needle-nosed thruster with black rubber footpads and what looked like a Grateful Dead logo. He struck a pose with it under his arm at the top of the steep sand bank carved out by the surge, waited for a lull between sets, then slid down the bank and charged into the water on the back of the last incoming wave. They watched him paddle strongly, duck dive under a line of soup, paddle, duck, paddle, and finally he was out with the others. No problem. "That kid could paddle all the way to Hawaii," his father said.

It was a long lull. The father sat cross-legged on the sand, eyes fixed, every muscle tense like a dog waiting for a Frisbee. His hair was thick and curly like his son's, and every once in a while he pulled the nail of his thumb across his lips. Like Belmondo in *Breathless*, Wendy thought. There was no mother in sight. Garth Murphy came over and sat down with him, pouring sand from one hand to the other and chuckling about Doyle. Farther down the beach, Curren was playing with his two-year-old son, sliding down the steep cutbank with him, then picking him up and throwing him back to the top just before the soup came in. Curren's wife or girlfriend, who looked forty years younger, was always there to grab him. Looking at the child, Wendy could feel a thought trying to sneak its way into her brain and blocked it again. But this was getting harder.

Another set came through, and Tommy picked up an inside wave and wailed on it. His style was as fluid and graceful as the old-timers', but his maneuvers were more like Marco's: cutbacks, off-the-lips, lay-backs. Opposite Marco, he made hard things look easy, and he did one or two things that looked entirely original. When he pulled out at the end, he and his board flew ten feet into the air, and everybody watching from the beach clapped, yelled, and waved. His father's face looked like he was in church. Wendy began to shoot his rides with growing excitement: she was getting something special, it was obvious. The torch was being passed right there in front of her camera, and she was privileged to get it all, five rolls and counting.

The first wave of the next set was a monster, bigger than anything she'd seen so far. Three of the five surfers dove off their boards halfway up the face, and two made it over, forcing their way through a curling lip that tried to grab them and hurl them twenty-five feet down onto rock-hard water. The abandoned boards bounced and flew around in the soup like matchsticks, and the heads of the swimming surfers showed black as they stroked for shore. One board had broken in two by the time it was thrown up on the beach. A couple of bystanders dragged the others clear.

As Wendy frantically reloaded, Tommy and Marco scratched over the tops of the next two and finally seemed to be in the clear. Marco took the deep position, with Tommy about twenty feet to his right. They sat and waited, rising and falling on the mountainous swells that made them look no bigger than terns. The telescopic lens determined who was who. "Marco's too far into the pocket," Garth Murphy said to Tommy's father. "Tommy's in the perfect spot. That's where I'd be. If I was out there. You trained him good."

"You were out there," Tommy's father said. "You got some good ones. That last one was sweet, the way you got around that section."

"Shit. I'm getting too old for this kind of thing. I wish I was Tommy's age again."

"So do I, baby." Never taking his eyes from his son. "So do I."

Then the two of them got to their feet, and Wendy swung the camera at them, clicked off a series, swung it back.

The little crowd silently watched the swell rise, standing out above the rest even at a quarter mile. The two tiny figures turned and began to paddle toward it. "Okay, now stop," Garth whispered, and the two figures stopped. "Tommy's wave." But both figures swiveled their boards as the face began to lift, and Wendy started the motor drive.

They rose slowly as if on an old-time elevator, the peak of the wave between them but closer to Marco, who started paddling two-thirds up the face. Wendy focused on him. "Sit it out, Tommy," his father said. "Let the asshole kill himself."

"Marco doesn't have a chance," Garth said. "Tommy could go."

"No," the father said. "There'll be other waves."

Marco took a few more strokes and popped to his feet, angling his board so his take-off was across the face rather than straight down it. The peak was beginning to jack. "He's going over the falls," Garth said. "Holy shit."

A count of two and the peak closed over him. He was gone. Wendy panned to Tommy, out on the shoulder, starting to paddle. He was on his feet, soaring down gracefully as Marco blew out of the tube toward him like a bullet, straining for every last bit of speed while the camera clicked away.

The empty wave continued to peel off perfectly as if in slow motion. The beach was silent. Wendy could see Curren running for his big board, charging with it into the water, struggling against the soup and getting thrown back on the beach, Garth grabbing the nearest thruster and slowly duck diving his way out, followed by two others. The father swimming, ducking, swimming, and getting nowhere. One head was showing in the creamy white water where the huge wave had first broken.

When the lull finally came, there were five rescue people in the water towing their boards by the leashes, diving, resurfacing, diving again. Tommy's thruster had washed up, cut cleanly in two as if by a Skilsaw. A little way south, Marco's red-nosed board, intact, floated just outside the shore break.

When Marco came ashore, Tommy's father was waiting for him. They rolled up and down in the breaking waves until a group of bystanders pulled them apart. The father kept silently struggling until four of them laid him on his back in the sand, one on each arm and leg. Even then he kept lifting his head to look out to sea. Marco got to his feet, glanced up at Wendy, still standing behind the tripod, and walked away down the beach to where his board was still floating.

Her tears came without warning, floods of them, shocking herself. She'd never cried this way before, at least not since childhood. Oh God, the father's face! Every time she got a grip, she'd see it again and start over. A small group of bystanders, mostly young men, were blaming Tommy for dropping in. Well, sure, others said, but he couldn't see into the curl. The odds were a hundred to one, against. How was he supposed to know?

And Marco had had time to change course and miss him. "The guy just kept going, straight as a fucking arrow. He could have cut. He *could* have. You know he killed a guy in a bar fight? One scary dude. You see him snake Curren's wave?"

"The father's probably going to file charges. Assuming the kid's . . ."

"Oh, he's gone. It's been what, an hour? They'll be lucky to find the body in this stuff. But fucking Marco will get off. We're in Mexico, right? And he's half Mexican. Plus his mother's married to a judge. Plus how do you ever prove he did it on purpose?"

One kid turned to look at Wendy and her camera, then they all were looking. One of them asked if she got the shot.

She shook her head ruefully. A no-brainer. She told him she'd run out of film right at the last minute.

As an onshore wind rose with the waves, one by one the searchers proned in. In an hour the break was impassable, a churning white cauldron as far out as you could see. No sign of the boy. Wendy walked back to town alone on the beach, scanning each incoming breaker and seeing not just the father's face but Marco's, as he'd looked up after the fight and seen her standing behind the tripod, watching.

A big day for sure, and now she was going to act on it. *You better act fast when you make a decision. It might be the wrong one.*

First thing Monday morning in the little phone booth, her gynecologist's voice from Encinitas seemed rudely loud. "Well . . . congratulations. But Jesus Christ! What took you so long to call?"

"Well, to begin with, my car blew up and I didn't want to leave it. It's still in the shop here, in fact."

"Your father's old Mercedes?"

"Yes. The fifty-six."

Her gynecologist didn't say anything. "Time passes faster down here," Wendy went on lamely.

"You're coming up on three months, Wendy. Have you seen anyone there? Any, ah, doctor?"

"No. I've been feeling okay."

"Nausea? Tiredness?"

"Well, yes. But that's getting better."

"How's your weight?"

"I don't have a scale."

"I mean, are you *showing* yet?"

"I don't think so. Nobody's said anything. But I definitely am . . . bigger."

The gynecologist was silent again. Wendy listened to the hiss of the connection and then said quickly: "I want to terminate it." She hadn't even recognized her own voice.

"*Terminate* it?" The gynecologist's voice had a frightening edge.

"I mean, I just can't—I've got to. Things, ah . . . It's not too late, is it?"

"Almost," the gynecologist said coolly. "You should have made this decision months ago. Are you absolutely sure?"

Tears were coming. Yesterday seemed to have loosened the floodgates. Crying felt weirdly good, she was discovering as she sobbed and sniffled into the phone. Cry your troubles away. Whereas a few months ago she would have despised herself.

"Wendy?" The gynecologist's voice now sounded a bit impatient. "How soon can you get up here?"

"What? Oh . . . I'll have to check the flights. It's not easy; there's only this one public phone and no directory."

"I've got a good travel agent here. Call me back in ten minutes, okay?"

Wendy pressed the phone's disconnect lever, but kept the phone to her ear so people outside would think she was still on the line. "Hello, Claire?" she said into the dead transmitter. "It's me. Is there something you wanted to tell me?" Listening. "Oh, *really*? Well, that's very . . . Thanks for letting me know. How long has it been going on?" Listening again. "Well, congratulations, Claire. By the way, I have some news of my own."

She was crying again, or maybe she'd never stopped. Dissolving in tears, like some teenaged girl, some . . . on and on. What could the people outside be thinking? Woman crying into phone, very natural. Finally she dried her eyes, squared her shoulders, put the phone on the hook, and left the booth. "I'm sorry, Pilar, we got cut off. Can you reconnect me to the same number?" Pilar nodding, with the same impatient, amazed expression she always had with Wendy.

This time, the gynecologist's voice sounded almost motherly. "Okay, Wendy. It's all set. You have a reservation from La Paz to LA at 8:30 ayem Thursday on Aero California. You'll have to buy the ticket, so get there extra early. The flight gets in at 11:35. You have a room at the Standard on Sunset because I know you like it. At two you have an appointment at the Pre-Term Clinic just down the hill on Santa Monica. You can walk there. I had to talk them into it, but one of the doctors is a personal friend and she'll do the procedure. You have five days reserved at the Standard. Okay? I'll come up to see you on Friday, the day after the procedure. I'm sure everything will be fine. But you're going to need to take it very easy for the rest of the time. You're no spring chicken, you know." She sighed. "You're very lucky, Wendy. Couple more days, and not even my friend would have done it."

She'd take the film with her, get contact sheets made, see what they showed. Assuming they showed what had happened, she'd get prints made of the incriminating evidence and get them to the father somehow. The negatives would go to her agent. He'd be floored.

Diving In

Claire's secret swimming hole was a three-hour hike up into the Absaroka-Beartooth Wilderness on the east side of Paradise Valley. The temperature on the valley floor was ninety-two degrees: a September heat wave had moved in during the night. We left Claire's Land Cruiser in a parking lot at the head of the trail and started climbing through baking pastureland, red-tailed hawks circling close on the roaring thermals.

It was pure beauty. But in a ridiculously short time, I began to wonder if I was going to make it. Breathless and dizzy, sweat pouring into my eyes, my navy blue tee shirt absorbing the heat and sticking poisonously to my body. Where my shorts stopped, the long grass cut my legs and made them itch and sting. My borrowed hiking boots (from a friend of Claire's) were half a size too small. I favored my back, but so far that was the least of my troubles.

Farther and farther ahead, Claire's long brown legs ate up the ground. Her light green hiking shorts ticked right and left with each stride and her yellow tee shirt fluttered coolly. She was carrying a day pack with lunch supplies, towels, and bathing suits (mine borrowed from the boot owner).

I sucked a mouthful of water from my canteen, swirled it around, and spit it out into the thick brown dust. Keeping up with her was impossible, so I slowed to a plod, and an ancient Irish folk tune struck up inside my head:

There was an old prophecy
Found in a bog
Lilliburlero bullen a la.
That we're to be ruled
By an ass and a hog
Lilliburlero bullen a la.

The song's rhythm was perfect for the pace. Losing myself in it, I watched my feet abstractedly until I heard her voice off to the left of the trail. "Well, don't kill yourself, big bro. Come take a breather."

She was sitting on a big granite boulder, in the shade of a thick stand of aspen at the top of the pasture, grinning like a champion. "Glad you stayed?"

"And fuck you too." I'd been eager to leave as soon as she'd told me where to go, but the first flight I'd been able to book to La Paz wasn't until Thursday. Claire had suggested I spend the three intervening days at her place rather than LA where the flight originated, and it had seemed like a very logical idea. Maybe even an inviting one.

But parting with that crucial information had changed things. I felt a little embarrassed to have gotten it, and she seemed to be having second thoughts about how wise she'd been to give it away. The first two days, she'd busied herself at the little art gallery where she worked while I had tried fly-fishing with the old split-cane rod she'd inherited from her father. Nary a nibble, even in supposedly some of the best water in the world. The gallery owner had joined us for dinner one night, and the next it had been one of the featured artists, a specialist in misty landscape. The dinners went late, too late to stay up and talk back at Claire's.

When the heat wave blew in, it was almost as if she'd been forced to take the last day off to show me the swimming hole.

I leaned against the boulder—if I sat on it, I might never get up again—and we looked out over the valley. Big western grasshoppers buzzed through the steamy grass. "How much farther?"

She laughed and tucked in a wisp of hair. "The worst is over, city boy. Isn't this beautiful?"

"Oh ya. How far up are we?"

"We climbed about a thousand feet. We're about seven thousand above sea level."

"Well, that explains it. No oxygen up here."

"There's oxygen. Wendy *ran* up here last spring."

"Christ. Good for her."

"You better get in shape, big bro."

"Hey, I just want to see her. I don't want to compete with her."

"Sure?"

"Absolutely sure."

"She'll be interested to hear that. She doesn't really know you very well, you know." She turned to look at me. "Like, right now she's probably thinking we're fucking our brains out. Ready to move on?" I watched Claire hiking ahead of me through bright panels of sunlight under the trees. Her look hadn't been friendly.

The trail through the forest was flatter, wider, and cooler. Walking together would have been pleasant, but Claire roared ahead at full speed. "Hey wait up, will you?" I called, and she stopped and waited impatiently while I caught up, panting. "What is this, the Iron Man?"

"Just going along like I always do." She was looking past me, not even breathing hard. "Sorry. Is your back bothering you?"

"No. Are you pissed off about something?"

"It's just when I get up here I like to move out."

"Okay. Tell me how to get to the swimming hole, and I'll meet you there. I'm a city boy, remember?"

"There are a lot of turn-offs. You'll never find them."

"Mark them, then. What do they call those piles of stones?"

"Cairns." Her nostrils flared slightly.

"*Cairns.* Is that Gaelic?"

She raised her chin. "Look, if you got lost up here, it could be serious. This forest goes all the way to the plains, and it's chock-full of grizzlies."

"Shit. I'm not scared of grizzlies. They only go after menstruating women, don't they?"

We stared at each other. I was ready to laugh, but she turned back to the trail. Huge ponderosa pines soared all around us and the light slanted down as if we were in church. Small, neon birds lit up the chasms. After a little while I realized she was easing the pace.

She'd been right about the turn-offs. I might have found some, but not all. Down through the pines I could see a creek catching the light as we followed it through a steep valley. Then the trail cut away from the sound of falling water and began a long zigzag up the valley side.

The last traverse ended on flat granite rocks over which the creek bubbled before disappearing into space. The rocks enclosed a large pool. "I guess this is it," I said when Claire unslung the pack, sat down in the shade, and began to unlace her boots. "Is it really secret?"

"I like to think so."

I walked to the edge of the pool and looked down. Pebbles on the bottom showed as clearly as if I were looking through air. "Wow. Must be twenty feet deep."

"And colder than shit." She started unloading the backpack.

I pulled off my wet tee shirt and dropped it on the hot granite. "That's what I need. I feel like I've been boiled alive in sweat."

She walked over barefoot and sank the bottle of Sauvignon in the freezing water. She was carrying our bathing suits and handed me mine. Testing the temperature with her toes. "Whoa. Better ease in. You could have a heart attack."

"What a way to go." I thought of the Trade Towers falling, people flying through the air. "You really believe she thinks we're fucking our brains out?"

"If she doesn't now, she definitely will when you show up. She'll figure that's the only way I'd ever tell you. As I say, she doesn't know you very well."

"I'd say that means she doesn't know *you* very well."

"Whatever." The nostrils again.

"You mean, I think of you as . . . family? Well, you're right. You even *look* like family."

"I look like your sister? The hell I do."

"From the back you do. That's mainly the view I've been getting on this hike."

"Sorry. I guess I was trying to work something out."

"Look. Telling me how to find her was the best thing you could have done. For her and me both."

She shook her head. "You know how she is. She'll never speak to me again. And God help me, she's my best friend."

"She'll be okay with it, Claire. She'll even thank you for it, probably."

"You know it was sneaky. Don't tell me you're not a little ashamed yourself. She trusted me, and I betrayed her."

"Claire. I had to see her. Have to. You made it possible because you understand."

She shaded her eyes from the sun with a hand, and smiled at me skeptically. "Do I really?" Turning away. "Come on. Let's get into that water." Walking behind a thick bush to put on her bathing suit.

I walked in the opposite direction to find my own bush. The borrowed trunks were a size too large, red and black nylon cargo baggies that hung to my knees. I had to pull the drawstring tight and tie it to hold them up. I left my underpants on because the trunks had no interior lining of their own.

She came out in a stylish low-backed black maillot. Trying to ignore her nipples pushing out the tight material, I stumbled as I walked over the rocks to the water and heard her laugh. I put my toes in gingerly, pulled them back, and looked up, shaking my head. She was sitting on her side of the pool, hugging her knees.

On her feet and headfirst into the pool in one motion. I could see her body receding slowly down to the bottom, turn, push off, and shoot back up in a cloud of bubbles. She laid an egg-sized granite pebble at my feet. "Your turn."

I seemed to be in air for hours, but when I hit, the shock was not quite mortal, a little death. I tried and failed to get her a pebble of her own. In the hot sun afterward, we opened the wine bottle and filled our tin cups.

That measuring look and a slightly rueful smile. "What'll we drink to this time?"

"I don't know. Fresh starts?"

"So be it. Fresh starts."

Our cups clanked. "Doesn't count," she said. "You didn't look at me. You have to look the person in the eye when you toast. Didn't anyone ever tell you that?"

We were sitting side by side on the smooth, warm granite rock surrounding the pool. When I turned my head, she'd lost her rueful smile and her eyes were oddly unfocussed.

We repeated the toast. I'd lost my own smile. I wondered how my eyes looked to her.

Waking on my back, on a thick pink towel under the dark blue sky and the arching light green aspen leaves, the creek bubbling and gurgling, Claire lying on her side on the other pink towel a few feet away, propped on an elbow

"Hello. Pleasant dreams?"

I sat up quickly to hide what seemed to be an erection. "Yes."

She giggled. "You were asleep for a good half hour. Anything could have happened."

"You mean in my dream? Yeah, wish I could remember. I was outdoors, that's all I know. And it was nice and warm."

"So who were you with?"

"Nobody," I lied. "I was alone."

The next morning, driving to the airport, enveloped by the smell of hay from the back of Land Cruiser, sipping from a sky-blue mug of coffee with white letters—BEST IN THE WEST—I asked her how she'd slept.

"Not well. And you?" She was wearing dark glasses, and her face was pale.

"Not well either. I could hear you tossing and turning."

"Sorry to keep you awake."

"I thought about coming in . . ."

"I thought you were going to."

"Would you have liked that?"

She didn't turn. "Betray your sister one more time? Oh yes, I would have loved it."

"For Christ's sake, Claire. I didn't mean it that way."

She lifted her glasses and rubbed at an eye. "I thought about it all night. I should never have told you. I really fucked up. And now it's too late . . . unless you don't go."

"Claire, I've got to go."

"But why?"

"You said it yourself. She's in trouble. She needs my help."

"You didn't know that when you came here. You still don't know what kind of trouble she's in, if any. As for your help, she's done fine without it up to now. And here's another question. Why did you fuck up the sessions? They were your big chance."

"Claire. I just said what I believed. I've got a right to say that, don't I? If Wendy does, so do I. What do you think our mother *did* to her, anyway? I mean, violence? All she'd say was something 'physical.'"

"And you basically said you thought she was hallucinating. That she was crazy. I don't know what your mother did, but I'll tell you one thing: it was no hallucination. And it went on for a long time. You lived in the same house. Didn't you notice anything?"

160

I shook my head slowly, thinking of the steamy bathroom.

We were coming up on the high pass between Livingston and Bozeman, and the temperature outside the car was below freezing. The sage alongside the road had a dusting of new snow, which caught the sharp sunlight like a hallucination. About a mile away, a tiny antelope crested a rise and stood outlined against the purplish sky.

Claire was saying something in a low voice. "Poor you. It hasn't been easy, has it?"

"No. Thanks for understanding."

"At least your sister had her hatred. And she finally made it work for her."

A patch of ice crunched under the tires. "I loved our mother, Claire. But without my sister, I can't even figure out why. I need her hate to feel my love. Yin and yang: that's us. You can't have one without the other. I guess that was what I learned in the attack. My little epiphany. So . . . here I am."

Standing in the soaring airport lobby, she took off her dark glasses and said forlornly, "I'll be waiting to hear what happens down there. I'm sure I won't hear it from your sister."

"I'll call you the minute I can." I put my hand lightly on her waist.

"I'll come down if you need me. That goes without saying."

"Of course."

"I'll be praying, even though I know it never works."

My hand was still on her waist when the flight was called. I was going to kiss her cheek but she turned her head and her lips were there instead. Uh-oh. We both pulled back in case someone was watching, and it occurred to me I had never seen a real flaming blush before.

Chubasco

At the Aero California counter in LA, a young Mexican woman smiled and told me the flight to La Paz had been canceled. "*Chubasco.*"

"What's a *chubasco*?"

"Like a *huracán*. Come in this morning."

"Jesus. So when will the flight leave?"

She shrugged, still smiling. "Maybe tomorrow. You can check."

"When will you know?"

"Tomorrow, *señor*." Now she looked surprised. "Maybe tomorrow."

It was late afternoon. I decided to spend the night at the Standard Hotel on Sunset Boulevard because Claire had told me my sister liked the place and usually stayed there herself. It might give me more of a connection to her.

But in the Standard's louche white lobby, a boy in a white dress shirt and white trousers told me they were fully booked. "But there was supposed to be a reservation," I lied. "Peter Davis?"

The boy checked the reservation list. "Nothing for Peter, sir. There *is* something for Wendy, though."

My scalp prickled. "Wendy Davis? Has she checked in yet?" Looking around the lobby.

"No, sir."

"What address did she give?"

"Crest Drive, Encinitas."

A couple of deep breaths. My fingers shook as they rested on the counter, and I put my hands in my armpits. "Well, great! That's all right, then. I'm her brother. We're sharing the room."

Looking out over the city from the room's little balcony, I reflexively tried to come up with a story for when she walked in. I'd been wooing a writer in Montana and had dropped in at Claire's for breakfast when she'd called. Then I'd gone on to LA, planning to stay at the Standard, but there were no rooms, blah blah blah. So surprise!

Fuck it. I'd tell her the truth and hope for the best. No, Claire and I had *not* been fucking our brains out. We missed her, worried about her, and wanted to see her. In fact, we both loved her.

But what was she coming here for anyway? Claire hadn't known about it. Right now she probably was tied up in meetings. Wasn't that what they did here? Maybe her book was making her a superstar.

The sun melted into the Pacific, and I ordered a bottle of Veuve Clicquot and a salmon caviar spread with blinis and sour cream because I thought she'd like it.

Suddenly it was clear. She wasn't going to make it. The *chubasco* most likely had scrubbed her flight out of La Paz as well as my flight in.

I thought about calling Claire, but it seemed too soon after our intense good-bye. Also a hotel call would register on the bill, and there was an outside chance my sister might see it (I oddly didn't consider the cell phone). When most of the ice in the silver bucket had melted, I opened the Champagne, poured two glasses, clinked them together, and drank a toast. Claire and Wendy. Wendy and Claire. I finished one glass and then the other, and found myself on the edge of tears.

The Champagne sank with the sun, and they both disappeared at about the same time. The first stars appeared over the city lights— *second star on the right and straight on till morning.* Her flight might have left just before the storm hit. She could still walk in the door.

I woke up to the phone, lying on the bed, still in my clothes, the empty Veuve Clicquot bottle and the remains of the salmon caviar spread, duck pâté, and a Caesar salad on the sideboard. "Hello? Wendy?" said a woman's voice doubtfully.

"This is her brother Peter. Who's this?"

"Jean Chin, her gynecologist. So how did things go at Preterm?"

"Uh . . . preterm?"

"The *procedure*." A pause. "That's why you're there, isn't it?"

"Ahm . . . ah, yes." I cleared my throat. "In the larger sense."

A long silence. "Is Wendy there?"

"No. She's not."

"Well, where is she, for Christ's sake?"

"I think her flight yesterday was canceled. There was a big storm in La Paz. They weren't sure when the service would be resumed."

"Oh my God," the woman whispered, and the line went dead.

Incriminating Evidence

It was still raining hard Friday morning after the storm, taco palms clattering in a hot and heavy south wind. She selected another shift, a purple one, from Isabel's bureau and stood at the mirror on the bathroom door holding it up in front of her. Her hair seemed thicker and had grown past her shoulders, making her face look sharper and more wary. She watched herself for a few more beats, then let the purple shift fall. A sight she'd been avoiding.

Her body looked like another woman's. Lush and rounded like a calendar girl from the fifties, that famous shot of Marilyn Monroe. But tighter. Her skin looked as tight as it felt, stretched to pale satin on the sides of her breasts and her undeniable bump. Undeniable, no question. How had it gotten that way without her noticing?

She turned sideways, put her hands on her hips, arched her back, and pushed out her belly. God! Forcing herself to hold the pose for a count of five. The image's expression was comically shocked, and she tried a smile.

The smile, tentative and questioning, was more comical still. She snickered like a voyeuristic high schooler, turned frontward, and shot a hip with a burlesque bounce of bosoms. Suddenly, she was laughing, head back, eyes closed. Laughing her thoughts away.

How long had someone been knocking? She pulled the purple shift over her head, dragged a comb through her tangled hair, and peered out the window beside the locked front door to see Clamato standing there in shorts and a soaked yellow tee shirt, water dripping from the tip of his nose.

"Did I interrupt something?" he asked when she opened the door and handed him a towel.

"Not at all. I was just thinking of you."

"Haw. Am I that amusing?"

"What? Oh . . . that was a whole different thing. Lemme see if I can find you something dry." She rummaged in Isabel's bureau and came out of the bedroom with a pink sweatshirt. When he pulled off his wet tee shirt and put it on, the word "PUSSYCAT" appeared in purple letters across the front. She patted the letters abstractedly. "Perfect!"

"Yeah?" Clamato sounded a little worried. "So how'd you get through the storm?"

"Okay. I just stayed inside mostly and ate up all of Isabel's supplies."

He wandered around the room, stopping in front of Wendy's portrait of Isabel, sitting nude at a table. "So when's she supposed to be getting back?"

"Today."

"Scratch that. Roads are washed out south and north. It happens every few years."

She couldn't stop a yawn. "And how long will it take to fix them?"

"*Quien sabe*. Could be a day or two. Could be a week. Could be two weeks. They say it's pretty bad this time."

No surprise. When the storm closed in, it had been pretty obvious she'd misread the signs. How strange. She'd been so sure to begin with. Well . . . not entirely. Another yawn engulfed her.

He stared out the window into the rain. "Want to come over and stay at my place? You can have the bedroom." Raising his right hand. "I solemnly reaffirm my vow of chastity."

"Why, Pancho!" She tried a smile. "Are you worried about me?"

"Well, maybe I would be if you'd gotten those shots." He grinned back. "But you're only pregnant."

"Wow. It's that obvious? When did you know?"

"As soon as I saw you in the park."

"I guess everybody in town knows, huh?"

"Well, not everybody. I heard Felipe Reyes defending your honor on my way over here."

She touched her belly. "Sorry, Felipe. A fallen woman. I finally made it. And do you know what? It feels kind of good."

Clamato laughed. "Now you're talking like a surfer. So you're going through with it, hey? Even if it's Marco's?"

"So it seems." She didn't feel like going into the missed flight, the appointment in LA.

"I say again. I think you should stay at my place until you can get out of here. Then you and Isabel can go to Mexico City or something."

"And get rid of it? It's too late."

"Not get rid of it. Just get out of town."

Shaking her head slowly. "I know it sounds crazy, but I can't leave without my Mercedes. Especially not to leave her with *him*."

Clamato blew out his cheeks. "Wendy, you have no idea what you're getting into. You've ditched this guy and taken up with a *woman*. You're pregnant with his kid. People are starting to notice, it's not just talk anymore. You're making him a laughingstock. His *macho's* at stake, dig it? He's a Mexican. This is Mexico. You know they have a saying here? *'La mujer, como el vidrio, siempre está en peligro.'*"

"A woman is like glass, always in danger? Well, he said he'd be finished with my car in a week or so."

"Yeah, and elephants can fly. He wants to keep you here. You're his property. If he can't have you, you're gone. He's a killer, you've seen that for yourself."

It was Wendy's turn to contemplate the self-portrait of Isabel. "Not only did I see it, Pancho, I got it all on film. I got every damn detail at 500mm, one exposure every quarter second. Practically a whole thirty-six-exposure roll."

Clamato looked more worried than she'd thought possible. "Holy *shit*. And nobody knows?"

"Well, I told the kids I missed it, of course. But Marco saw me with the camera when he came out of the water. That was a pretty strange flash."

"What do you mean, strange flash?"

"I don't know. . . . The way we looked at each other."

"Fuck." Clamato slapped his forehead. "Okay. Here's what we do. You give me the photos. I tell our friend that if you don't get your car in a week they go right to my buddy at *The Surfer's Journal*. You get your car, and you drive on out of here, then when you tell me you're where you want to be, I'll let him have them. It could work."

"Sorry. I've got to give them to the father."

"Wendy, this is Mexico. The photos wouldn't help him. He'd lose the case anyway. But this just might be your ticket out of here. You and your car both."

She thought for a minute. "Why would you have to give Marco the photos after I called? Why couldn't you just get them to the father?"

Clamato shrugged and showed his piano key teeth. "Elementary, my dear Wendy. He'd kill me."

He was probably right. He *was* right: the photos could get her clear. But for once there was no question in her mind about what she should do. Her last sight of the father's face took care of that. She had made some mistakes in her life, that was for sure. But she was not going to make one here.

The bathroom door was open, mirror showing, and she moved in front of it for the second time. The shape of things to come was obvious.

A decision had been made. She should get clear to honor it, but paradoxically, the condition she was in made that impossible. Her feeling for the father, her absolute need to help him, seemed to flow directly from her condition. Maybe, just maybe, she hadn't been a very good person before.

"The father's still here, isn't he?"

"He's camping out at the break. Even during the storm he's walking the beach. They still haven't found the body."

"I'm taking the roll out to him. It's his. Hopefully he'll give it back to me when he's finished."

"Wendy, for Christ's sake, you don't know what you're doing."

"Oh, but I do. I finally figured it out. Is Marco going to kill me for doing what I have to do?"

"He could. His stepfather will protect him. He could do *anything he wants.* That's what you don't fucking understand. They're going to find you out on the beach someday, and they won't even be able to tell it's you. You think he cares about the kid? You're wrong. What he cares about is himself."

He stood there panting in the pink sweatshirt. Pussycat! He'd made her see it, that image, a little pile of clothes and flesh turning into a skeleton on the vast beach, alongside the bones of whales, dolphins, pelicans, seagulls, and parts of wrecked ships.

In midafternoon, after the rain had stopped, she walked down the mile-long sandy two-track from the Barrio San Ignacio to the beach. Someone was beautifully whistling a tune that she knew she should recognize, but couldn't quite. She was wearing her jeans, tee shirt out to cover the fact that the top two buttons were undone. The film canister was in her left-hand pocket.

From the high dunes the ocean looked almost black, punctuated with whitecaps by the strong south wind. Curlicues of dry sand streamed in front of it, mixed with rolling strands of dried seaweed. The beach ran north unbroken for a hundred miles to Magdalena Bay. Clamato was sure there were secret breaks along the way and thought it could be driven with the right vehicle.

Carrying her Adidas, she walked down onto the hard damp sand near the water and began the three-mile hike to the break. Better to avoid the road, and whoever might be on it.

On calm days there would be a few mackerel fishermen swinging their lures around their heads like bolos, letting them fly, then pulling them in with the complicated sign language of hand-lining. Now there was no one. Broken, irregular waves occasionally frothed up around her legs, and she thought about removing her jeans but decided against it.

One bare foot advanced and then the other. The usual song danced its way into her head.

> *Grab your coat and get your hat*
> *Leave your worries on the doorstep*
> *Life can be so sweet*
> *On the sunny side of the street.*

Her brother would love this beach; it was all perspective, sea on one side, land on the other almost as far as you could see. And at the beginning of the perspective where the lines faded into the mist, wasn't that a figure?

It was a man, not a woman. You could tell, even though the figure was just taking shape.

The father! She waved eagerly and picked up her pace. She wouldn't have to do the whole three miles after all.

The figure didn't wave back. It seemed to be just standing there in the haze, looking in her direction. Waiting for her.

She slowed down and finally stopped. The beach was noisy and confusing with wind and waves. How far had she come? If she turned around and started running back, could she make it? The last time she'd tried running, she'd felt a cramp like an ice pick in her belly and hadn't tried again. Swim back? Not against the wind. Inland, except for the two-track, there was nothing but empty desert all the way to Garth Murphy's ranch. But surprisingly, walking over the dunes from that desert, was another figure—a familiar one in loose white clothes and a straw cowboy hat. "*Aquí estoy,*" said Felipe Reyes when

170

he got close enough to be heard. In Spanish, it sounded exactly right. Here I am.

She nodded and smiled and couldn't think of a word to say in return. The figure up ahead hadn't moved.

Felipe's eyes were shadowed by the hat, and his sad smile was nowhere in evidence. He looked where she was looking, and his hands hung loosely at his sides. "Do you want me to walk with you?"

"Please."

"I will walk with you then."

They continued down the wind. Blowing sand made her feet and ankles sting, and conversation was impossible. Felipe was holding his hat on with one hand, his loose clothes flapping like flags, hair over his face. The figure was no longer visible, if it had been there at all. She resisted an urge to take Felipe's arm, but could feel the warmth of his body anyway. He was between her and the ocean and beyond him the whitecaps rolled by.

The break was deserted, no tents, no campers, no one out. She and Felipe sheltered from the wind behind a small dune and Wendy suddenly felt weak and dizzy. She sank down on the sand, legs folded underneath her like a fifties college girl at a faculty tea. Looking up at Felipe and trying a smile. They hadn't said a word to each other since the beginning of the walk.

"Are you tired?"

She just nodded and lowered her eyes.

"Of course. You need to rest a little."

"Yes. Just a little. Thank you for walking with me. And how did you ever find me?"

"It was no problem. I always know where you are."

She could see only his sad smile. "Felipe," she said softly. "Please will you take off your hat? I'd like to see your eyes."

Where There's a Will

My fate these days apparently was to be given bad news in airports. Sure, I could rent a car, the girl at the counter told me in La Paz, but I couldn't get to Paraíso in it. The roads had been washed out in the *chubasco* three days earlier.

"When will they be fixed?" I watched as she drew in her breath and started to smile.

"That's all right. Forget it." I took a taxi into town and at the driver's advice got a room in a rustic set of bungalows off the *malecón*: Las Cabanas de los Arcos. The big Los Arcos Hotel was just up the street, and I headed there to try to pick up news.

In the lobby, a burly gringo in a Hawaiian shirt, hair down to his shoulders, and a Pancho Villa mustache was addressing a group of tourists, telling them how to find their bus, where they were going, what to expect when they got there. It was a kayaking trip; they'd spend the next week paddling and camping in the lagoons of Magdalena Bay. The roads up there were okay.

I stood around waiting until the burly gringo was free. Apart from the basic details, the man rarely responded directly to the kayakers' questions. He answered with jokes, sometimes off-color. The kayakers were thrown off-balance, and they ended up forgetting their concerns. He looked a little like Slim Pickens, but with more of an edge. They called him Timo.

When I asked about Paraíso, Timo just looked at me and raised his chin. He had small, very clear violet eyes.

"They tell me you can't get through," I said.

"What do you want to go there for?"

"To visit my sister. It's kind of an emergency."

"Huh." Timo fluttered his lips thoughtfully. "Your sister drive an old Mercedes?"

"An old Mercedes?" My head whirled. "She just might."

"Weeell . . ." Flapping his lips. "Got something you might be interested in, if you want to take a little ride."

Timo drove an old Toyota Land Cruiser decorated with beach debris. The windows were nonfunctional, and the back was filled with ancient dolls: "People who've done me wrong. I stick pins in 'em every once in a while. That one there ran off with my wife." We turned off the main road into an alley, bumped over a high curb, and stopped in front of a wooden gate.

He tossed me a key and drove inside after I'd opened the gate. The big, overgrown lot was a graveyard of boats, trucks, and machinery. Timo pointed with his chin. At the far end, under a tar-paper lean-to, I could see an engine hung in a frame between two huge, inwardly cambered tires, like something out of Donald Duck. Closer up, I saw it was an old Volkswagen with the engine exposed, the fenders gone, the body stripped down, and rear tires maybe from an airplane. Timo called it a Bug.

It made my heart beat faster. "How does it run?"

"Cool."

"Would it get me to Paraíso?"

"If you go by the beach."

"How much do you want for it?"

"Shit. Just go ahead and borrow it." He sucked the ends of his mustache. "I didn't pay anything for it. In fact, it's not even mine."

"Well, thanks. Very generous of you. Mind if I ask why you're doing this?"

Timo shot me a straight, hard look. "If your sister's the one I've heard about, I think she'll be glad to see you."

"Christ. What have you heard?"

"Aw, just grapevine stuff. Something about a mechanic she got in wrong with, trying to fix her car."

"Really? How did she get in wrong with him?"

"Good mechanic. Bad guy." Timo had to hurry to catch the bus with his kayakers. The Bug started right up with a blast of straight pipes, and he backed it out from under the lean-to. "Tell you what," he said, climbing from the cockpit. "If it breaks down this trip, you take it off my hands, okay?"

"I guess. Do I have any choice? How much?"

Timo unfurled a crocodile smile. "Three thousand US should cover it."

I breakfasted on *huevos rancheros* just after dawn at an open-air restaurant on the *malecón* and blasted my way out of the city, catching more than a few eyeballs. Timo had told me to take a left on the first dirt road to the west twelve miles north of La Paz, then straight on to the beach. The Bug ate up the rough road beautifully as thick, green, aromatic scrub closed in around me, and after a few miles I stopped to take a pee.

The desert had seemed about as far away from my beloved Costa Rican jungles as you could get, but in its own way it was a place of plenty. Flowers were out on all the cacti. Even the huge cardons had blossoms the size of old phonograph horns, and the buzzing of bees slowly filled the vacuum left by the silence of the engine. Between the cacti, a floor of talcum-fine red dusty soil patterned with the prints of what looked like cattle, coyotes, snakes, lizards, foxes, raccoons, badgers, roadrunners, quail, and deer.

A big eagle-like hawk with a white head and bright red legs inspected me from the top of a cardon, and a glowing black wasp as big as my thumb wandered along the sand flipping its red wings. I recognized it from *National Geographic*: a female *Pompilidus* with the habit after mating of stalking and overcoming a tarantula with a series of nonfatal but paralyzing stings and gluing a fertilized, opalescent egg onto its hairy helpless belly. It then carefully buries the immobile but quite conscious tarantula, and after a while the egg hatches and the grub begins to feed.

The wasp spread its wings and disappeared. What was my sister planning? What was she thinking? For all I knew she loved her mechanic.

She might not laugh when I rolled up in this comical contraption. Maybe she'd call the *policía*? Like before.

The road turned north at a low bluff overlooking a beach like nothing I'd ever seen before. Cloud shadows rolled down it on a light northwest wind, and the breaking section of the angled waves traveled south in constantly changing light. The perspectives took my breath away. My mother would have loved them.

A little way along the bluff I found a steep straight track to the beach. Apparently other vehicles had made it down, but there would be no going back. The incline was more than forty-five degrees, and the surface was loose sandy soil and gravel.

No choice. I eased the Bug over the edge and skidded it down, rear wheels locked most of the way. I'd been afraid it would slew sideways and flip, but it did beautifully. What a machine!

Now the whole beach lay ahead of me. The Bug floated over the soft undulating sand like a dream and I couldn't resist flirting with the waves, swooping down onto the wet sand after they'd pulled back, up again at the last possible moment when they broke and rushed in. I heard myself laughing wildly over the blat of the exhaust.

Halfway to the horizon was a spout, a jet of steam as if there were an undersea volcano. Two spouts. A pelican surfed the wave tops with the tips of its wings actually making grooves in the glass. A mixed flock of seagulls, pelicans, terns, ducks, and cormorants swirled into the air from a low berm as the Bug bore down on them.

After a few miles, the bluff above the beach steepened and turned to rock. The beach began to narrow, and I went around a steep headland on nothing but a yellow ribbon between the black rock and the blue sea. Beyond the headland was a long cove backed by cliffs, and the narrow beach continued on around a second headland about three miles away.

Halfway there, hoping that around it I'd find the same broad beach as before, I noticed a gray fin in the surf—a dolphin playing in the waves. I stopped to watch as a bigger than average wave caught the animal, washed it up on the beach, and receded, leaving it high and dry. It flopped there helplessly for a while, until another bigger than average wave came up and pulled it back.

Too close for comfort. Anyway, it was safe now.

I put the Bug back into gear and was about to let out the clutch when the fin appeared again in the creamy white water just inside the break.

This time I turned off the engine and just sat there. The dolphin wasn't just playing in the waves; it wanted to die.

Just a matter of time before a jumbo wave swept the creature up onto the dry sand and left it there, shining gray and glossy. But still it flopped and seemed to be trying to save itself, so I had to help it.

Its tail felt like the hard rubber sole of a hiking boot. When it flipped, it would knock me off my feet. The whole creature weighed about three hundred pounds, but as long as it didn't flip I could inch it by the tail slowly down the sloping sand toward the water. And after a while it seemed to appreciate what I was trying to do and lay still.

A big breaking wave shot up the beach and slammed the dolphin into my legs while I struggled to keep it from being stranded again. Then we were rolling in the soup, one on top and then the other.

I'd stripped down to my boxers for the rescue, and the inert dolphin was smooth, hard, and cold against my skin. Panting and exhausted, I could only hang on to its fins and try to keep it headed out to sea. Once I got a look at a black shiny eye watching me calmly from smooth gray folds of blubber.

Finally, we were in waist-deep water, just short of the break. Before another wave could come, I pushed the creature out to sea with my last reserve of strength, and it disappeared.

Would it strand itself again? I sat dizzily on the sand knowing that this time I'd have to watch it die. The prospect was terrifying.

But the waves continued to roll in dolphinless. I waited and watched and finally lay back and closed my eyes.

I opened them again when a wave washed over my bare leg. Jesus! The sun seemed a lot lower in the sky.

The whole beach was narrower. Now with the larger waves, there were barely twenty feet between the water and the cliff. The far headland appeared to meet the water with no beach at all. Impossible!

But as I drove the Bug closer, I could see this was the case. The beach around it was gone. Reversing frantically to get turned on the narrow strip of sand that was left, I roared back toward the first headland as fast as possible, the vehicle almost leaving the sand on the sharper rises. Too late.

PART FOUR

Meanwhile, Back at the Ranch

Claire was not sleeping well. She hadn't heard a word from Wendy, and the last she'd talked to Peter had been from the LA airport, three days after the storm, while he waited for the first flight to La Paz. He'd told her that as far as he knew, Wendy had made no further reservations either at the hotel or at the clinic. Her name hadn't been on the incoming passenger list.

Claire had been shivering as she listened. She and Peter had talked every day since he'd left, sometimes more than once, and she found herself trembling at the tone of his voice and his inflections. His own voice had sounded just as shaky, or was it her imagination? Claire had ventured that a lot had gone down in Montana, and Peter had said it sure had.

But this was a little different, this shivering. She had come up with a theory. If Wendy had decided on having the procedure, a storm wouldn't have changed her mind. Unless the storm had delayed her too late to have it.

There had been a silence on the other end while Peter had digested this. "You're right." Finally. "She would have been on that flight if she was going to go ahead."

"And now she's trapped." Claire had gasped with another insight. "The mechanic that's working on her car? I'll bet you anything he's the father. It'd be just like her. Oh, Jesus, now I'm really being indiscreet."

"It's okay, baby. Aren't we in this together now?"

"Yeah? Oh shit, Peter. Why am I not going with you?"

A slow beat of five. "You are."

Claire invented excuses to stay home during the day in case the phone rang (she didn't trust her cell phone's reception in the valley), and never went out in the evening. She read, cooked, drank, and retired to bed around nine. The writer called to invite her out to his ranch again, but she took a rain check.

She found herself thinking a lot of pregnancy itself. What did it feel like to be pregnant? To feel a new life *burgeoning* inside you like an idea? Her ex-husband had made a fetish of condom-wearing, so luckily she'd avoided it there. Now she was right in the middle of her cycle, her fertile period. Another wasted egg, and she didn't have that many more left.

The fourth night she tried smoking a little dope before bed, hoping it would make her sleepy, but it had the opposite effect.

Her left nipple had always been more sensitive than the right. How strange! The right felt prickly and irritated if caressed, and the feeling went nowhere. Whereas the left bloomed like a rose and put out roots.

A useful fantasy involved walking down a city street late at night and becoming aware of someone following her. She would test this awareness by making some turns. Whoever it was would make them too. Scary and exciting.

She'd arrive at her apartment, unlock the door, and hurry inside. In the fantasy, she never had time to relock it. From her bedroom she'd hear the slow footsteps approaching, see the faceless dark form, struggle against it, but inevitably feel the silk cords binding her wrists and ankles to the bedposts, the silk gag in her mouth. Skirt up, panties down, irresistible entry and mounting excitement until *AAAHH-HHH* . . . panting for breath, snapping on the light, and lying there damply staring at the clock: only 11:00 p.m.

Her ex, Tom, had been smaller than she but strong and wiry as a top climber needed to be. He believed in stock market charts and numerology. Everything happened for a reason; it was all interconnected. A tricky ascent required getting all your ducks in line, psychically, physically, and environmentally. Chance should not be part of the equation at all. Only a perfectly prepared climber could prevail.

Before they met, Claire, in her late twenties, had been living an aimless life in Bryn Mawr, outside Philadelphia. She'd gone to high school in Bryn Mawr, then to Bryn Mawr College, majoring in English. She was helping run a bookstore in Bryn Mawr. She was a member of a women's rowing club down on the Schuylkill River near Bryn Mawr and had represented it in the Head of the Charles Regatta in Cambridge in the fours class. The men she knew bored her to tears. Talk about stuck! When she saw an ad in *Outside* magazine for mountain climbing in the Tetons, a bell rang in her head.

Tom had been the lead guide for her party of six in a two-day ascent of the Grand. His precise, almost automaton-like climbing had impressed her mightily and had made her feel wonderfully safe. His hands felt dry, warm, strong, and very capable. His blue eyes had a faraway look geared to wide-open spaces. He didn't smile very often. The men she knew in Philadelphia were always smiling.

The best part of the climb for Claire had been a three-hundred-foot rappel down a vertical granite cliff. Only one other member of the party (a nineteen-year-old boy) agreed to do it; the rest took the long way. The green-and-yellow Dacron rappelling rope reached all the way to the bottom, passing in a figure-eight pattern through a descender ring for friction. The ring was attached to a harness that the rappeller sat in, letting the rope slide through the fingers to control the rate of drop. Tom demonstrated how you push away from the cliff with your feet as you let the rope slide, dropping as you swing out and back in, and then push off again in a series of moon-man bounds. It gave Claire the rush of her life. Tom had been waiting at the bottom with one of his rare smiles. "Looks like you have a talent for this."

Six months later they were married in the mess tent of the climbing school, a local Episcopalian minister officiating to appease her family, and Claire started working to fulfill Tom's ambition to make her the country's top woman climber.

She loved the mountains, and she loved the teamwork of climbing, the feeling that each person was totally dependent on the rest. Ultimate stakes and crystal-clear goals in a spectacular setting. And wonderful sex at the end of the day.

Solo climbing was something else again. No one to talk to, no one to laugh with, no one to rely on but yourself. A terrible, often terrifying loneliness, and the triumph of reaching the top couldn't be shared. But as Tom kept saying, it was the quickest way to make a name. Quite a few ascents remained to be climbed for the first time by a solo female, and she did a couple of the easier ones for him. She knew they were only warm-ups, and that seriously compromised whatever good feelings she might have had about them.

Some years passed, and finally the hot August evening came when he looked at her with that rare smile and said, "Know something? I think you're ready."

Heart sinking. "Ready for what?"

They were standing just outside their tent in the climbing school campground. He pointed at the 13,770-foot granite peak of the Grand Teton, spiring up practically in their backyard. "The North Face. This is the right year, too. Hot and dry like I've never seen."

"What makes you think I'm ready?"

"You're hot right now. You whipped up Space Shot like it was a gopher mound. Even Kim was impressed. You're on a roll, kid, this is your year. By the end of the season you'll be famous."

"If I make it."

He took on his holier-than-thou guru look. "Don't ever start thinking that way. You'll always make it. I'd never ask you to try something you couldn't do. Trust me."

She was getting tired of these speeches. "Tell me something, Tom. Why does this mean so much to you?"

"Oh, come on, baby. You've got it. You can be the *best*." He rubbed his right thumbnail back and forth along his sunburned lips (they'd just gotten back from climbing in Utah, and the sun had been fierce). "You, uh, have an obligation to realize your potential, you know. Everyone does."

"Yeah, but you didn't answer my question."

"Why does it mean so much to me?" With a thin smile. "Well, I figure that's my role in life. To help you realize your potential."

What about *your* potential, she was going to ask. But she thought better of it.

Someone had scored some primo bud, and Tom and Claire shared a few tokes just before bed. In the dark, when she felt Tom's hand drift onto her bare breast (the sensitive one, as he knew from much experience), she said, "You know, I don't think I'm ready."

Tom didn't take his hand away. "Awww, come on. We haven't fooled around for days."

"No, I meant the North Face. I'm not ready to climb it. I don't even *want* to climb it."

She could feel the hand on her breast tense, and then it was gone. He rolled onto his back, and she could hear him breathing through his mouth. She waited for him to say something more, but he'd never been a big one for talk. Finally, he rolled away from her, pulled up his knees, and pretended to fall asleep. Or so she thought.

She could hear her heart beat loudly behind the dope. . . . about eighty-five beats per minute, quite a bit faster than her usual resting pulse of forty-five. Did she really not want to make the climb or was she just being rebellious? It wasn't that hard—Alex Lowe had soloed it in the middle of winter not too long ago—but it was two days' lonely climbing, the weather was unpredictable, and the rock was weathered and treacherous in places. Worst of all, she just didn't like the place. She didn't feel at home there. The crags were dark and forbidding.

The spirits of the place were unfriendly to her.

Now Tom was pretending to snore faintly, but she was sure he was as wide awake as she was. Years ago, there had been a dramatic rescue on the North Face: a climber's leg had been badly fractured by falling rock; he'd had to be lowered thousands of feet down on a stretcher. There was a documentary film about it, and the rescuers became heroes.

Something bad would happen to her on the mountain, and Tom could come to her rescue. Perfect! His little puppet. She was beginning to understand why he was so involved. In the end, wasn't it all for him? Maybe he'd been planning this thing for years.

And after years of apprenticeship, that was what climbing was turning out to be: not happy teamwork but a struggle of monumental egos for fifteen minutes of fame. It was a stoned epiphany.

So Claire did not solo the North Face that summer, and Tom became eerily malignant. She was scared. She saw her shrink friend (who'd hosted the earlier sessions with Peter and Wendy) in Jackson during the winter, even had a fling with him, and in the spring she moved to Livingston.

As she'd been doing since Peter left, Claire woke before dawn the next morning and walked over to the river to watch the sunrise. The painter from her gallery was fly-fishing in a molten silver riffle downstream, and they exchanged waves. The writer was his close fishing buddy, she knew, but luckily he wasn't in view. Back home after granola and espresso, she dialed the shrink's number in Jackson. She left her name and number with his secretary, made herself another cup of espresso, and sat back down to read the *New York Times*, which had just started delivery in Livingston.

Almost two weeks after the attack, the body count had stabilized at a little over one thousand. The flood of wounded expected in the city's emergency rooms had never materialized; only bodies had been recovered, but rarely whole ones. Some of the debris had been moved to Staten Island, where people picked through it, looking for parts. An invasion of Afghanistan was obviously in the works, but Claire had a suspicion that bin Laden never would be killed or captured. That wasn't how the twenty-first century was going to go.

To hell with the twenty-first century. She was part of the twentieth, and she just might have a shot at some long overdue happiness. But she didn't want to *dwell* on it too much, because that could jinx the whole thing. The weather had suddenly turned warm again, steam rising off the damp asphalt, so she carried her coffee outside and sat on the stoop in the sun, smelling the wet leaves and listening to the shouts of children in the playground at the Montessori school on the next block. In one of their phone conversations, Peter had told her about the feeling he'd had waking up on her pull-out couch. *The right place at the right time.* Why hadn't she told him it had been right for her too? She'd been scared of a jinx, that's why.

The shrink's name was Daniel. She'd forgotten how dry and nasal his voice was, or maybe it had changed. He was eager to tell her about his new life: he'd turned New Age, drumming, chanting, vision quests up in the Wasatch. He and his wife had had a child.

"Really! That's wonderful! Boy or girl?"

"We named him Spruce. After that one I planted in front of the house. You should see it now."

"I'd like to. I remember it perfectly."

"What's up with you?" he finally asked offhandedly. "I heard you and Tom are no more."

"We are no more," she agreed. "I've been holed up here in Livingston since last spring. It's nice. You'll never guess who passed through the other day."

"Who?" She heard him tell his secretary that he was going to need a few more minutes.

"Peter Davis. Wendy's long-lost brother." She wondered if he could hear anything significant in her voice, but when he didn't answer, she went on, "Remember them? You saw them a while back. Before me."

"Ah yes! How are they doing?"

"Not too good. Listen, Daniel. I've got a favor to ask you. It's kind of an emergency: Wendy's in trouble."

"Sorry to hear that." There was a drumming sound, as in pen on desk.

"She's in some kind of hot water in Mexico. Her brother has gone down to try to help. He came here right after the attack to find out where she was, and I told him. So now I'm involved, you know? The trouble is, ah . . ."

"Well, I'll be happy to see her again. And her brother. Anytime."

"They haven't talked since you saw them the first time. As you know."

The shrink didn't say anything.

"They blew up before they made it to their big issue, you know. The one they originally came to see you about. They never got past the mother stuff—what she might have done to Wendy as a kid. At least that's what I hear from both of them."

"Claire . . ."

"The issue they never got to is pretty simple, to refresh your memory. She thinks he ratted on her about her affair in Briarcliffe. You remember, with the director? He says he kept her secret, and you know what? I kind of believe him. He thinks there just might have been someone else involved who blew the whistle. I thought maybe you could shed some—"

"You know I can't discuss any of this, Claire," the shrink cut in. Talking through his nose. "It's doctor-patient."

"It was years ago. Isn't there a statute of limitations or something?"

"No, there isn't. Plus, I couldn't really remember." He asked his secretary for one more second.

"You must have a file, though, right?"

He didn't say anything.

"What do they say about compassion and understanding in the New Age, Daniel?" God, she was losing it! "I'd love to see your tree again. And your boy. Suppose I drop by this evening?"

"Claire . . ."

"Who knows what'll happen in Mexico. The truth could save their lives."

"Claire, I've got to go. I've got three patients stacked up out there."

"I'm on my way. Shouldn't be more than four hours or so. I haven't seen Susie in a coon's age either."

"Claire, what you're asking me to do, I could lose my license."

"I won't tell a soul. Do you think I'm crazy?" She had to laugh.

He didn't laugh back. She could almost hear him thinking. "Didn't you tell me after the blowup that the mother had made it clear to Wendy that her brother was responsible?"

"But what if she'd found out some other way, someone else had tipped her? That she just wanted the brother to be blamed. You know she died in a car wreck a week later and Peter's sure she killed herself. Wendy was in no shape to take notice. The mother was a *psychopath*, Daniel. She knew she'd wrecked her children's lives and she couldn't live with herself. I'd like to set it straight after all these years."

He sighed. "Look. I'll go through the file, Claire. If I see anything in it I think could help you, I'll let you know."

She let out her breath gently. "Well, thanks, Daniel. Give Susie my best, okay?"

Her excuses for staying at home had worn thin, and she spent the rest of the day at the gallery. New Age the fuck indeed! She was sure she'd never hear from the shrink again and was amazed when she got home to find his message on the answering machine.

Before he had agreed to see Wendy, Daniel had taken the unusual precaution of consulting a lawyer. He'd be dealing with a well-connected Eastern family. Who knew what kind of legal mine-field he might be stumbling into?

The lawyer made some inquiries. Apparently, there'd been a law-suit filed against the trucking company after the mother's death. The papers would be a matter of public record. As far as Daniel knew, neither child had been informed of the suit—understandable not to upset them with it. It never came up in the sessions, and it wasn't his business to tell them. Very possibly there was nothing there. But he thought checking the papers out for clues might be worth the trouble.

Claire walked to the bathroom and stared at her image in the mirror. Cocking her head and trying a smile. A frown. The smile looked better. The weather lines in the corners of her eyes were get-ting deeper but weren't unattractive. What was she doing? Getting in deeper and deeper. So the mother had killed herself. Maybe. A piece of the puzzle, but only a piece.

Claire began to think maybe a little junket to Philadelphia would stop her brooding about Mexico. Why not? A least she'd be doing something, not just sitting around waiting for the phone to ring. How long could it take? Three days at most. Things were slow at the gallery. She knew from college an associate curator at the Philadel-phia Museum of Art, and she could drop by with some slides by the misty-landscape artist the gallery was featuring. Her mother had moved to Florida after her father died, but she still had friends in Bryn Mawr. Maybe she could hang out a little. She could see what had happened to the Davis place.

I, Wendy Davis

The desk clerk at the Hotel California stared at my damp, disheveled clothes, grinned, nodded, and told me where my sister was living: left on the dusty little road that slants down behind the church and the town square into the valley, across the valley floor past a little mud and wattle restaurant, through big old cottonwoods and eucalypti, orange and avocado groves, and chili and onion fields. When the road starts up the other side, it'll be on the left-hand corner in a grove of taco palms. You can't miss it.

I walked it in twenty minutes, knocked on the door, and called her name. Gave it a slow count of ten and called again. Taco palms rustling in the afternoon breeze, a rooster crowing, a dog barking, kids playing in the schoolyard a little farther up the street, an unmuffled truck approaching from that direction, clattering past, and receding down into the valley where I'd come from.

Omigod! What are you doing here? Your school doesn't get out till Friday.

Well, there was a fire, so there.

A fire? Was it a dorm or something? Was anybody hurt?

No, it was the chapel. Burned to the ground.

The porch featured a hide-covered rocking chair flanked by a small wood table with a paperback face up: Faulkner's *The Sound and the Fury*. I peered in a window to a small white room full of what looked like Indian art.

Then a deep bass bellowing started up beyond the taco palms: *eeee-eeee-eeee*. A contented sound, more of a mooing than a bellowing. As it got louder, I could hear the crunch of footsteps on the dusty road.

A big man was walking toward me backlit by the sun, so his face was in shadow, walking loosely as if not entirely in control of his arms and legs and making that sound. Nearing the porch, he waved and made a louder noise that sounded like *eeeep*.

The man stopped and turned slightly so his face came into the sunlight. So empty you couldn't look at it for more than a second. A black hole of a face that you could disappear into if you looked too long.

His hand came out, large but smooth and boneless, and hovered in the air to heavy breathing. It was only money he wanted. He was used to getting it from my sister, now he'd get it from me. Rich gringos, the two of us.

I pulled my soggy wallet from my back pocket, selected a dollar bill, and put it in the pink, soft hand. For a minute there was silence. Then a real bellow, a roar. The bill fluttered to the ground, and the hand it had been in clasped the other hand and wrung it in despair. Bellow on bellow with almost no interval for breath.

The man's open mouth was huge and his teeth looked perfect: not one filling in sight. His tongue was thick and pink like a crying baby's in a cartoon. I moved backward a couple of steps so that the man wasn't bellowing right into my face and tried to figure out what to do. Two women had come out of the house up the street and were standing there watching and talking to each other. A *campesino* on his way to the fields stopped with his hoe over his shoulder and a lunch bag slung on it. The big man watched me out of his empty eyes as the bellowing continued.

Then a young girl in a dark blue school jumper ran up the lane and handed something to the bellowing man. The noise stopped as suddenly as it had started. The man began peeling the paper wrapping

192

off the thing that had been handed to him, and I saw it was a Hershey chocolate bar with almonds.

"She always gives him chocolate," the girl said. "Every day he comes for it."

The man was holding the Hershey bar in both hands like a squirrel, taking little nibbles and smiling as if nothing had happened. "I just gave him a dollar," I said.

She laughed. "A dollar? Where in the United States do you come from?"

"Filadelfeeia." Was that how you pronounced it in Spanish?

"Really? That's where *she* comes from. You look a lot like her."

"Because I'm her brother."

"Yes, I knew it. But how did you get here with the roads gone?"

I told her about the Bug, the beach, the dolphin rescue, the tide, watching the Bug disappear beneath the waves, and my rescue the next day by a boatload of fishermen. After my stint in Costa Rica my Spanish was good, but Mexican Spanish is much purer. I wondered what she thought of my accent.

"You needed to see her very much." The girl nodded gravely. "I understand."

"So, where is she?" The big man was nibbling the last of the Hershey bar and following our conversation like a dog watching a ping-pong game.

"I don't know. Not far, *claro*. Jefe, go away. There's no more chocolate. The chocolate's finished. No more today, Jefe. All gone. Are you worried about him?"

"Jefe? Why?"

"I mean, for your sister. You don't have to worry. They operated on him a few years ago. He's calm and tranquil now, see?" She giggled. "*Pobrecito*. He can't remember. Listen, do you want to wait for her here? She'll be back soon. I can get a key from my grandmother, it's our house, you see."

"I'd feel like I was trespassing."

193

She looked shocked. "But she's your *sister*. She would want you here, no? And she is alone now, too. *La artista* will not be back until the roads open." She seemed to be about to say something more, but thought better of it.

"*La artista?*"

"From Mexico City." Was the girl blushing? "She went back for a little while. They are sharing the house, you know?"

She left to get the key and Jefe drifted away, bellowing softly. The sun was just beginning to hit the edge of the porch; sitting in the rocking chair, I took off my damp shoes and socks and just sat there wiggling my toes in the warmth, waiting for my pants and shirt to dry, and feeling weirdly comfortable for the second time in a little more than a week.

The girl came back with the house key, unlocked the door, and showed me into the little white living room–kitchen with its adjoining gallery. She kept her back to the portrait of Isabel the *artista* . . . *una loca*, she explained, who had once played the accordion *desnuda* in the *teatro*.

I was no expert, but the art looked impressive. Colorful, wild, and original, like Elizabeth Murray. In the tiny guest room, my sister's photographic gear on the little unused cot, folded clothes on the shelves along with a dolphin skull, sea snake skeletons, shells of oysters, abalones, pectens, driftwood shapes.

The girl paused awkwardly at the doorway of the main bedroom. "Well, I have to go now. My grandmother's making tortillas." After she'd left, I stood there looking at the rumpled double bed with its Mexican blankets, wondering if my sister had ever made love with her best friend, Claire.

I waited on the porch while the sun slid behind the taco palms and the high cirrus clouds turned neon. After dark I went inside and heated a can of chili for dinner with a shot or two of Sauza Reposado tequila from the bottle on the shelf over the sideboard. Then I found myself gravitating to the bed.

A reading lamp clamped to the head of the wrought-iron bedstead cast a yellowish cone of light over my upper body as I riffled through *The Sound and the Fury*. Caddy the wayward sister and Benjy the idiot. When I stopped reading and let the book slide off my chest onto the floor, I realized my entire body was under tremendous strain. I tried to relax the muscles one by one, like someone turning off the lights in a bedroom for the night, with a disturbing mixture of musk and Chanel No. 5 from the bed sheets wafting up around me.

Finally, the tense muscle on the inside of my left thigh began to cramp. I pushed from the bed onto my feet and paced up and down the dark room, stretching and kneading the muscle. Yellow light from the weak reading lamp projected an enormous, misshapen shadow on the wall.

In that diffuse light, on a ledge above the bed, I could now make out a notebook—the kind of composition notebook our mother always bought for us before we were sent away to school. The notebooks had black-and-white-marbled cardboard covers, stitched (not glued) pages, and they lasted forever. The shadow reached out its twisted arm and took the notebook down.

Many entries were in the form of letters—some to me. I read with my heart thumping, my face burning, and my ears tuned for the crunch of her feet on the sandy road, turning into the yard.

Set off from the other entries, at the end of the notebook, I came across the following:

LAST WILL AND TESTAMENT

I, Wendy E. Davis, being of relatively sound mind and body, do hereby submit this Instrument as my final Will and Testament, superseding all others in the event of my Death.

I hereby place all my financial holdings now under management by Marlowe M. Gregers, Esq., of Pasadena, California, and any other financial holdings I may possess in any form whatsoever anywhere in the world, or that I may possess at any time in the future, in Trust under the following conditions:

1. My brother, Peter A. Davis, of New York City, is hereby appointed sole Executor, Trustee, and Conservator in perpetuity. He is also charged with distributing my personal possessions to whom he sees fit.

2. In the event I am survived by Issue:
a. If Issue still be minor, I appoint my brother sole legal guardian, and I would beg he adopt same as his own, trust monies to provide all due appropriate support.
b. If Issue has attained majority, my brother will use trust monies to provide same with the best education possible and nothing more.

3. He should make all due provision for the support where necessary of Isabel Martinez Contreras, of Mexico City, DF, Mexico, and her issue, should she have any.

4. For Augustine Nuñez Delgado (aka Felipe Reyes, amigo del pueblo), of Paraíso, Baja California Sur, Mexico, he should make all due provision for facilitation of good deeds, and realization of noble dreams.

My brother, in his infinite wisdom, will determine when these conditions have been fulfilled. The remaining monies will then be subsumed into a subsidiary Trust in the name of our mother, Ava C. Davis (deceased), to be administered for the benefit of abused and/ or molested girls.

Should my brother, Peter A. Davis, predecease me, I leave all above holdings to Claire Barstow, of Livingston, Montana, with exactly the same provisions as those listed above, except for my personal possessions, which I leave to Isabel Martinez Contreras.

If predeceased by both my brother and my Issue, such holdings will pass directly to the above referenced Ava C. Davis Trust.

ADDENDUM:
In the event I am unable to tell him in person

The document ended there. It was after midnight. I put the notebook back on the ledge and went out onto the porch, carrying the copy of *The Sound and the Fury,* which I replaced on the table. For once it was quiet—not a dog, not a rooster, not a truck, not a note of music. The stars illuminated the landscape with no differentiation, no shadows, but with everything clearly visible, even the mountains.

Foul Play

The sound of whistling woke me just before dawn, a run of clear notes that didn't sound local, possibly not even Mexican. More like an *oud* number from the Sahara.

Gray light seeped through the windows of my sister's house. Through the open door I could see the outline of a taco palm silhouetted against the sky, with one fading star caught in the topmost fronds. Slow footsteps crunched past on the sandy road, doves cooed, and the strange whistling continued.

I needed to see who the whistler might be, so I got up, put on my still-dampish clothes, and went out into the gray yard. Cool air penetrating my lungs, carrying a sharp herbal smell. Wood smoke rising from the house down the lane where the schoolgirl lived with her grandmother.

But the whistling had stopped. Nobody in sight. The cool air was making me shiver, and my sister still had not come back.

I was swinging the handle of the manual coffee grinder when I heard a car pull into the yard outside—crunch of tires, engine purring, then stopping, door opening and closing with an oddly familiar heavy *chunk* . . . a kind of aural déjà vu.

A Mexican man, nicely dressed in pressed jeans, a striped long-sleeved shirt, and wearing a black Western hat, was walking up from my father's old green Mercedes. When I opened the door and stepped out on the porch, the man stopped and just stood there. His green eyes registered nothing, like a cat's.

198

I had the high ground. I waited for the man's eyes to shift, and when at last they did, I said in Spanish, "I think I know that car."

"Oh really? Where from?" The man spoke uninflected California English.

"It used to belong to my father."

"It's a piece of shit." The man grinned. "I've been working on it for four months. Only just got it running."

"What was wrong with it?"

"Just about everything. Would have been easier to scrap it and get a new engine."

"Total rebuild, hunh?"

"Pretty close."

"What happened? Water in the oil?"

The man nodded approvingly. "Rust pinhole from the water pump. The pump was integrated right into the engine block. Less than a quarter inch clearance. The worst design I've ever seen, and I've seen quite a few."

"I bet you have." I nodded back. "It's lucky my sister was able to find you. You're probably the only guy in Baja who could have done this work, right?"

The man cocked his head and ignored the question. "So you're the brother? I've heard a lot about you."

"I've heard a lot about you, too," I said.

Neither of us spoke for a while. "Well, where is she?" the man said finally. "I've come to take her for a test drive." He walked to the foot of the stairs and called her name. Waited for a count of five and called again.

"You're wasting your breath," I said.

"What the fuck do you mean?" The man was up the stairs and into the house. "Wendy? Wendy!"

I waited on the porch, listening to the man move through the rooms. Sunlight was just beginning to hit the tops of the taco palms, and the mountain range behind the town marched off to the south in exquisitely modified shades of blue.

When the man came back out, I shook my head as if confused. "You say you want to take her for a *test drive*?"

The man picked up the copy of *The Sound and the Fury* and riffled the pages. "William Faulkner," he said. "I don't know him. It's your book?"

"No, hers."

"What's it about?"

"A family."

"What kind of a family?"

I just shrugged.

"Speaking of families." The man replaced the book, face down. "I'm half Mexican. Look at it this way. Your sister's and my kid will only be a quarter Mexican. You'll hardly be able to tell."

Jefe appeared at the gate and stood there watching silently. Both of us ignored him.

"She told you she was pregnant, didn't she?" Chuckling and patting his stomach. "It's getting hard to miss."

"I haven't seen her. I thought she might be with you."

The cat's eyes narrowed. "When did you get here?"

"Yesterday afternoon."

"You've been here ever since?"

"Ever since."

"How the fuck did you get here, with the roads out?"

"Flew." I watched the eyes widen and braced myself. The man moved like a cat, but I had him on weight and height. Suppose he had a knife?

So be it.

"You look like a straight shooter," I told the man, thinking of Wendy's last will and testament. "So let me ask you a straight question. Did you ever threaten my sister's life?"

"Is that what she says?" The man didn't seem surprised. "She's deluded. You know how women are in her condition. She's carrying my baby. Why would I want to kill her?"

200

"You tell me," I answered.

The man held up his right arm and unrolled the sleeve of his shirt to exhibit a red crescent scar on the forearm. "A love bite," he said. "One of many. She makes love like a *tigre*. Only I know how to really handle her."

"I bet you're a *tigre* yourself," I said. "Did you take anything out of her room just now?"

"Are you calling me a thief?"

"I heard you in there. Now you have something in your pocket."

The man pulled out the film canister and flourished it. "This? These are photos she took of me surfing. See? She's written my name on it. She was going to make me prints. You can tell her I picked them up myself. Okay? I'll save her the trouble."

Jefe had come into the yard and was standing near the Mercedes. Slowly he reached out a huge hand to touch the front fender.

"Jefe!" The man's voice cut like a whip, and Jefe jumped back. "*Vete!*" He ran out of the gate like a frightened child.

"Why is he so scared of you?" I asked.

"He took some of my tools a while back. Just wandered away with them. He'll never take any again."

"Well, anyway," I said. "Thanks for bringing the car over. How much do we owe you?"

"We? I thought it was your sister's car."

I didn't say anything.

"There's still a lot to do," the man said. "This was only a test drive."

"That's all right. We'll take it as is. How much?"

"I can't let you have the car in this condition." The man walked down the steps into the yard, me following. "What if it broke down again here in Paraíso? I'd be a laughingstock. Nobody would respect me anymore."

The Mercedes's front window on the driver's side was open, and I leaned down and put my head inside. The familiar smell of oil and leather made me light-headed. I noticed the dashboard clock, mounted on the walnut door of the glove compartment, had stopped at 11:11. The urge to open the door, wind the clock, and reset it was almost irresistible.

A hand on my shoulder. "Excuse me," the man was saying. So I turned to face him.

I'd been concentrating on the eyes, and the foot came out of nowhere straight into my crotch, seeming to lift me a couple of feet into the air. The sky split with a screaming white lightning bolt.

I was a throbbing heart of pure pain at the center of the universe, radiating glowing sizzling red waves into darkness with a single high note focusing. A violin stretched beyond the highest register, bowed by a maniac.

Strong Current

I just feel a little tired," Wendy said to Felipe. She was resting on a canvas cot in Felipe's little cabin up the Sierra de la Laguna, where he harvested his honey. It had been almost five hours of steep, rough climbing, on and off the horse, and her belly was a little crampy. Nothing serious.

Felipe smiled and nodded from the grate, boiling water for damiana tea on a mesquite fire. Wax honeycombs in wooden frames decorated the dark little room and there was the cot, a rough table, a kind of window-ledge settee, a sink with a bucket of water from the well, shelves of cooking utensils, mugs, and plates, and the cooking grate. The cabin was among tall pines on the edge of a grassy meadow, set with white-painted beehives. It could have been in Maine.

"But I did pretty well for someone in my condition, don't you think?"

He concentrated on pulling leaves from a damiana stalk, looking out the small open window over the sink. "Yes, *doña*. Do you like it here?"

"It's lovely, Felipe. How long have you had it?"

"Oh, it's not mine. I just use it."

"Whose is it, then?"

"I don't know. No one ever comes here but me. The trail is too bad."

"But don't you get lonely here by yourself?"

"I'm not by myself, *doña*. Up here I'm closer to God."

She didn't know how to answer.

"And," he went on, "I have my horse and my *chaquaca*."

He went outside where she could hear him whistling softly and came back with a California quail perched on his forefinger. The little cock was a perfect creation—dawn gray breast, egg brown wings, black head with its sassy shako, canary yellow bill—he'd found wandering alone as a chick and brought home.

"Hold out your finger," he said. He held out his alongside hers, closer and closer until the two fingers touched and the quail stepped nonchalantly from one to the other. She wondered if it had felt the strange spark of energy between them. The quail's eyes were black, and its feet, wrapped securely around her finger, were pink. It cocked its head and seemed to look into her soul.

"Does he have a name?"

"Of course."

"What is it?"

"Ah, that I don't know." He smiled and shook his head. "I just whistle and he comes. He is never far away."

She passed the quail back, testing the current. It made her wonder what kissing him would be like.

Crazy. She was losing it up here on the mountain. Raging hormones, et cetera. And everything so strange and unconnected. He had meant to rescue her, surely, and it was a perfect escape: hole up for a few days until the roads were fixed and Clamato could drive her out (he hadn't been around when she and Felipe had gotten back from the fruitless mission to the break). But here they were, a man and a woman alone in a remote cabin. He might be in another place completely. You just couldn't tell. Those eyes. That smile. A long, thin, dark, warm finger with a clear, strong nail, the finger connected to a strong, dark hand, the hand to a sinewy wrist that disappeared into a white, long-sleeved shirt.

She ran a hand lightly over her belly. "Felipe. You know I'm going to have a child, don't you?"

"*Claro.*" His eyes undifferentiated black, like the quail's eyes.

"Do you know who the father is?"

"*Claro que si.*"

"Of course you do. That's why you brought me up here, isn't it? Not just to see the bees."

"Yes." He moved his finger to the window ledge, and the quail stepped onto it. Then he poured the boiling water into the pot of damiana leaves and tamped them with a spoon. "Damiana will make you strong again. Is it all right? No problems?"

"I don't think so. I just feel very tired."

"You should have ridden more. We should have gone slower. I'm sorry. The trail is very ugly."

"The trail is beautiful. Everything is beautiful up here. I feel like I've seen it all before."

"Well, maybe you have."

"My brother and I tried to get here when we were children. We ran away together."

"Ah. You knew where you were going. That's good."

"You'd like him, Felipe. He loves to dance."

"Does he look like you?"

"I haven't seen him for a long time. But he used to."

Felipe poured out a cup of tea and handed it to her reverentially.

"Thank you, Felipe." The damiana tasted bitter and potent. "I wish I knew what you were thinking."

"I'm thinking of you, *doña.*"

"Really? What about me?"

"Of how beautiful you are. And how blessed."

"Why, thank you." She shook her head and smiled over the cup's rim. "I don't feel very beautiful right now. Or very blessed."

"And how pure."

She lowered the cup, on the verge of laughter. A veray parafit knight erroring, indeed. As if Dulcinea had been pregnant into the bargain.

He just stared back. He had used the word *pura. Que pura.* Didn't *La Purísima* in Mexico refer to the Virgin Mary? The Holy Virgin.

My God! He'd said he knew who the father was, and that was the reason he'd brought her to the cabin. God the Father! Could it be possible?

How could she put the question? No, it was too much. The more she thought about it, the less she wanted to know the answer.

"You know, I'm very far from being worthy of you, *doña*," he said finally.

"You're wrong, Felipe. It is I who am not worthy of you."

He shook his head. "God will judge in the end, *doña*. Only He knows what is in my heart."

El Farolito Sings

A wizened but rugged old gringo looped my left arm around his neck, levered me onto my feet, and half-dragged me to the porch. My body felt paralyzed but tenderized, as if stung by a *Pompilidus*. Sometime during my red trance of pain, I'd felt a liquid shoot forcefully from my mouth. What had *that* been? I could barely sit on the edge of the porch without falling over. "And you must be Peter," the man was saying. "What happened, you forget how to fly?"

While I told him, the man arched his back slowly, hands on his hips, and looked at the sky. "Where was Wendy in all this?" he wanted to know. "Didn't you come to spirit her away?"

"She wasn't around when I got here yesterday. The girl down the street gave me the key and said to wait, she was supposed to be back any minute. I waited for her all night. That mechanic . . . what's his name? What's *your* name, while we're at it?"

"They call him Marco Blanco. They call me Pancho Clamato."

"Well, thanks for your help. He thought she was going to be here, obviously."

"Ob-vee-ously."

"So did you. So where the hell could she be?"

"Well, she probably went out on the same road you came in on. They got it fixed, right? That's pretty fast work."

"Wrong."

Clamato was amazed to hear of my trip down the beach. "Wow! So you lost the Bug, hunh? Guess I won't be tryin' that myself. See any good waves?"

"They were big, that's all I know." I propped myself with an arm to keep from slumping sideways. "Maybe I better lie down for a while."

Clamato got me inside and onto the bed, and then paced around, stopping in front of Wendy's portrait of Isabel. "You know who this is?"

"Yes. The girl told me. A crazy artist who once played the accordion naked in the local theater."

Clamato nodded. "I was there. She wasn't bad."

"What do you think?" I asked. "I mean, about her and my sister."

"I think it's good. They're happy, and Isabel's a tough lady. Your sister needs all the help she can get. She always been bi?"

"I haven't talked to her for a while." Thinking of Claire. "It's possible."

"A *while*?" A stagy double-take. "Well, the Peter and Wendy bit must have been tough. You guys couldn't wait to get away from each other, right?"

"It's a long story," I said.

"I bet it is." He favored me with the sight of his teeth. "You'll have to tell it to me sometime."

Clamato said he'd ask around while I had a chance to recover. Flat on my back was the only semibearable position, and oddly enough the mortal ache in my balls centered my mind on the Mercedes.

Our mother is at the wheel. My sister next to her in the middle, and I by the window, which I'd cranked open in the heat. Our mother in a light blue sleeveless shirtwaist and us in shorts and tee shirts. We are just going, maybe on one of those aimless drives to the open country at the foot of College Avenue or over to the Montgomery estate along Darby Paoli Road or out Goshen Road to the Radnor Hunt country. Early summer, and the color is fresh green, like snow peas.

My sister's arms and legs are covered with fine blond hair. I have no real hair of my own except on my head, so hers makes me envious. In fact, I envy the comfortable way she inhabits her whole body (she can easily do things that I can't: handstands, handsprings, arches, one and a half gainers and backflips off the diving board, et cetera). Suddenly, I want to make her less comfortable, so I start jostling against her extra hard when we go around corners. She jostles back, and then we begin to giggle.

"Stop that, you two," our mother says. "Driving this wretched car is hard enough without you playing the fool."

"If you don't like this one," my sister says, "why don't you ask Daddy to buy you another one?"

Yeah! Why hadn't she done that long ago? Why does she keep driving a car she hates? Instead, I ask: "Mummy, why is Wendy so hairy? Is she going to get hairier and hairier?"

"I wouldn't be at all surprised."

"When she grows up is she going to be as hairy as a dog?"

"We'll just have to wait and see."

"I am not," Wendy says. "Peter's going to get hairier and hairier, because he's a *boy*."

"Well, maybe I made a mistake," our mother says, smiling. "Maybe I mixed you two up when you were born. Nobody's perfect, you know."

We drive on for a while, and the Mercedes seems so full of thoughts it's hard to breathe. Finally, I reach out, grab a few of the long blond hairs on my sister's forearm, and pull them back against the grain. Not too hard, but she screams extra loudly just to be obnoxious. Our mother jumps and swerves but manages to swerve back nanoseconds before she hits a telephone pole.

Her face is red and excited, like at a party or after she'd been arrested and released, and her voice sounds pleased. "If we'd hit that pole, we'd all be dead."

"Would you be happy, Mummy?" my sister asks.

"Of course not."

"Well, we'd be together in heaven, wouldn't we?"

"No. You'd be in hell because you made it happen."

"Peter would be in hell too, because he pulled my hair. Daddy would still be alive. So you'd be stuck in heaven with all the other angels." She giggles. "If Hannah was there, she could cook heavenly meals and you could have a party every night."

The Mercedes swings left, over the little bridge at the start of Goshen Road, and roars up the steep hill past Earle's Woods. Through a couple of stop signs, and we're on a straight stretch among plowed fields doing over 100 miles an hour on the speedometer.

"How much farther are we going?" The wind sucking my words out the window.

And our mother hissing, "We're going all the way to *hell*."

I put my arm around my sister and watch the landscape fly past. Her body is shaking as she snuggles against me. Her eyes are closed.

In the early afternoon, Clamato reappeared carrying a greasy brown paper bag and two bottles of Pacifico beer. "Fish tacos from Pilar's. Just the thing for swollen nuts. How do they feel?"

"Like bruised peaches."

"Youch." He took down two plates from the shelves and put a taco on each. Handing me a plate and one of the beer bottles and sitting on the foot of the bed with his share. "*Salud*."

The fish taco was light, flaky, and tangy with salsa verde. "Delicious," I said to Clamato. "Have you ever been kicked in the nuts?"

"Hasn't everyone?"

"Not me, until now."

"You must have had a sheltered childhood. Don't worry, you'll live to love another day. Hey, I got a lead on your sister, or at least a theory."

Clamato had learned that Felipe Reyes's honey cart was not in its usual place, and nobody had seen Felipe himself for a couple of days. Very unusual: he was generally a fixture on the plaza. "He's got kind of a thing for your sister. You know the story of Don Quixote?"

"Yes." I'd been on the verge of asking, Doesn't everyone? I remembered vividly the entry in my sister's journal about Felipe's rescue attempt on the beach. Who was rescuing whom?

"Yeah, well." Clamato raised his beer bottle. "Here's to noble intentions. Felipe has a place up in the mountains somewhere where he gets his honey. Maybe it's better than nothing." The problem, he went on, would be finding Felipe's place in the virtually trackless sierra. A perfect hidey-hole.

"You probably figured out that Marco had a few more reasons for coming over here than just a test drive." He told me about the surf incident, and Wendy's series of photos. "She was going to give them to the father, but he'd already left when she got out there. I know because he came over here to say good-bye. Marco must have known it too."

"Well, now Marco has them," I said. "He went in the house and got them out of her room. The canister had his name on it. He showed it to me."

"Shit . . . that's gotta be a blind," Clamato said. "She wouldn't be dumb enough to leave a labeled canister in the room where he could get it. He knows that too."

There was one person in town who probably knew how to get to Felipe's place in the mountains, but that person wasn't a friend of Clamato's (he'd go into that later) and probably wouldn't tell him. I'd have better luck trying it on my own, as soon as I could walk.

After Clamato left, I found myself reflecting on all the bad things that had happened to my body in the current chapter of my life. Hot sake in the eyes, a beating by a lobsterman, incapacitating back spasm, and now this. Was someone trying to tell me something?

I decided I was on the right track. No pain, no gain, so they say. Each installment was worse. My balls had come to feel like bruised grapefruits, but the pain seemed somehow talismanic.

In the late afternoon, I got up and tried walking. It was bearable if I supported myself with my hand, unbearable if I just wore my boxer shorts. On a whim, I went into the little room where my sister's things were laid out neatly on shelves.

Was there something here I could use? Leafing through a stack of filmy underclothes until, at the bottom, I came across two pairs of white cotton Carter's briefs like the ones our mother used to buy for us. I held one up to check the size. They'd help get me into town, at least.

"I was expecting you," the guitar player said. He was sitting on a low wall across the street from the Hotel California, holding his guitar, dark glasses reflecting the sunset. "You're the brother, no?"

"I am. My name is Peter. Maybe you can help me. I'm looking for a friend of yours, Felipe Reyes."

El Farolito was silent for a long time, then struck a chord. "Felipe Reyes. Did you know he wrote your sister a song?"

I shook my head, then remembered Clamato had told me the man was blind. "No, I—"

"Oh, yes. He asked me to sing it to her as a favor, because his own voice is so bad. I hadn't sung a note for years, but he's my closest companion and it was such a good song I tried one night outside her house. Well, I was nervous after so long and had too many drinks to relax myself. It was a *desmadre* . . . but I can try to sing it for you now, if you want to hear it."

"Of course, I do."

"At least I'm not drunk now. But forgive me. I am still very out of practice and my voice is rusty."

El Farolito hummed and tuned his guitar, and people passing on the street stopped and stared. A little crowd started to collect. He struck another chord, played a run of notes, tilted his head back and began to sing in a plummy, Latin voice like Plácido Domingo.

> *Calla, calla, princesa*
> *—dice el hada madrina—*
> *En caballo con alas*
> *hacía acá sé encamina,*
> *En el cinto la espada*
> *y en la mano el azor,*
>
> *El feliz caballero*
> *que te adora sin verte,*
> *Y que llega de lejos,*
> *vencedor de la Muerte,*
> *A encenderte los labios*
> *con su beso de amor.*

By the time El Farolito had finished, it was early dusk. A star or two out, one dim streetlight on in front of the hotel, another way down at the end of the street where it turned south out of town. When he took his hands from the guitar and bowed his head, people in the now sizable crowd began to clap. A few men called out things like *olé*, *bravo*, and *otra vez*.

"What a miracle, Farolito," another man said. "You're singing and composing songs again! And by God what a song!"

"Thank you, my friend," El Farolito said. "I'm happy to sing this song, but I didn't compose it."

"Well, who was it, then? Where did it come from?"

"Who knows where from, but it came to my friend Felipe Reyes." El Farolito laughed. "While he was eating in the Santa Fe restaurant."

A short silence. "What did he say? What did he say?" one woman repeated. Finally, a man asked loudly, "What was Felipe eating in the Santa Fe?"

"I'm not sure," El Farolito said. "But I think it must have been the pigeon pie." And suddenly everyone was roaring with laughter.

After a while the crowd split up and wandered away, some of them staring at me and whispering: *The brother, look, the brother.*

"Do you want to join me for dinner?" I said to El Farolito. "I was just on my way to the Santa Fe."

Someone had put a lot of money into the Santa Fe, beautifully refurbishing one of the brick nineteenth-century sugar baron residences that fronted on the square. The menu was impeccable, northern Italian dishes with fresh local ingredients. Even the margaritas were special, made with a local liqueur distilled from the *damiana* herb instead of the usual Triple Sec.

El Farolito and I were seated outside in the courtyard, our table hidden by exotic plants. I ordered a round of margaritas, and after they were half gone the blind man reached out his hand in my direction. The hand was large, dry, and soft.

"*Con permiso.*" Touching my face. "I just need to understand who I'm talking to, you know?"

A waiter arrived, and El Farolito ordered the pizza. When I ordered the pigeon pie, he smiled sadly. "It was only a joke," he said. "I don't really know how that song came to Felipe. He didn't tell me. He just came to me one day, took me down into the *huerta*, and sang it for me, and begged me to sing it to your sister. If only she could have heard it."

"Well." I suddenly felt chilly. "I'm sure some day she will."

"I'm sure some day she will," he repeated. "*Calm yourself, calm yourself, princess, says her fairy godmother. On a winged horse, with a sword on his belt and a hawk on his wrist, comes that joyful*

214

horseman—he who adores you without seeing you and who journeys from afar, the conqueror of Death, to set your lips afire with his kiss of love. My God, how did that come to him?" He carefully finished off the last of his second margarita. "Will you tell me about your family?"

"Well, there's just my sister and me. Our parents are both dead, and we have no close relatives. We grew up in, ah, Philadelphia. Do you know it?" I had a vision of El Farolito sitting on a bench in Rittenhouse Square, where many of my parents' friends lived, playing his guitar and singing Felipe Reyes's song.

"I've heard of it. It's where they signed the Declaration of Independence, isn't it? So your ancestors were revolutionaries? Founding fathers of the republic?"

"More or less."

"They fought for their freedom and then they got rich, no? Isn't that the American way?"

"Not so rich."

"Rich enough for a Mercedes, anyway."

"A very old Mercedes. Which is now broken down."

"And which your sister decided to drive to Mexico. What did she hope to find here? Or was she just tired of Philadelphia?"

"To tell you the truth, I don't know. Maybe she'll tell me, now that I'm here. If I can find her."

The Italian chef himself brought out the dishes. The pigeon pie was five inches in diameter with a light flaky crust over the casserole, so tangy, rich, and delicious I couldn't believe it.

"We usa little *chile de campo*, give some bite. Nize, ah?"

"It's magical."

"The pigeon from inna mountains. Very beeg. Gotta red feet." He kissed the tips of his fingers.

We ate hungrily without talk, washing our meals down with a bottle of Santo Tomás vino tinto. "Listen," the blind guitarist said finally when the food was gone. "At this very moment your sister is with my friend Felipe. But not the way you might think."

I didn't say anything.

"I swear to you on my mother's grave that he honors and respects your sister more than anything in the world."

"Well, I'm happy to hear that." The chill again.

"I can assure you she is safe with him. And content at last. Because she has finally found what she has been looking for, *señor*."

"Really? Can you tell me what that is?"

"Why, perfect love, *señor*."

His face was expressionless, just his mouth moving. His glasses watched inscrutably. His hands rested on the table on either side of his empty plate.

"Where is she, then?" I asked, feeling chillier than ever. "Can you please tell me how to find her?" I took hold of El Farolito's right hand with both of mine.

That Bird Will Eat You

Clamato stopped the Land Cruiser at the top of the rise and set the handbrake. A huge blue misty valley opened between us and the sierra—you could see the rough track curving around outcroppings and into gullies on its way down. Dry bouldered riverbeds at the bottom led up into the canyons of the sierra on the other side, and tiny dots of vultures moved slowly over the gray-green trees and bushes. Now you could see the vegetation change about two-thirds of the way up the range, darkening to forest. The bare granite had a salt-and-pepper look. Twenty years earlier they had tried to build a road across the range, Clamato said, but never got through.

Back the way we'd come, the desert rolled down to the ocean in a long straight slope broken by rounded cactus-covered hills. The slatey Pacific in the far distance was mottled with cloud shadows the color of gun metal.

Clamato locked the hubs into four-wheel drive, and we started down. Each of the gullies had a mild washout, but one had almost destroyed a ten-foot section of the track, which fell away at a forty-five-degree angle over the edge into space. He tromped the *accelerator* and yodeled while the Land Cruiser crashed into the washout, slewed sideways for a second, and clawed its way out the other side. "Just like surfing, man. You gotta get around the sections."

The valley floor was fragrant with manure, and the sound of cowbells echoed through the scrub and medium-sized trees. We crossed

217

the bouldered drywash on a sandy patch, drove past an empty corral, and pulled up next to a black Toyota truck at a group of woven stick buildings on the hillside, connected by a palm-thatched ramada and surrounded by a stick fence. Piglets, chickens, and two huge tom turkeys moved lazily out of the way as we walked across the yard toward an old woman, watching without expression from beneath the ramada.

"Don Yeyo is inside with the *gripa*," she said after Clamato made his explanations. "There have been some problems."

Don Yeyo was longer than his cot. His hard brown feet protruded from beneath a many-hued blanket and looked capable of carrying him into the mountains without shoes. "Well, he took La Paloma." Coughing and propping himself on an elbow. "I was too sick to stop him."

Clamato squatted down beside the old man. "Who? Felipe?"

"No, no! It was that green-eyed *cabrón*. He took her because she knows the trail to Las Abejas."

"Marco, you mean?"

"I don't know his worthless name. That green-eyed *mierda* asked my wife if the horse knew the trail, and like an idiot she told him. Then he put a saddle on my poor little mare and rode away on her."

"How long ago?"

"Not long. An hour, whatever."

"Well, he'll be back. He left his truck outside. That is his truck, isn't it?"

"Yes, may the Devil fuck him up the ass."

"Have you seen any other trucks?"

The old man shook his head. "Felipe and La Purísima came on a horse. Or rather, she came on a horse and he was leading it. Like Joseph."

"La Purísima?"

"Well, she's pregnant, isn't she? Even I could see that. If you know Felipe like I do, you can be sure he thinks she's the mother of

God. Who is this *gringa embarazada*? Do you know? Why is that green-eyed *chingadero* following them? Why are you worthless gringos prowling around here like coyotes? What the fuck is going on, anyway?"

Clamato knew all the local Spanish idioms and jokes, and finally was able to calm the old man down. He explained that I had come all the way from New York to find my sister and take her home with me, and that the green-eyed man was the father of her child and wanted her too.

"Mother of God," the old man whispered.

"Is there another horse we can use?"

"No. La Paloma was the only one, God damn his soul of shit."

"Christ, that sucks." Clamato looked more upset than I could have believed possible. "I was counting on that horse. I've got a bum knee—I just couldn't make it up there on foot. It blows everything."

What to do? There seemed to be only one option. "Can he tell me the route?" I asked.

"What did he say? What did he say?" the old woman asked.

Clamato translated. "You're out of your mind," he added in English to me. "You can't go alone. . . . That bird will eat you alive. Let's wait for him to come back down to his truck."

"Well, does he have any water?" the old man asked.

I shook my head. "No water," I said in Spanish.

"For God's sake, get him some water," the old man yelled at his wife. "You can put it in that old goatskin of mine." He turned back to me. "Are you going to kill him, my friend?"

"I don't know."

"Well, if you do, can you bring my little mare back to me?"

I nodded. "Of course."

"Get him a fucking blanket so he doesn't freeze to death up there," he yelled, reaching down to the bare earth floor beside the cot and scratching some lines with his forefinger. "Look, my friend. The trail turns off here, about three kilometers along the river. Go up the ridge till you can see Paraíso down to the west. Then turn off here, toward the saddle. When you get over the saddle, turn here and follow the side of the mountain to the left. At the open place in the forest with the big rock, turn here. The trail goes down through the pine trees, and you will meet some pigs. They will be able to tell you how to go from there." He was laughing. "Look. Be careful right here. That turn is very easy to miss. It's right after the big *madroño*. You know what a *madroño* is, my friend? Do you have them in New York?"

"You can't miss it," Clamato said. "The branches are all red and snaky, and they're shedding their skin. They make one hell of a cocktail out of the fruit."

"Thanks," I told him. Back to Don Yeyo. "How long will it take to get up there?"

"It depends on how fast you go, my friend." He coughed and cleared his throat. "I can make the whole trip in three hours. *Oye, mujer!* Get him some venison *machaca* and tortillas. And my fucking *mochila* to carry his things in."

The Trail

The trail ran alongside a mostly dry riverbed set with small pools of standing water. Huge wild fig trees snaked their way down the canyon sides, forking around boulders, doubling back, and rejoining themselves like something out of Dalí, their bark a smooth vanilla, their leaves big green ovals the size of footballs, leaving shadows moving on shadows in a light breeze fifty feet up in the clerestory.

I passed a large bush or small tree covered with white flowers. Each flower was alive with multicolored butterflies: white, yellow, black with red and white stripes, blue and black, orange and black. They were in the air around the flowers in a thick, fluttering cloud.

The pools in the riverbed grew and became connected and finally formed a small river: grassy banks, cattails, a few giant cottonwoods and tall, thin, straight palms. Small fish hung in the clear water, water striders indented the surface. Kingfishers flitted up and downstream, two wing beats and a dive. Big yellow and black orioles hopped and preened in the willows, a small flock of ducks arrowed up the canyon, but the big, red-footed, delicious pigeons the Italian chef had raved about were nowhere to be seen.

Farther along, the river ran through deep cuts in the rock interspersed with big deep pools, when I could see it. The trail hung high on the canyonside above the river or doglegged away in switchbacks through a dry thorny forest hung with yellow, red, blue, and purple flowers and pulsing with white-winged doves.

The configuration was very like the secret place Claire had taken me to, and when I finally emerged on a plateau of rock enclosing a large pool with a small waterfall at one end, I took it as a sign.

No, it was all too perfect, a mirage. A vision of life beyond.

In an hour or so, I could be food for the buzzards. Couldn't I? *To be a gringo in Mexico; that is euthanasia.* Ambrose Bierce wrote that before he disappeared.

I needed to concentrate on something practical: the dull pain in my balls that persisted as I slowly put one foot in front of the other, the thought of Claire's gray eyes, her laughter on hearing *I'm flat on my fucking* back. *Meanwhile the* world *is coming to an end.*

A few hundred yards past the pool, as Don Yeyo had diagrammed, I turned off on an almost invisible trail zigzagging up the steep side of the canyon, full of loose rocks that twisted and rolled underfoot. Where the trail curved around outcroppings, the view was all the way out into the Pacific. In some of the gullies, running water had hollowed it into a six-foot-deep trough. In places there were grassy banks set with wildflowers, in others the thorny scrub closed in so you could barely see the sky. I climbed in stops and starts, sweating, panting, seeing bright spots move through the thin air in front of me and wondering if I was about to crumple from a heart attack.

Every once in a while I'd see a footprint. There were two sets: one made by hiking boots, the other a tire tread of *huaraches*. No sign of a third track. Marco must be riding (there were plenty of hoof-marks), although it was impossible to imagine that any horse could carry a rider up here.

Not far away, a bird that looked like a very colorful robin preened and perked on a large plant with a thick, woody trunk that divided about seven feet up, then exploded in two big cascades of thin, long leaves like arboreal fireworks. Beyond lay nothing but thousands of feet of blue, empty air. The scary drumbeat of my heart.

As I toiled up a forty-five-degree ridge toward a saddle in the high escarpment, the scrub slowly turned to pine, oak, and dark red, snaky *madroño*, which Clamato had perfectly described, all twisted in strange shapes. Approaching the saddle, I was in light green forest. Spanish moss began to hang from the tree branches and brilliant red and green lichens appeared on the rocks. Ferns brushed against my legs, flocks of white-winged doves whistled through the trees, and a small kestrel jagged past, setting up a twittering from invisible warblers hidden in the moss.

I was in the clouds. The tiny town of Paraíso appeared through rents in the mist, then disappeared. The ground leveled out, and the world contracted to a twenty-foot gray circle. The mist that formed this circle swirled and roiled in a familiar way, like a part of my mind.

A faint track led off left into the cloud forest, corresponding to Don Yeyo's turnoff to the saddle. A little way along it, the outline of a mist-colored horse gradually filled itself in, tied by the reins to a small tree. La Paloma. The mare nickered and tossed her head gently as I rubbed her nose and then shifted her weight with a strange lurch, favoring a front foot. When I knelt to look, I could see the foot dangled limply, with blood and white points of bone showing in the mist-colored hair.

Then I noticed reddish swollen welts along the flanks and rump. The leg must have broken where the trail was steep and rocky, maybe somewhere along the ridge up to the saddle. Marco had had to beat her hard to make her keep climbing after that. There had been no third set of footprints anywhere along the trail.

I began to loosen the cinch to La Paloma's saddle, rubbing the side of the mare's neck with one hand. The mare's skin twitched where I touched it, and she swung her head looking for a handout. Or just looking. Stamping a hind foot and blowing out her nostrils when I swung the saddle off and threw it aside, then bending her head and nibbling leaves from a low shrub.

Her mane tickled my nose when I put my arms around her neck and laid my cheek against it. *I'll get him.*

God the Father

She woke in dim light, not knowing where she was. "Peter?" He was somewhere around. Not far. Just down the hall. "Peter? Can you hear me?"

Her brother and she are sitting cross-legged opposite each other in the hayloft of the barn outside Philadelphia. There's a little hay left over from when their parents kept cows, enough to cushion them, but they're sitting on the bare wood floor because of fire hazard. This is the summer before his school chapel burned to the ground and they took off for Mexico.

They're both wearing khaki shorts and tee shirts, hers white, his dark blue. In a month and a half she'll be proudly showing him how to make a Hula-Hoop climb up her body in the middle of an August thunderstorm, her wet shirt showing off unmistakable breast buds.

They're sitting in vague evening light through the open loft door, which faces west. An ancient sleigh, a plow, a butter churn, scythes, pitchforks, other old implements too dim to make out off in the shadows. He's demonstrating technique: how to roll a joint between thumbs and fingers so it doesn't come out loose and messy or lumpy and wrinkled, big in the middle, narrow at the ends. He doesn't tell her there's a critical moment in this process where you just have to trust to luck.

It comes out perfect: long, thin, straight, and tight. "Now that's how you roll a joint," he says with pride and relief, passing her the makings. "You try."

Easy enough, until the critical moment, the moment when you lick the gum and start the final roll. *Keep calm, take your time.* Her third try is a lot better than her first, though he seems happy to point out it's shaped more like a barrel than a cylinder. He tears them down and pours the makings back into the baggie.

How to take a long deep toke and hold it till the last minute, how to pass the roach, pushing it from forefinger to forefinger, then clamping it with the thumb. He shows her these things, and the roach goes back and forth between them until it's gone.

"Okay," he says. The edge of the setting sun is just beginning to shine through the open loft door, backlighting her brother's hair. The shadow of his face, and the darker shadows in the corners, are tinged with electric blue. "How do you feel?"

"Pretty much the same." She runs the fingers of her right hand lightly along the top of her left forearm, where the blond hair is thickest. "How am I *supposed* to feel?"

"Good. Just . . . good." He picks up a dried grass stem and brushes her knee with the feathery tip. "More sensitive."

"Well . . . maybe. Yeah."

"Actually, this stuff is primo sinsemilla. You should be *flying* pretty soon."

Neon red sunlight gradually invades the electric blue shadows. She flaps her arms like wings and giggles. "I do feel lighter. *Voom.* Can you really fly?"

"Sure you can."

"Will you show me how?"

"It's all in your mind," he says. "Just *think* yourself up. See? Look how high I am." He reaches down to her and she takes his hand. "Come up here with me."

His pupils are enormous.

"We'll go a little higher now, okay?"

"Okay," she says faintly. "Not too far." She's holding on tight.

"Here we are up in the rafters. No problem, right?"

She doesn't answer.

"Okay. Now we'll drift along toward the door. Take a look outside."

She tugs back on his hand. "No!"

"Why not? Look, the sun's almost down. Look how beautiful!"

"Let's stay here. Please!"

Suddenly, she's terrified. Of what? Out of control. She's never felt like this before. She feels him floating away toward the open door, his hand slipping out of hers. He's gone. She curls up in the hay, eyes closed, face toward the wall. Someone is saying something faintly, a woman's voice, her mother's, whispering in her ear.

"Wendy. *Wendy*. Are you okay?" Her brother is back beside her.

She just curls up more tightly. Feels his hand on her shoulder. "Oh God, I hear something horrible. *Horrible*."

"What is it, Wendy? What?" But he only sounds half present.

"Oh, Peter, you left me up there. Why did you leave me?" Now she's sitting up, bits of hay in her hair and sticking to her clothes. Looking into his face.

"I didn't leave you, Wendy. I'm right here."

"You are?"

"You can see I am." But he's not. She can feel it.

She sighs, puts her head in his lap, closes her eyes, and clasps her arms around one of his crossed legs. The leg is smooth, solid, and warm. If she holds on tight enough, she can bring him back.

The cabin door opened, silhouetting a tall, thin figure in a straw cowboy hat against a gray, foggy background. "Have you seen my brother?" she asked Felipe. "He seems so close."

"Your brother? Why, no." He came inside and shut the door. "Did you sleep all right, *doña*? How are you feeling?"

"A little strange."

"Of course. What is happening to you is a miracle."

226

She took a deep breath. "And what is happening to me, Felipe? I'm frightened."

"Don't be frightened, *doña*. You are walking with God."

"God is frightening sometimes, isn't he?"

Felipe stepped closer to stand beside the cot. "Listen, *doña*. Did you know that once I tried to kill myself?"

"My God! What happened?"

"A long time ago, in Culiacán, where I grew up. I loved a girl, and I thought she loved me, but she went with someone else. I didn't want to live without her, so I cut my throat."

She touched her own throat.

"I was down in the *huerta*. Somebody found me and got me to the hospital. When I woke up everything was white, the rooms, the people. I thought I was in heaven. The doctor told me that God had made sure I used a knife that was so dull it only wrecked my voice."

"My voice and my songs had impressed that girl and made her love me for a little while. But I couldn't write and sing enough songs to keep her, so my voice was driving me crazy. It wasn't good enough."

"Without my voice, I could see God wanted me to live for another purpose, so I began a journey to find out what it was. I arrived here in the summer, and the flowers were full of honey bees. The first man I met was a blind guitar player who greeted me as if he'd known me all my life. He told me I was alive to do good deeds and to gather honey, and the minute he said it I knew it was true."

She put her hand on his arm. "To do good deeds and to gather honey. What a wonderful life!"

"*Claro*. So God was good to me, not frightening." A small, sad smile. "*Solo uno problema*: it's not so easy to do good deeds. I've had many failures, and I know the people laugh at me. But I keep trying, and I believe that one day I'll succeed."

"You're succeeding right now, Felipe."

"Do you think so?" The smile faded. "I am not so sure."

"Felipe." Squeezing gently. "Felipe. I have to tell you something, and you must believe me because it frightens me very much if you don't. God is not the father of this child."

"Oh yes he is, *doña*." Felipe's dark face was suddenly glowing. "I'm sure of that, at least. He is the father of every child."

In the Mist

A coppery, blue-spotted tree frog with little round suction-cup feet and a white belly sat in the exact center of a heart-shaped leaf. It didn't move as I bent down to get a closer look into its black-striped golden eyes. I could have picked it up and held it.

The mist did not break.

The trail curved left, around the side of the mountain, with occasional vistas into valleys or across them to the peaks of the southern range. Silence. Had the mist muffled all sound, or was there just no sound to be heard?

Sometimes the trail forked, and I began constructing little cairns to mark the way out. I passed the big *madroño*, and turned where Don Yeyo had indicated. The oak trees twisted and writhed, and I thought I might have heard a footstep or two behind me. Quick and soft.

I strained to hear through the silence, looking back along the twenty feet of trail at gray shapes on the edge of visibility. Looking into the forest. Shivering in my thin clothes. The mist had beaded the ends of the hairs on my forearms.

I went on, stopped, listened, went on again. And stopped again. Still silence. If there was anyone behind me, he or she was stopping too.

I crept into a thick bush beside the trail and hunkered down. Outside the bush the mist curled . . . questions with no answers, a little boy standing at the door of a steamy, illuminated bathroom trying to make out what is inside.

All I could see was a black hat. The rest was muffled, shrouded, indistinct. The soft, quick footsteps had stopped. It seemed that the hat had swiveled toward me.

Hey, Marco, I thought. But I didn't say anything. I didn't move. Marco was looking right at me, probably, though I couldn't see his eyes. Couldn't see his face. Couldn't make out what he was wearing.

Maybe Marco could see *me*. But my shirt was khaki (a poplin safari shirt I'd bought in Montana), and it blended with the background.

I could move, walk toward my enemy, but I stayed frozen. Then Marco turned away, took a couple of silent steps off the trail, and was swallowed up by the forest.

How had he gotten behind me? Without the mare's guidance, he'd probably taken a wrong turn, doubled back, and had seen the cairns. I strained my senses while occasional droplets of condensed atmosphere splatted on leaves.

If I waited hidden and soundless, he might eventually continue on down the trail. Meanwhile, he no doubt was waiting for the same thing. Mexican standoff, though I had the advantage of a good sighting.

After what seemed like hours, a bird trilled somewhere very close. The mist both amplified and diffused the sound, so you couldn't tell where it was coming from.

Claire had said I'd changed. Maybe she'd just been testing the water. No, she must have believed it, even though I hadn't really believed it myself.

Now here I was, huddled in the mist, trying my best to keep absolutely still so my enemy wouldn't hear me. Talk about change. Who could have imagined, a couple of weeks ago before the attack in New York? I was sitting on my left heel, hugging my right knee—not the most comfortable of positions. My left leg was prickling and the sensation, along with a faint ache in my balls, strangely recalled my feeling for Claire.

Suppose I had gone into her room that last night when I'd heard her tossing and turning? The man I was now would have gone without hesitation. Maybe I'd never have another chance!

The bird trilled again. Or was it a different bird? Sounded derisive. I now had an Enemy. That was something new. *That bird will eat you alive.*

My leg was completely numb. Something had to be done. I uncoiled from the bush and stepped out onto the trail. "Forget it, Marco," I heard myself shout. "She doesn't have what you're looking for. Why don't you go back and put that horse out of its misery. You have a knife, don't you?"

Silence. I picked up a lemon-sized rock from the side of the trail and hurled it as hard as I could at the place I'd last seen the hat. I heard it smash through shrubbery and hit the ground with a thump.

"What's the big deal, Marco?" I called.

After a few beats, a light, nondirectional baritone began to surround me.

> *Volver, volver, volver*
> *En tus brazos otra vez*
> *Estaría donde estés*
> *Yo sé perder*
> *Yo sé perder*
> *Quiero volver*
> *Volver, volver . . .*

The notes receded back into the mist, succeeded by a conversational voice. "That's her favorite song, bro. She loves me to sing it for her. 'I know I am lost, and I want to return to your arms again, wherever you might be.'"

"She hates you." I realized I didn't have to shout.

"That's bad talk, bro. Be reasonable." There was a rustle in the bushes twenty feet away from where I'd hurled the rock. "She didn't have to have my baby, you know."

I walked slowly toward the sound. "Come out and talk it over."

A low laugh that made the back of my neck tingle. "I think you got my message the last time. Go back to New York and leave us in peace. You're the one she hates. What did you do to her, anyway?"

I hurled a second rock and heard it smash through the thick, damp foliage. There was no answering rustle, no further sound. I yelled and charged blindly into the cloud forest until the vegetation stopped me.

My enemy was lost. I'd forgotten that. But I myself had been told the way.

Run as fast as you can. Go now!

Back on the trail, I ran steadily for what felt like a mile through the mist, then jumped into another thick bush. And waited, panting, trying to see. But there were no footsteps, no shapes.

Running, walking, listening, running again. Surely by now I should have gotten to the open place in the forest with the big rock. But the trail seemed to be curving around a shoulder and rising. Impossible! But yes, it was rising, the mist was clearing, the vegetation was thinning, and then I was above the mist on a rocky slope with nothing above me but a towering crag standing out in hallucinatory relief against a dark blue cloudless sky. No plants, no birds, no life of any kind. Like the face of the moon.

Where I'd Like to Be

In a shed not far from the cabin, Felipe had showed her a wooden tub made from oak slats and shaped like a barrel laid on its side and cut in half lengthwise. He filtered his honey into this tub. It held the entire summer's supply, infused with a special herb that allowed it to age without crystallizing and to develop its unique sharp flavor until he bottled it and hauled it down to be sold. The tub was about seven feet long and four feet wide.

"It's very *tranquilo*, isn't it?" Felipe had said, as they stood on the filtering platform looking down into the golden depths. "Sometimes I just look for a while, and it makes me calm again."

"I know what you mean." But she wasn't sure she did.

She'd heard him continue in a low voice: "This is where I'd like to be. When my life is over. Do you think it's possible?"

He'd been staring at her when she turned. No smile. *Do you think it's possible?* "Why, of course, Felipe," she'd said as lightly as she could. "What a wonderful idea!"

She had read somewhere that Alexander the Great had had himself embalmed in honey. So it was definitely possible. An unsettling image came into her mind of Felipe floating peacefully and weightlessly in his final resting place, preserved down through the centuries. And smiling.

***

Now it was early afternoon, and Felipe was off tending his hives. A warm slant of sun through the window touched her lower leg. She ran a hand over her belly: it felt extra large and sensual in a strange way. She thought of Felipe's strong brown hands. Raging hormones.

Are you sick? You're sick, aren't you?

Her brother did feel close. Suppose he never saw the letters to him she'd written in her journal. Suppose she never saw him again. She should have brought her journal with her. There was nothing to write in up here; she had nothing but one change of clothes, a toothbrush, and the film canister.

It was time to leave. She was feeling more and more certain that she and Felipe should not be alone together here for another night. They could get down at least to the *rancho* before sunset if they left now. "Felipe," she called. "*Felipe!*" With relief, she heard his steps on the wood slats leading up to the door.

Opposites United

A watery sun had burned off the mist by the time I'd doubled back down and found the right trail, though shreds of it still hung in the top branches of the pine trees bordering the meadow. The edges of the meadow were set with white beehives, and the air buzzed lazily. Swallows cut back and forth over the knee-high yellow grass, and two blue-black ravens croaked and preened beside a stream.

There was the little shed with the chestnut horse tethered outside, and there was the cabin. I walked toward it cautiously, up the stairs, listened for a second, and pushed open the door into a dim room. A slant of light showed a wooden cot with someone sitting on it cross-legged, knees covered by a colorful Mexican blanket.

Suddenly, I was looking into my own eyes. My own eyes looked back. My sister and I were enclosed by a circle, room for nothing else, carrying us silently back through time.

Omigod, what are you doing here?

My sister strained forward on the cot but didn't get up. She seemed bound in some way, hands behind her back. *Marco?* I mouthed the name and raised my chin. She nodded. I moved to untie her hands, but they were shackled with a pair of antique handcuffs around the cot's low wooden back brace. Her hair had a familiar soap smell as I bent to whisper in her ear. She'd grown it long again, like when she was a girl.

"Where is he?"

Putting my own ear to her mouth, feeling her warm breath. *"Out-side somewhere. Looking for Felipe."*

"When did he get here?"

"Half hour ago, maybe."

"You okay?"

"Yes. He'll be back any minute."

I moved to the cabin window in time to see Marco come out of the shed, stand in the sun for a short time, then walk toward the horse, which drew back to the end of its tether, shaking its head.

I selected an iron skillet from among the cooking things, looked at my sister, put a finger to my lips, and eased behind the open door. Her eyes stayed with me.

Sooner or later, the steps outside creaked and Marco's bulk cut off light through the door. He stayed just outside. "Your brother show up yet?"

"Where's Felipe?" Her voice was shaking.

The boards creaked as he stepped in. "I didn't see him. Maybe he left."

"What are you talking about?" Straining forward. "Is the horse still there?"

"Yeah, tied outside the shed."

"He'd never just leave. What did you do to him?"

"I told you. I didn't see him. Look, he's got hives all over the place, he could be anywhere."

She bowed her head. "You have the negatives. You got what you came for. Will you please go away now?"

Marco knelt, moved the blanket aside, and put his hand on her belly.

"Please, Marco. What else do you want? Do you want the car? For Christ's sake, you can have it."

"That's my child in there. You could have gotten rid of it, but you didn't." I could barely hear his words, they were so soft.

"I . . . I was going to."

236

"But you chose not to."

"I didn't choose . . ."

"Do you really hate me, Wendy? Your brother said you do."

"No, Marco. I don't hate you."

"Well, good." He moved behind her and unlocked one of the cuffs. While she slowly rubbed the free wrist with the shackled hand, he swept off his hat and bent his knee. "Will you marry me?"

I set my feet to leap, and a board creaked.

I wasn't prepared for Marco's reaction, turning to see me crouched with the skillet raised: a barking laugh. It made me freeze.

"Haw, shit," I heard him say. "I'll take mine over easy, okay? And don't overdo 'em, for Christ's sake."

I took a step forward. "Take those cuffs off."

Marco uncoiled to his feet, hands shoulder high, palms facing out. "Relax, bro. Everything's cool." Tossing his head toward Wendy. "I think they look good on her. You know what they call them down here in Mexico? *Esposas*." Keeping his eyes on me. "So Wendy my dear, what do you say? Will you be my *esposa*?"

Wendy's face was completely blank. It gave nothing away, no matter how carefully I looked. Finally, she nodded slowly. "Yes. All right."

Marco clapped his hands. "*Que milagro!* The *padrecito* is a special friend. He says he can do it tomorrow."

"Marco, I just had a cramp. I'm frightened. Can we please go down now?"

"You've just made me the happiest man in the world, *mi amor*. Sure we can go. Tell your brother to put down that frying pan before he hurts somebody, okay?"

"Peter." Was there a ghost of a smile? "Will you put down that frying pan?"

I carefully set the skillet on the counter.

"Hey, bro," Marco said. "Not that I don't trust you, but can you put it back on the shelf where you got it?"

I did.

"And step away from it?"

I obeyed. "*Vámonos*," Marco said, and Wendy stood with an effort, faded red tee shirt barely covering half-buttoned jeans. Without thinking, I went to her and put my arms around her. I felt her arms go around me in turn. Her belly was hard against me as I heard a metallic ratcheting and the handcuff tightened on my wrist.

Marco had locked our opposite wrists together, so when we separated we were both able to face him. "What are you doing, Marco?" Wendy asked.

"Just a joke, don't worry about it." He was grinning. "I just wanted to get you two back together. I'll take them off if you want."

The three of us just stood there.

"Peter and Wendy." The grin widened. "Nobody ever read me that book. How does it end?" When no one answered, he went on: "What did he do to you, anyway?"

He walked to the door and looked out. I became aware of my sister's arm against mine and looked down to see the familiar thick blond hair shading the tanned skin.

Marco turned. "He fucked you over, right? Well, now he's a different man." Grinning. "He's been through a lot to get back to you. I know for a fact."

I shifted my handcuffed wrist slightly, and the links connecting me to my sister jingled.

"Same with me," Marco went on. "I'm a different man myself."

"How is that, Marco?" I heard my sister ask.

"Well, having a child on the way is a whole new ballgame. I definitely never wanted to get married before. I was never even in love before. Didn't know what love *felt* like."

"How does it feel?" I asked in spite of myself.

"There's no way to describe it. Maybe in Spanish . . . No, it's something you have to feel for yourself, bro."

"Like sex?"

"They don't call it 'making love' for nothing. And then a kid comes out of it. I know I'm not saying this very well."

A block of bright sunlight suddenly forced its way through the window and lay on the board floor between them, dust motes circling above it. "I've done some bad things. I know that. I wish—"

"You want to put those behind you," I said. "You want to start over."

"Don't you?"

"I do indeed."

Marco nodded at Wendy. "It all comes down to her, doesn't it? How do you feel about that, Wendy? Suppose we have your brother be best man?"

"Marco. Please."

"You're not going to marry me, are you?" Suddenly his face had gone blank. "You have no fucking intention of marrying me. You and your brother would like to see me dead."

He had us walk in front of him out the cabin door toward the horse. What was happening? Anything could happen, I thought. Nothing I could imagine was outside the realm of possibility.

Whatever happened, my sister and I were together. When my arm swung, hers swung with it, warm skin lightly brushing on warm skin, shoulders occasionally touching. We were even in step.

Sisters

The first bus from La Paz to Paraíso since the storm left at 8:00 a.m. from the Calle Bravo market. It was full. Claire was sitting at the window about halfway back on the left-hand side next to a handsome, hefty woman, with long dark wild hair, about her age. The woman used a heavy, almost musky, perfume that Claire found not unpleasant.

The woman had smiled at her in a friendly way when she'd sat down, but Claire's Spanish was terrible and she hadn't felt up to trying to speak it just then.

No word from either Wendy or Peter since that last airport phone call before he boarded the Aero California flight to La Paz, and she was worrying about what she'd find. Time was suddenly of the essence; what she had to do was very clear. She'd flown straight to LA from New York, taken the first available flight to La Paz, and had stayed in the Los Arcos Hotel for the next four days, rising at dawn and heading to the bus station for word about the road. At first she expected to find Peter in the small crowd, but he must have found another route. The word was always tomorrow. Finally, a few minutes ahead of departure time, it was announced that the bus would leave on schedule. Claire was close to the head of the line.

On the outskirts of town, the woman spoke to her in English. "First time to Paraíso?"

"Yes."

"I saw where you were in the line. You must have gotten here very early."

"About six. For the fourth day."

"Ay, *Dios*! So what does our little town have to offer you, to put in so much work when everyone else goes straight to Cabo?"

The bus rolled out of the city up onto the high green desert and sped along the straight level highway with a comforting diesel purr. Passengers were in a good mood, finally going home, laughing and chatting. It felt like a rolling coffee shop, made for cozy confidences.

In no time at all, Claire and Isabel filled in the backstory between them. Wendy's pregnancy, Isabel's support, the Marco situation (complete with incriminating film canister), the sessions, the estrangement, Peter's final departure to see his sister and Claire's role in it. So fast it was dizzying.

Finally Claire drew in her breath. "So do you really love her? Or is this just a . . ."

"*Lujuria?*" Isabel smiled and shook her head. "First tell me do you really love the brother, what's his name again?"

"Peter," Claire said.

"You do, don't you? From the way you said it."

"Ummm . . . much too early to know." Her face felt warm. "But, hey . . . I was asking the questions here."

Isabel put her hand over hers. "Okay, I'm happy to answer. Yes, I love her. It's real, *mi amor*. I want to help her with the child. I want our lives shared together for a long time."

Why, they were practically sisters!

"So, anyway," Claire said before she had really thought it out. "You'll never guess where I'm coming from."

"Montana, no?"

"No. Philadelphia."

"Ah, where *she* comes from."

"Exactly."

"Did you go see the famous house?"

"I knew it from before. On my play dates with Wendy when we were little girls. And I went back to see it again."

"A real castle, no? With the wicked witch?"

"The wicked witch. Didn't Wendy ever talk about her?"

Isabel looked past her out the window at the desert. Mountains were beginning to appear on the horizon. "No, *mi amor*. She didn't talk about the mother much at all. She hated her, no? She wanted to forget her. Wasn't that why she was in Paraíso? *Dios mío*, I didn't even know she had a brother until now. And what was the problem between them, *mi'ha*?"

"Their mother was the problem," Claire said. "Let me tell you what I found back East."

The case file, in the moldy basement of the old marble Delaware County Courthouse in Media, in the Philly suburbs, contained two interesting depositions on behalf of the defense, Nu-Car Carriers.

The company lawyer had worked hard. First, he'd found an eye-witness to the crash who'd heard the mother apologize, that she shouldn't have pulled out, that it had been her fault. Then he'd gone to the hospital and talked to the head nurse, not the doctor, because the doctor was a family friend.

The head nurse was very experienced, very capable, had trained at Mass General. She said that the mother's life could easily have been saved with a blood transfusion, but she'd refused it. Without her signature on the release, the doctor was legally prohibited from giving it to her.

The mother had tried to refuse just about any kind of treatment, the nurse continued. Even the most basic, like sponge baths. She'd ordered her husband to leave her alone and go to a dinner party the night before she died. "A hostile patient," the nurse concluded. "That's what we call that kind."

The final ruling in the suit was hard to decipher from the file. At last Claire had carried it up to the clerk, who looked at it briefly and announced: "There was no ruling. The family settled the suit, I don't think for very much. The depositions were too damaging for them to take it to trial." He closed the file and looked up at Claire. "Where do you fit in, may I ask?"

"Just a family friend trying to help right a wrong."

The clerk nodded. "Don't quote me, but I'd say the mother might have been tired of life."

"So," said Claire to Isabel. "Peter was right, you see. The mother probably killed herself."

"*Dios mío.* You gonna tell Wendy?"

"Of course."

"*Pero que fisgón!*"

"*Fisgón?*"

Isabel tapped her nose with a finger.

"Okay. So, I'm nosy." Claire shrugged and scratched her own nose. "Here's another question. Why did the mother want to die?"

The bus lurched over a speed bump at the beginning of the Paraíso main street, throwing Claire and Isabel together, then hurling them apart. Baskets and suitcases flew from the overhead racks, and everyone was laughing as they careered around corners and finally screeched to a stop in front of a row of food stalls. Isabel straightened her dress and nodded at the smirking young driver. "*Luciroso pendejo.*"

"My Spanish is terrible. What does that mean?"

"Show-off of a pubic hair. You'll come to my place, right? Then we can fine out what's goin' on." She hauled herself into the aisle and reached up for her suitcase, one of the few still there. Claire couldn't help noticing the swell of her breasts.

Walking from the bus stop to the house, they stopped at the little plaza in front of the church and looked out over the valley to the sea. Still too early for the wind, and the taco palms and mango trees stood quietly over luminous fields backdropped by a blue silk ocean. Someone was whistling.

Claire sniffed the air. "It's a magic place. I can smell it."

"Ha. Probably the Santa Fe kitchen." Pointing across the street at the old theater. "And that's where I sang naked with my accordion."

"Wow. Wish I'd been there."

"Well, you couldn't see much with the hair and all."

"What color was the accordion?"

"Red, with white and black trim."

"Perfect! What did you sing?"

"Oh, you know. Some *corrido*. I was modest in those days. But I wonder where is Felipe. He always here with his honey. Every day."

"Who's Felipe?"

"Ah. Who indeed? Let *her* tell you."

The door to the little house across the valley was padlocked. Isabel opened it and stood aside for Claire to enter. The art and the nude portrait (which she recognized as Wendy's) left her oddly breathless. As they stood there silently, they could hear the sound of running feet, and a girl rushed in on a torrent of Spanish.

Finally, the girl was crying and Isabel had her arms around her. "She says they are all up on the mountain."

"Who, for heaven's sake?"

"Everyone. Everyone that matters."

After the girl departed, Isabel filled in the blanks for Claire as best she could. But she'd been away for two weeks, there were many things she could only guess at, and the girl's account had been all over the lot.

In the end, all they could do was wait. *Like women did*, Claire thought. They decided to wander down to the beach because it was Wendy's favorite place.

Halfway along the sandy two-track, they both took off their shoes. Isabel picked a sprig of crimson-flowered San Miguel vine from a fence post and handed it to Claire with an unreadable smile. "Welcome to Mexico, *fisgón*."

Sniffing the blossoms. "Hey, I wasn't prying. I just added things up."

"*Bueno*." The smile focused itself. "As you were saying before we went over that *pinche* bump? About why the mother wanted to die?"

In the head nurse's deposition, she stated that she'd gotten a phone call from the daughter's therapist, a man named Philip Sternberg, saying that the daughter wanted to talk to her mother. Would that be possible? Sternberg personally thought it might be a good idea. But when the nurse asked the mother, she closed her eyes and pretended to be asleep. She died the next day.

There must have been somebody else. Sitting in her rental Corolla outside the Media courthouse, Claire placed a cell phone call to Briarcliffe and asked for Phil Sternberg. "He was a staff therapist there in the late seventies. Under Dr. Reiger. He . . . ah . . . worked with me back then. My name is Wendy Davis."

Sternberg was no longer there, and Reiger himself had moved on years ago. The secretary asked for a couple of hours to check the files. Maybe there was an address for Sternberg. "People do like to stay in touch, don't they?"

Claire drove the familiar roads to Haverford, turning right off Darby Paoli Road onto College Avenue, past green lawns and big maples with tasteful homes nestled discreetly in the background, past the Piaseckis' white Italianate mansion, and down the hill toward the trolley tracks and Haverford College.

Just before the bridge over the tracks, she turned left onto the asphalt driveway bracketed by low whitewashed stone walls ending in boxwood hedges, up a rise under big shade trees to where the stately house waited for her: three stories of whitewashed fieldstone and green shutters, fronted by a brick-terraced, white-columned porch. On a slope to the right, an orchard. To the left, a sunken garden with a fish pool down flagstone steps through a slope of rhododendron. A spreading catalpa sheltered a stone and glass greenhouse with formal beds of roses beyond.

Nothing had changed since she'd last seen the place. Absolutely nothing. It gave Claire goose bumps.

She stopped the car under an overhanging roof off the porch, got out, and waited. It was about 12:30, almost lunchtime. In a minute, Wendy's mother would come out of the front door and down the steps.

She'd be dressed in a bright floral print by Lily Pulitzer, her short dark hair up in its usual Queen Elizabeth coif, a circle of curls like a wreath around the sides of her head. Her smile would be wide and friendly, showing many of her large, uneven teeth, and her little eyes would be almost invisible. "Why, there you are at last, you naughty girl. What took you so long? Come in now, quick. We're all just sitting down."

At the circular table, in a Savile Row houndstooth tweed jacket, would be Wendy's handsome father, eyes twinkling. Peter would be away at school. Tee-shirted, blue-jeaned Wendy would be smiling crookedly to his left. Claire would be on the right and the mother opposite. "Now tell us about your morning," the mother would say as Grace brought in the soup course. "Did Bill fall off his horse again?" Some days she might rip off a fart, and the father would pretend to look shocked. "Now, dear. We have guests, you know."

Or if she arrived in the afternoon, and Wendy was late getting back from wherever she'd been, the mother might invite Claire upstairs, through the formal sitting room into the inner sanctum, where she lay watching *As the World Turns* at high volume from the same bed her invalid mother had taken to thirty years before. Who knew what mood she might be in? Cozy and confidential? Weepy? Bitter and angry?

She might say things like "Oh, dear, I'm not cut out to be a mother. I think I've ruined my children's lives. Wendy hates me, you know."

And Claire might answer: "Oh, no. Don't worry. She can be moody sometimes."

"But she says such awful things to me. This morning she said she wished I was *dead*."

And Claire would keep silent because Wendy might have told her the same thing earlier. "She's such an angry creature," the mother would say. "Where does it all come from, anyway? Peter was never like that. You like him, don't you?"

"Sure."

"But he's so *distant*. I never know what he's thinking. It's so hard being a mother. Wait till you try it."

During one of those sessions, the mother had given her a gift, an old clothbound copy of *Heidi* by Johanna Spyri, with color illustrations, the mother's favorite book as a child, a kind of talisman. Her maiden name was written childishly on the flyleaf.

Heidi was a little Swiss orphan in the late Victorian era who'd been sent by her aunt at the age of six to stay with her grandfather up in the Alps, where he lived as a hermit in a remote chalet. Heidi grew to love the mountains and the pastoral life, and her grumpy old grandfather grew to love her, but after a few years, to make some money, her aunt billeted her as a paid companion to a rich girl her age who lived in a big gloomy house in the city and was confined to a wheelchair.

"The invalid's name was Klara," the mother said. "Her parents never paid the slightest attention to her and put her under the orders of an evil governess, Miss Rottenmeier, who never allowed her any fun and was crushing the life out of her. Every year she got more sad and sickly." She shot Claire a glance. "I had one of those myself, you know."

Claire didn't know what to say, so she kept silent.

"Luckily for her, Klara had Heidi. Heidi was finally able to get her out of there, up to the Alps with her grandfather, where she got better." With a second quick look.

Claire just sat there.

"I had to hide this book, or my governess would have taken it away and burned it." The mother now had a confusing little smile. "I would have given it to Wendy, you know, but I'm sure she'd never read it. I wanted to give it to someone who'd love it as much as I did. And after all, you have almost the same name."

Wendy herself was only vaguely aware of these sessions, and generally didn't seem to care that her hated mother liked her best friend. Par for the course. Claire had no idea why the mother had taken such a fancy to her. She was a strange lady. Claire still had the book and took it out every once in a while to leaf through it and wonder.

Instead of ringing the doorbell, Claire strolled to the end of the brick porch and stood in the sun looking out over the rose garden. Down the stone steps, past a wisteria trellis and a rock garden, the ground sloped gradually to a grove of birches beside a little pond with an island in the middle supporting a wrought-iron heron. Who took care of all this now? The place seemed at attention, waiting with its ears pricked. How did she look, in her navy worsted tight-skirted suit, low black heels, pearls, cream silk blouse? Did the spirits approve?

She took off her heels and sauntered barefoot over the dry September grass toward the trellis, through the rock garden, down the slope toward the pond. Setting her shoes down on the grass, taking off her jacket, folding it neatly beside the shoes, venturing onto the red wooden bridge over the stream below the pond, striking a slightly defiant pose with her shoulders back, head raised, hands on the railing, the wood warm under her hands and feet.

She felt like she belonged here. As if she, not Wendy, had been born and raised here. As if she knew every secret nook and cranny. As if she, not Peter, had wandered down here on an early spring morning just after sunrise and seen the mother picking her way through the daffodils on a parallel path without noticing her.

Her cell phone rang: it was the Briarcliffe secretary with information that Dr. Sternberg was now in private practice in Greenwich, Connecticut. She even supplied his phone number and office address. Claire called the number and left a message with the secretary that she'd been a close friend of Wendy Davis's since grade school at Shipley in Bryn Mawr; she happened to be in Greenwich for the afternoon, and wondered if she could meet Dr. Sternberg for coffee after he left his office. She had some important news.

A dark-haired man about her age, in a blue Oxford shirt, khaki pants, and Topsiders, was waving and smiling his way down the slope from the house toward her. "Well, well! Where have *you* been all my life?"

He turned out to be the new owner, but looked confused when Claire said she'd been a childhood friend of Wendy's. "She used to live here. Wendy Davis?"

He'd never met the Davises. They'd sold the place to the Eisenbreys, and he'd bought it from them. He grinned. "Kind of a fire sale."

"Fire sale?"

"Wendy didn't tell you?" The man smoothed back his hair. "Strange story. A year or so after he bought it, Eisenbrey sued Mr. Davis, claimed the place was *haunted*. He spent heaven knows how long trying to prove it in all kinds of different courts. They all ruled against him. I got it for a song."

"God! Was it the mother? The one that was killed?"

"What?"

"The *ghost*."

"No . . . no ghost. Things would just *fall* for no reason, Eisenbrey claimed. Clocks, paintings, trays, anything. He had witnesses in court: 'That tray of dishes just fell. We were on the other side of the room. No one was near it. And that priceless vase on the mantel.'"

"Things just *fall*," Claire repeated. "Doesn't that bother you?"

"I haven't noticed anything falling since I moved in." He laughed. "Unless I knock it over myself."

"What about your family?"

"Don't have one." He put a hand over his heart. "I'm still on the market."

"This is a pretty big place for a single man, isn't it?"

"Oh, I don't plan to live here permanently. I'm a developer." Snapping his fingers. "*Condos*. Start off with the main house and the garage, then subdivide and put up matching structures. You know, tasteful, traditional, solid. Just got the permits a few days ago. The plans are inside, if you'd like to see them." Now he was smiling.

"Actually"—returning the smile as best she could—"I've got a long drive to make. But I'll tell Wendy you're doing a great job. Can't wait to ask her about the falling objects."

Now it was just before two. She should be able to make it to Greenwich in three hours or less. Shrinks were punctual about office hours, she knew. From Haverford, she crossed the Schuylkill River and got on the Pennsy Turnpike to New Jersey. While she was crossing the George Washington Bridge, her phone rang. The shrink, probably to tell her he could not meet. She didn't answer. By 4:30, averaging about seventy and hitting ninety-five whenever she dared, she was in Greenwich.

The shrink worked in a small office building on a leafy side street convenient to downtown. Should she go in and announce herself? That might give him a chance to sidestep. She parked her car opposite the building in the shade of a big elm, turned off the radio, and turned it back on again for the five o'clock news. George W. was declaring he'd make sure that bin Laden was brought to justice dead or alive.

Her left elbow was cocked out the open window, the wedding ring on her dangling hand sizzling in a shaft of sunlight. She found herself turning the heavy, solitary ring slowly around her finger, clockwise, she realized. To the right. Right is tight, she'd learned as a girl, screwing and unscrewing nuts. She changed direction to turn the ring counterclockwise, slowly up over her knuckle until it was off. Tentatively, she opened the car's glove compartment, put the ring inside, and closed it again.

She decided she hated George W.'s voice. The cocky braggadocio. The phony Texas accent. The slightly hoarse good-ol'-boy timbre. And most of all, the way he emphasized certain words, like in a comic strip. But she too would like to see bin Laden brought to justice.

A fiftyish, mustachioed man dressed like a boarding school teacher, tweed jacket, khaki pants, and loafers, came down the stairs of the office building and headed up the street past her.

Straightening her hair, opening her door, stepping out, and calling across the street: "Dr. Sternberg?"

The man stopped and looked over at her with such suspicion she had to laugh. "No, I'm not a process server. I'm a friend of Wendy Davis's. From Briarcliffe? I called you earlier." She started across the street toward him.

He seemed on the verge of turning to run, then he drew himself up and put his hands in his jacket pockets like Jack Kennedy used to.

They ended up in an espresso place a few blocks away, drinking cappuccinos and eating biscotti. Sternberg kept looking distractedly around the room, anywhere but right at her. He had fake tortoise shell–framed glasses that he put on and took off several times and finally cleaned with a handkerchief from the breast pocket of his jacket. He'd crossed his legs and was jiggling his free foot.

"The cappuccino's perfect," Claire said encouragingly. "I love it when the foam's nice and creamy like this."

"I don't come here that much." Sternberg put his glasses on and looked at her for almost the first time.

"How long have you been in practice here?"

"About twelve years."

"Ever since you left Briarcliffe?"

"Pretty much. So . . . you were Wendy's childhood friend?"

"From seven years old. Grade school. We had our own club."

"And did the club have a name?"

"Wonder Girls. Our motto was, Be Kind to Animals."

Sternberg leaned back in his chair and smiled indulgently. "So. Are you now a wonder woman? Tell me about yourself. What brings you to our little town?"

"Not much to tell. I'm just passing through. On my way to Boston. I have a legal practice in New York and I'm going to a conference up there."

"Indeed." Licking his lips. "And did you stop just to see me?"

"I did."

A long silence. "You said you had some news about Wendy?"

Claire gave him her best smile. "Don't worry. It's good. Her new book just came out, and she wanted you to know. She would have told you herself, but she's in Mexico."

"Wonderful," Sternberg said warily. "What's it about?"

"Sports. She's a sports photographer now, a really good one. And not a bad writer. She wanted you to know that she's doing okay. Blowing the whistle on that thing with Reiger definitely turned out for the best."

Sternberg said he would buy the book ASAP. Then he shook his head. "That thing with Reiger?"

Claire sat up straighter and narrowed her eyes. "I'm sure you know what I'm talking about. She's blamed her brother for the last twenty years. They've hardly spoken. It's a real tragedy after they were so close as children."

Sternberg raised his cappuccino, took a careful sip, then wiped the foam off his mustache with his napkin.

"Even *she* would say it's all turned out for the best," Claire went on. "But she still blames her brother for ratting. I mean, how do you work it out? Do *you* have any ideas?"

Sternberg took his glasses off again and massaged the bridge of his nose. "All this is pretty much outside my territory."

"Well, the head nurse at the hospital where her mother died said that you had called the day before to ask if Wendy could speak to her."

"Really? How do you know that?"

"The family filed suit against the trucking company that owned the vehicle that killed the mother. Your name was in the head nurse's deposition."

"You've reviewed the papers?"

"This morning. In the Media courthouse. How did you know she was in the hospital? Reiger himself didn't even know."

A long silence.

"Did you know that the mother told Wendy that her brother had blown the whistle?" Claire asked. "Why would she do a terrible thing like that? I mean, it completely estranged them for the rest of their lives." She put her fists on the table on each side of her plate. "At least up to *now*."

"It was the wife." Sternberg spoke so softly she could barely hear him.

"The *wife*? Whose wife?"

"Reiger's wife. Apparently, he'd done this kind of thing before. Many times. That's why he left Austria. The mother had to promise not to sue. The wife was trying to save his ass. I was supposed to follow up with the mother when she came for that last visit. And afterward. Reiger wouldn't see her."

"The *wife*." Claire shook her head. "I was sure it was you."

"I would have lost my job. In a heartbeat. Reiger would have found out. Plus, I really didn't know for sure. Though I had my suspicions."

"But . . . why did the mother tell Wendy it was her brother?"

Sternberg spread his hands. "There you have me."

"You know she killed herself right after that visit. That car accident wasn't an accident."

He cleared his throat. "I don't think suicide was ever established."

"When Wendy was a child, the mother used to *do* things to her, you know. She never told me what they were, exactly. I wonder if . . ."

The doctor slowly raised his hands, palms toward Claire as if to ward her off, and shook his head.

Claire was back in the mother's bedroom, being handed her favorite book as a special gift . . . a gift that Wendy should have gotten. "I think she was like someone out of Shakespeare. A tragic figure. She wanted so much to love and be loved, but she didn't know how. So it drove her crazy."

Sternberg leaned back and gave her another smile, much less indulgent than the first. "Very perceptive. Maybe you missed your calling."

Claire and Isabel had been walking side by side on the parallel sandy tracks, heads down, lost in the story. When the words stopped, they kept walking and didn't look at each other. Now they were almost at the beach.

A little farther on, the track began to climb a high beige dune. They left their shoes at the bottom and silently slogged their way up through deep dry sand. The summit looked out over the huge beach on one side, the green valley, the little town, and the high sierra on the other.

"They're up there somewhere." Isabel pointed. "God only knows. You think your Peter can—?"

"He's on the right side. That counts for something, doesn't it? I wish I could have told him all this stuff before."

"Yes, the truth at last. It would have made him stronger. But you don't know Marco. Maybe we ought to say a prayer for them."

"Maybe we should. Do you know any?"

"In Spanish, *claro*."

"Go ahead, then."

Their hands touched and clasped as they faced the mountain and bowed their heads. After Isabel had finished she cleared her throat. "And now she's going to be a mother herself, *si Dios quiere. Qué raro, no?*"

"*Qué raro*. What does that mean?"

"How strange. It is strange, isn't it? How things turn out?"

"Could be the best thing that ever happened." As soon as she said it, Claire knew she was right.

Isabel released Claire's hand and turned to the ocean. A midday breeze was coming in from the northwest, turning the light blue water darker. "Hey, are we too old to run?" Then, like a young girl, she was tearing headlong down the dune toward the creamy breakers. Claire, in good shape from the mountains of Montana, could hardly keep up.

Honey on the Mountain

As we walked past the shed toward the horse, Marco moved ahead to untie its lead. I felt my sister's fingers curl around mine and squeeze. When I looked at her, she cut her eyes to the shed and back. I understood what she wanted, and why, as well as if she'd told me.

As a perfect unit, we were running together to the shed's door, hearing Marco yell, hearing his pounding feet behind us. Wendy pulled the door open and we were inside. Marco was there in a second, and then the only sound was our hard breathing.

Felipe seemed to be smiling. My sister knelt beside him, ignoring the terrible wound, cradling his head with her free arm.

"Cut his own throat," Marco was saying. "I didn't want you to see that, Wendy."

And she staring up at him.

I knelt myself, to take the strain off her arm.

"He tried it before, you know," Marco said. "Because of a woman. Everyone knows that. He was a little crazy that way."

"He didn't have a knife," Wendy whispered.

"You're wrong." Marco's hand went to his pocket and removed a large rosewood-handled folding knife with heavy silver caps on the ends. "He had this, Wendy. It was lying next to him."

"Oh God." Wendy dropped her head. "You're so *evil*."

"You think it's mine, don't you?" He opened the blade and tested the edge with his finger. "Christ, it's sharp. An old *cuchillo* Barcelona,

256

real quality. They don't make them like this anymore. This comes from Spain, it probably belonged to his father." He refolded it and returned it to his pocket. "I'll keep it safe, don't worry. Maybe I'll present it to the Casa Cultura."

Kneeling beside my sister, I could feel my body humming like a dynamo. Surely she could feel it herself. The artery pulsing in her neck I'd seen before, in the waiting room at Briarcliffe. Felipe's blood, seeping into the earth beside him, smelled like old brass.

"Okay, I believe you, Marco," I heard her say. "After all, you want to marry me, don't you? But anyway, he told me where he wanted to be after he was . . . gone. Isn't that strange?" Tears tracking her cheeks. "So he must have been planning something, mustn't he?"

"I'm glad you see it that way, Wendy." Marco looked stagily relieved. "It makes me very happy. So where did he want to be? Maybe it can be arranged."

He didn't remove our cuffs, but with Wendy and me on one side of the body and him on the other, we were able to lift the shoulders up onto the wooden filtering platform beside the big vat of honey. While Wendy and I kept the torso in place, Marco lifted the legs until the entire body could be rolled onto the platform. It lay face up, one arm dangling. Wendy lifted the arm gently and crossed it over the chest.

The platform was about waist high, with a ladder at one end. "I'll roll him in," Marco said, turning away, putting a foot on the first step, slipping, then staggering, and ending up with the rim of the tub against the small of his back.

No thought. Just instinct and rhythm, togetherness and action. As in a dance step, our shackled arms went over Marco's head from behind, one on each side so the links of the shackles were across his throat. He raised his hands to grip them, but our two arms bent him backward over the rim.

Marco's body was now arched radically over the vat as we strained with all our strength from the opposite side. He couldn't twist free while we forced his head back, hands clawing at the links. I was aware of my sister's eyes, a choking sound, the humming dynamo feeling in my body, and that was about all.

The choking stopped when the face went below the surface. Sometime after that, the body stopped straining and twisting. Finally, we removed our shackled, honey-coated hands and stared at each other like children who have just done something very bad.

Peter and Wendy

The key to the handcuffs was in Marco's left trouser pocket as he lay where we'd let him slump on the bare earth near the vat. The strain of forcing his head under had stripped skin from both our cuffed wrists, and when we were free we stood there exploring the raw patches and massaging the bruises. It distracted us from looking directly at each other again.

"You feeling okay?" My voice echoed self-consciously. "That was . . ."

She just nodded. I could feel the sixteen-year-old girl I used to know flitting in and out. In and out. "Where's the knife?"

"In his other pocket, I guess."

"Can you get it?"

Marco was lying face down. Not looking at the head, I knelt, reached into the right trouser pocket, and worked the big knife out.

"Can I see it? Open it first, okay?"

I checked the blade's edge with my finger the way Marco had and handed it to my sister, handle first.

The blade caught the dim light as she turned the knife slowly. "It *is* sharp, isn't it?"

"You think Felipe cut his own throat? Why would he do that?"

"Like Marco said. Because of a woman. Because of *me*. He was tempted, and it was my fault. I did it. I tempted him. I couldn't help it."

"So he killed himself? Wendy, it's too weird. Listen, I don't think the knife was Felipe's. That's not a beekeeper's knife. Marco was lying."

"A lot of weird things happen in this world, Peter. A lot of weird people . . . That's one thing I've learned after all these years." Glaring at me. "I've met my share, you know, but Felipe was only trying to save my honor. And that's the weirdest thing of all, isn't it?"

I couldn't look at her anymore. She hurled the knife away, sat down with her back against the wall, and rested her head on her knees.

It was time to make a move. She insisted on taking Felipe's upper body, though it was much heavier, while I got the legs. Never looking up as we inched him to the edge of the platform over the honey vat.

So that he'd lie face up, the upper body needed to go in first, but when I came to help she'd already started. "Just hold his feet straight." The artery on her neck pulsing as she strained to move the weight. The left arm went in, then the shoulders. The honey slowly closed over the face and sealed the wound on his throat. "Now." Breathlessly. "For God's sake hold him straight." Breathless myself, twisting the legs so the torso stayed face up, I performed my task. The body was absorbed millimeter by millimeter.

"All right?"

Was Felipe smiling?

She didn't answer. Kneeling on the platform, staring down, thick hair obscuring her face. I left her there, climbed down the ladder, and headed for the door.

On the way out, my foot struck something that skittered glinting into the light through the doorway. The open knife. I picked it up and carried it outside into the afternoon sun.

Now I could see the trademark stamped into the flange of the blade: SCHRADE. So the knife wasn't from Barcelona after all, and probably not that old. Like my sister had before me, I turned it over and over in my hands and finally noticed faint spidery italic letters engraved into one of the silver caps: MW 1982.

So I'd been right. A present, probably, from his father or something. Marco had been lying.

When I went back into the shed, she hadn't moved, still kneeling by the honey tub staring down. I climbed the ladder and touched her shoulder. "Wendy. Please come outside. I have to show you something."

She showed her teeth when she turned her face. "Get your hand off me."

"Wendy, you were wrong. I can show you."

"You *fuck*. Is that why you came here? To tell me I'm wrong again?"

I waved the knife. "No, for Christ's sake. *This* is what you were wrong about. *This*. Just come out into the sun while it's still bright enough to see."

She got slowly to her feet. Outside, when I showed her the initials and offered her the knife, she wouldn't touch it. "Oh, Felipe," she whispered finally. "Thank God."

There was a shovel inside Felipe's cabin, and I used it to dig a shallow grave in the soft soil at the edge of the meadow. By the time we put Marco's body into it and filled in the earth, it was too late to begin the trip down. The sun was hanging in the tops of the big pines, and the bees seemed louder than ever . . . unless the sound was inside my head, I was so exhausted.

"Sure you're okay?" I asked my sister again.

"Okay, I think."

She sank into the long grass in the last remaining patch of sun, feet stretched out in front of her, braced on her arms, looking ahead at nothing. The buzzing continued.

After a while I sat down beside her, copying her position. Neither of us spoke for a long time. It helped to be more tired than I'd ever been before. "You know there was a fire at school," I said finally, facing straight ahead.

"What?"

"In case you were wondering why I came."

Out of the corner of my eye, I could see her shake her head. "I wasn't wondering. I was just being very thankful." Now she turned to look at me with a little smile. "Thank you for coming, Peter."

I turned to look back. "I'm glad I got here in time."

She reached out and closed her hand softly over mine. We sat that way while the evening came slowly down.

"Now that you mention it," she said into the dusk, "how *did* you happen to come? A fire at school? What are you talking about?"

"Don't you remember? That's why we ran away in the first place."

Her fingers tightened. "My God, you're right. It seems like another lifetime."

"Well, there was another fire. In New York. I heard you were trying to reach me."

"Claire must have told you, right?"

"Yes. She was the first person I called after the towers fell. Then I went to see her. She told me where you were."

Drawing her hand back. "Did you two get it on? Is that why she told you?"

"Of course not. I think she felt sorry for me."

"Why?"

"I think you know."

"She always had a crush on you. She refused to believe you ratted on me."

"Well, she's right, goddamn it. I never did rat."

She finally turned toward me. I turned to face her and she shook her head sadly. "Oh, Peter. You wrote so many letters about that."

"Which you never answered. I wasn't sure you ever got them. Or read them. Anyway, Claire told me why you thought I'd done it."

She just waited.

"Because our mother said I had, right? And you believed her."

"Look." Turning away again. "It had to have been you. You were the only person who knew, other than Karl and me."

"No, Wendy. No. It was awful, what Reiger was doing. But I never would have betrayed you."

"How do you know what Karl was doing?"

I thought of Ellen's face, just before the hot sake. "Well, I don't. Of course I don't. All I know is that you were in love with him. Weren't you?"

In a whisper. "Yes."

"Well, wasn't he, um . . . ?"

"Fucking me? Taking *advantage* of me? Actually, if you want to know the truth, I enjoyed a lot of it." She rested a hand on her belly, sighed, and turned my way again. "Peter? Let's just go on from here?"

"Are you forgiving me? Well, thanks, but there's nothing to forgive. Our mother was lying." I hated the whining sound that had come into my voice. "There must have been somebody else who knew. Can't you remember?"

"Peter, I've spent twenty years trying to forget all that. I hated our mother, but why would she lie? What would she get out of it?"

"Well, here's my take, and I promise I'll never talk about it again. She wanted to separate us . . . for good. And when she realized how successful she'd been, she drove in front of a truck." My sister slowly got to her feet without saying a word and walked out into the darkening meadow, long yellow grass rising up around her. I watched her as she receded and finally was lost in the pine trees on the other side.

Gone. I struggled up to run after her and suddenly understood that she'd be back. And that nothing else mattered.

Our mother had failed. We were together. I arched my back, tilted my head to search the sky. Still too early for stars. Then I put my hands in my pockets and sauntered slowly in the opposite direction from my sister, toward Felipe's cabin looming in the dusk.

I climbed the rickety stairs and pulled the creaky door open for the second time that day. Lit the kerosene lantern on the shelf with the matches that were beside it. Filled the woodstove with dry twigs from the kindling pile and a few pieces of mesquite *leña* on top and lit them too. Filled a pot with water from the clay jar and put it on the grill. On the sideboard were some potatoes and greens that looked like broccoli rabe that Felipe must have gathered earlier, and I started to work on them.

The buzzing outside had stopped. Through the window above the sink, I could dimly see a quail pecking at seeds in the yard, topknot bobbing. Everything fitted. I'd come out the other side of tiredness into a vast comfort.

First Star on the Right

Framed by the window, I could see my sister slowly approach the quail, squat down, hold out a finger. She seemed to be glowing in the reddening gloom. Time stopped. Her hair hid her face. The quail watched her without moving. It was a tableau, a still life full of meaning. I held my breath.

At the last minute, the quail hopped aboard. I breathed out, then in.

She gently carried it in through the open door. "What are we going to do?" Smiling anxiously. "Isn't it past his bedtime?" The quail looked from one to the other of us with his bright black eyes, topknot bobbing.

"Is it Felipe's? What's his name?"

"Felipe didn't know. But he said he has one."

"Huh. Probably John." My favorite Lost Boy.

"Why John? That's not even Spanish." She started searching the cabin. "Well, now it's up to us to feed him. Got to be something around."

There was indeed a loaf of stale bread on one of the shelves. Wendy broke it into crumbs and scattered them on the floor. "Wow, look at that. He *was* hungry."

"I bet you're hungry yourself," I said. "I know I am."

She walked to stove and looked into the steaming pot. "I'm starving. Let's eat, for Christ's sake. Then we can tell each other the story of our lives."

"Okay. Or maybe we can just skip that part."

Laughing felt terrific.

"Yeah! Why don't we just skip it. Great idea."

I watched her sit on the rough wooden cot and look around absently at first, then more and more sharply. The cabin. The kerosene lamp. The quail pecking on the crumbs. The water boiling on the stove, me working on the greens. She gave a little cry, put a hand over her eyes.

"Wendy! What is it? What's wrong?" Had I said those exact words before, in exactly the same tone of voice?

I could barely hear her answer: "I just had a flash. You know, a déjà vu. Being here in this cabin with you."

Slowly, carefully putting down the chopping knife as she dropped her hands and stared back. "Really?" I shook my head, not because I didn't believe her. I might have been smiling.

She didn't smile back. "I wouldn't lie to you, Peter. I have them all the time, but this was a doozy. Super dooper. What do you think it means?"

"Well, some people say it's the soul hiccupping."

"Don't be so goddamn patronizing."

"Okay. Maybe it *would* have happened before if we'd actually made it."

"Well. Nice thought."

"A déjà vu of possibility?" Now I was grinning. "Take it another step. Maybe this is the place we were trying to get to."

"God! Wouldn't that be something!"

I'd said the right thing. In fact, maybe I actually believed it. With pupils expanded so her eyes looked black, she was taking me in as if she'd never seen me before.

After we finished eating, the quail flew up to spend the night on a rafter. It was that time. We silently watched it ruffle its feathers, fluff itself out, and tuck its head under a wing. My sister giggled. "Flip for the cot?" We used to flip for things a lot.

I felt in my pockets, grinning. "No change. You go ahead and take it."

"Poor Peter. What are you going to do?"

"Looks like there's two blankets. I'll take one. I'm so tired I could sleep on a bed of nails."

She handed me the extra blanket, lay on her side on the cot, and pulled the other over her, watching me spread mine on the floor, put another log on the woodstove, blow out the kerosene lantern.

I lay down on my back, wrapping myself in the rest of the blanket. The mesquite popped in the stove, and the flame flickered. I could hear my sister breathing, she was so close. Just a few feet away, in fact.

Her name came out on one of my own breaths. As natural as that.

"I'm here," she whispered.

"Are you really?"

"Yes, Peter." She stretched out her arm, and I groped for her hand and held it for the second time that day.

"We made it. It's real this time. Isn't it?"

"I think so."

A couple of beats. "And are you really pregnant?"

"You mean, am I going to go through with it?"

"I guess that's what I mean."

"Looks that way. Actually, I want to."

"Okay. . . . Can I help?"

"Yes." She squeezed my hand and let it go. "Please."

"All right."

A searing image slowly came into focus. I had to go on. "Speaking of pregnancy, can I tell you a very strange story about our mother?"

A long silence, and a feeling of falling. Had I blown it?

Finally: "Do you really have to?"

"No, I don't have to."

"But you want to. You need to."

"Yes."

"Go ahead, then. Tell me."

"Okay." I breathed in. "You know when our mother was pregnant with you, I was only two. But I have this one strong memory. We were sitting on the sofa in her sitting room. She was wearing a blue top with white polka dots and buttons down the front. I was rolling a toy truck down her belly and then slowly she unbuttoned the top and offered me a boob."

"A *boob?*" Strangely, she didn't sound surprised. "Okay. Why are you telling me this?"

"Because it didn't stop. After you were born, she nursed me instead of you. I got the milk that you were supposed to have."

"How long did that go on?"

"I don't know. Years, maybe."

"Yeah." I heard her sigh. "Yeah."

"What?"

"I knew that, on some level. But thanks for telling me." A slow beat of five. "And now can I tell *you* a story about our mother?"

Oh God. "Of course." Did she notice I could hardly get the words out?

"Do you remember walking in on us, me, in my bathroom when I was about six?"

"Yes, I do." So here it was. "I *do.* I can't get it out of my mind."

"What did you see?"

"Well . . . it was so steamy I could barely see anything."

"But did you see what was happening?"

"No! At least I don't think so. I can never get it straight." I turned away from her, toward the window. Now it was pitch dark outside, and through the open window I could see a single bright star showing above the pines. "You were lying on that white wooden table. She was somewhere in the background. That's all I remember for sure."

"Did I have any clothes on?"

"I don't *know*. I swear to God."

"It was always the same." Her voice was flat. "Like a dance we did. In the middle of the night when everyone else was asleep. She'd say I was sick, and she was going to make me feel better. *Much* better. It was always hot and steamy, and I'd be half asleep myself. She'd be wearing that pink wrapper of hers and smiling as if she really loved me. She'd fill her thing up and lay me down on the table to get ready. And that's when you came in. I could see your eyes. . . . You were looking at us, Peter. I could see you, and you could see us."

I'm moving through rooms in our old house that I thought I knew and seeing them freshly, as if a filter is gone. I see that my sister has by far the best, big windows facing east and south, a porch overlooking the rose garden and farther on the little stream that flowed through the bottom of our property. My room is isolated and much smaller, off by itself down a long corridor in the back part of the house. That's okay. Our father's huge fragrant bathroom: bay rum, English soaps, talcum, cabinets of toiletries, an extra-large claw-footed tub, and an open rain-head shower, where he performs his morning and evening ablutions and emerges as groomed as a prize-winning show horse.

Turning the knob on our mother's door and, amazingly enough, it isn't locked. In the sitting room I see the cream damask-covered sofa she'd sat on while I rolled a toy truck down her pregnant belly and she opened her blouse. In the bedroom, the big TV at the foot of what I now see is an invalid's hospital bed with a black electric motor underneath to control its various angles. A few books on the bedside table: Truman Capote's *The Dogs Bark*, Tom Wolfe's *The Kandy-Kolored Tangerine-Flake Streamlined Baby*, and *The Poetry of William Blake*. I'd given her all three for Christmas on successive years and inscribed the flyleaves. The inscriptions are there when I check. At least she'd loved Capote and Tom Wolfe. I knew because I'd hear her talking about them to friends.

On a shelf under the table is a locked red leather-bound diary dated 1976. The year my sister and I took off for Mexico. Should I cut the strap and open it?

No.

Out the door again and across the landing at the top of the big staircase. Left down the long hall that leads past my sister's bathroom to my bedroom. Stopping at the door to that bathroom and slowly pushing it open.

Everything inside seems crystal clear and sharp as if lit by a halogen bulb. There's the white wooden table with the pull-out section. There's the claw-footed bathtub and the Crane porcelain toilet. White tile walls, and hexagonal tiled floor. Glass shelves in a polished zinc framework beside a bevel-mirrored medicine cabinet. On the shelves, the accoutrements of my sister's toilette, each one standing out in stark relief. The room smells exactly like our mother's bathroom, foreign and indescribable.

The players are not around, but I can imagine them going through their dance. Just as my sister described it. I can almost see them.

"Please tell me. What happened after I came in?"

"I thought you were saving me, but you only stared for a minute and then you were gone. I think you slammed the door. She made me promise never to talk about it. 'It'll be our little secret.' In her coziest voice that she hardly ever used."

"But what was going on?"

"Guess. You know. You do."

Then she was sobbing, dry, heaving sobs that shook her body under the blanket, almost as shocking as what our mother had done to her. I got up and knelt beside her cot and put my arms around her until she stopped. I was going to say something more, something about the fog lifting and beginning to see clearly, that kind of stuff, but realized she was asleep.

Straight on Till Morning

The sharp whirr of the little quail's wings wakes me as it flies down from its perch on the rafter and lands with a little thud on the sideboard. I watch it wander around pecking at crumbs and finally fly out the lightening window into the gray dawn. I'm lying on my back, and the wood floor beneath my thin blanket feels very hard and cold. But kind of reassuring. It holds me up.

No rising slowly out of sleep as usual. I'm totally awake. Calm and sharp like I've never been before, or at least can't remember being. A few birds are starting to sing outside, maybe one of those big yellow and black orioles? A warbler or two? Somewhere in the distance a dove is sounding off, answered by another closer in and a third farther away. The pungent air through the window smells of pine, flowers, and damp meadow with a touch of wood smoke from the stove. Straight above me, the rafters intersect the weathered roof boards at intriguing angles, clear as an Eliot Porter photograph. A fly buzzes slowly from one side of the room to the other, sounding like a human voice so soft you can't make out the words. And then lands on the counter, where I watch it wander around and finally drone out the window.

When I roll toward the cot where my sister lies, my body feels tenderized as a piece of hammered meat. My right shoulder, side, and hip take up their own painful but reassuring contact with the wooden boards. My right wrist smarts with the handcuff burn. She's still there, I can see her shape beneath the blankets, facing away from me so I can't hear her breathing. But of course she's alive. And so am I. Never more so.

On my back again, stretching my stiff, bruised arms and legs as far out as they'll go, enjoying the pain, engulfed in a delicious dog-like yawn, thinking about Claire tossing and turning in the next room, wondering whether or not to go in, then doing it, her blond hair spread on the pillow, her warmth rising, her eyes unreadable as they mostly are. No words. Arms reaching toward me as I bend down? Where is she now? What is she doing?

Tenderized or not, I know I could carry my sister down the mountain if I had to. Face whatever music I may have to face about the death of Marco, my enemy. His knife's still in my pocket; I felt it when I rolled over. Incriminating evidence. Have to take care of that.

Sooner or later, there will be five of us: my sister, Claire, Isabel, the baby, and me. Full house. *Si Diós quiere*, as they say here. If God wishes it, things will work out.

I have a feeling they will. Had it since I first woke up. You know? That feeling of sureness you get once or twice in your life?

After a while I can hear the cot creak as my sister rolls over toward me. "Peter?"

"I'm here."

"Peeterr . . ." She draws out my name in a new way that makes me very happy. "Listen. I wonder what happened to the film. . . . I gave it to him, you know."

I remember I'd felt something else in Marco's pocket when I reached in to extract the handcuff key. God, do I have to mention it? It's moot now, after all.

I decide I'd better go ahead and tell her, even if it means I'll have to dig Marco back up again.

FIN